Rancid

James Hawes was born in 1 ... from University College Swansea, where he lectures in German. His first novel, *A White Merc with Fins*, was published in 1996 to great acclaim and is being translated into nine languages. He lives in Cardiff with his wife and son.

by the same author

A WHITE MERC WITH FINS

Rancid Aluminium

James Hawes

JONATHAN CAPE
LONDON

To Teresa and Owain, with thanks for their help to: Steff; my mother Janet and brother Robert; Tim; Richard; Jim B; Norman/Christine/Chris; Jüri Gabriel; Dan Franklin, Pascal Cariss and Sophie Martin at Cape; Peter Howarth and Natasha Marsh. Also variously to Isia Tlusty-Sheen; Anoop; Menna; Tamsin; Noel, Phil & the Magadalen XI of 1982; Simon Heaven at BBC Wales; Rhys Williams.

First published 1997

3 5 7 9 10 8 6 4 2

© James Hawes 1997

James Hawes has asserted his right
under the Copyright, Designs and Patents Act 1988
to be identified as the author of this work

Part of Chapter 1 first appeared in a
different form in *Arena* magazine

First published in the United Kingdom in 1997 by Jonathan Cape.
Random House, 20 Vauxhall Bridge Road, London SW1V 2SA

Random House Australia (Pty) Limited
20 Alfred Street, Milsons Point, Sydney,
New South Wales 2061, Australia

Random House New Zealand Limited
18 Poland Road, Glenfield,
Auckland 10, New Zealand

Random House South Africa (Pty) Limited
Endulini, 5A Jubilee Road, Parktown 2193, South Africa

Random House UK Limited Reg. No. 954009

A CIP catalogue record for this book is available from the British Library

Papers used by Random House UK Limited are natural,
recyclable products made from wood grown in sustainable forests.
The manufacturing processes conform to the environmental
regulations of the country of origin.

ISBN 0–224–04396–X

Typeset by Deltatype Limited, Birkenhead, Merseyside
Printed and bound in Great Britain by Mackays of Chatham PLC

Contents

Prologue: PR and Firepower

A betting man would have said blind that a Lada had brought Stefan Szymanski's coffin to the market at Otradny this morning. Money for nothing: because everything in the ten-acre medieval chaos that submerges this biodegrading ex-Red Army parade ground each Sunday has come in, or has been towed up by, one of the Ladas corralled in the muddy yard beside the white-and-orange church of St Maria of the Sorrows.

And the customers too. They have come from a hundred miles about, whole families of them stuffed into Ladas, clutching their ferociously saved hard currency to hunt down the objects of their long, slow dreams. A western trader, or a western customer, the hardest-bitten of either, would stand out here with their wonderful shoes and fat, pampered eyes like a being from another world.

This is where the First World ends and Lada Heaven begins.

And what makes a coffin so different? So Stefan Szymanski died of an overdose of 5.65mm bullets, what is so special about that, these days? A coffin gets a Lada too: a black stretch Lada with extra chrome.

The black stretch Lada stands out among the other Ladas by the church. Most of them are pale grey, like the unrendered breeze-block walls of the houses. A good few are a washy brown, like the high-sulphur coal-smoke which pukes from rusting factories and tin-roofed shacks alike (brown coal is the only alternative here to the electricity coaxed irregularly from the terrifyingly decrepit Chernobyl-series nuclear power-station only too visible twenty miles away on the horizon). The rest are that peculiar shade of dull mustard yellow that shouts Early Eighties in your face.

They gather at first light, belching untuned fumes into the wet, flat morning.

Some of the traders' Ladas have sneaked, bribed or even fought their way for days across the ancient, lawless caravan-routes that still lead from Eastern Europe to Asia; others have merely bounced and groaned up the hopeless local trackways with whatever their owners could find, steal, or grub up from the soggy ground. Lada Heaven has gone freemarket.

And so here they are, all gathered, ready to do trade, and this is what they have brought: bootleg CDs and copyright-busting hi-tech games from China; thin, bright clothes from Taiwan with counterfeit labels; plastic trainers from Malaysia and economy Walkmen from Singapore; stacked Marlboro and Kent cigarettes that have crossed half the world to escape taxation; shower attachments from christknowswhere, building blocks knocked off from ex-Soviet contractors, home-brewed off-the-scale schnapps, pungent heaps of cabbage and swede, racks of scraggy chickens.

Except the black one, which has brought a coffin, of course.

The black stretch Lada was the sort of hearse a postman or a minor official might have got in the old, safe days. Cheap, now. But then Stefan Szymanski's mourners had obviously spent the real money on the show that mattered: the mass of flowers that lay piled, waist-high, in shocking waves of wet colour, re-framing the framed photograph of the dead man that stood propped at the foot of the coffin. The whole spectacle was positioned in front of the double-sized sausage-and-coffee caravan that has served as a focal point for the market at Otradny since before the walls came down.

The men gathered around this funereal display might have seemed, to a romantic westerner, to be holding a wake for Stefan Szymanski, guarding his departing soul against the wiles of evil ghosts. They were all drinking schnapps of some kind from yellow, scratched little Pyrex glasses, and talking without eye-contact in the low, hollow voices of mourners everywhere. As their narrow gazes flicked around the market, the hands cupping the rain away from their cigarettes swung in fast little arcs from lips to chest-level to lips again, like censers. Thin grey whiffs of smoke rose and entwined around the coffin, settling as a hanging miasma of high-tar breath to grease the heavy air.

But they were also carrying shotguns on slings, even the odd ancient rifle or two could be seen here and there. They were not waiting for any spirits that might impede Stefan Szymanski's progress to the next world: they were waiting for the men who had ended his tenancy of this one.

They were waiting for the black Mercedes.

They did not have to wait any longer than any normal Saturday: at eight o'clock sharp – the stereo recording of the church bells was playing from the new Sony speakers in the tower of St Maria's – a gang of boys ran into the square and shouted at the men, who lit new cigarettes and looked each other in the eye, trying to gain courage and conviction from each other. To no-one's surprise, a couple of shabbily armed policemen hitched in their beer-guts and walked, without looking at each other, over to their very own red-and-white Lada, in which they chugged blatantly off towards the town centre.

The black Mercedes was breasting one of the long, gentle undulations that pass for landscape hereabouts: against the flat greyness where the world and the sky joined imperceptibly, it seemed to be rising slowly, vertically, from the earth itself.

Everyone knew the car. Each Saturday for two years it had appeared at eight a.m. to pick up the rent from the stalls. It was so regular that it had come to feel like a part of nature; no-one even bothered to ask any more by what right Golebiowski collected his dues.

Except Stefan Szymanski.

When they hiked the rates yet again, he had asked, publicly, with the courage that is not courage, but just the simple knee-jerk of a man who knows he is being pushed inexorably over the edge. He had shouted his question into Golebiowski's face. Everyone had quietly slipped him a drink that night, when the stalls were folded and stashed away and the flat night was falling with the rain.

The next morning they found him already stiff in his riddled brown Lada.

And now they were gathered around his coffin, with their old shotguns and Second World War rifles, and they watched the black Mercedes floating fully into view. But presently they also saw the two Range-Rovers wallowing along behind it; soon they could make out the sunglassed men leaning from the windows, and the stubby little machine-pistols in their hands.

The women and children minding the stalls looked at their men. The men looked at each other. Someone turned, stubbed his cigarette into the mud, and walked stiffly over to his stall, the set of his back challenging anyone to call after him.

In thirty seconds, the only person left at Stefan

Szymanski's coffin was his widow, crying silent tears of helpless rage as she watched the black Mercedes coming up.

Except then there was a crackling roar from behind a new breeze-block wall beside the church. A cloud of thick black diesel smoke fired vertically upwards; the wall burst open like a dam and out into the square bounded a small armoured car.

Small, for an armoured car. Small and fast.

The Mercedes and the Range-Rovers hardly had time to slow up, they just drove head-on into the 20mm cannon-fire that stuttered up the road and gutted them. The stallholders did not hear the shells hit: they had their heads down low, they just felt the detonations in their guts, in the hollows around their hearts and in the big veins of their necks.

The silence that followed was like before time began.

Then the world started again, cautiously, and they looked up and saw the Mercedes simply flattened out, like a squashed beetle, steaming. One of the Range-Rovers was still trundling along, off the road, its wheels tracking the ridges of the scrubby potato-field, except that there was nothing left above the bonnet except clouds of black smoke; the other was on its back, burning orange. They could feel the bloom of heat on their faces. The armoured car circled, like a sheep-dog, until the dying Range-Rover sagged over in the field and disappeared in its own pyre. Then it gunned its engines and bounced off towards the distant power-station, which was also, as everybody knew, the place where the local Interior Ministry troops were based.

And then they saw an even bigger, even blacker Mercedes come nosing up from the back of the church.

It was so black that it shone almost purple: the windows were black; the rear-light clusters were black;

even the headlights were tinted black by some miracle of Germanic technology. It made a bow-wave of silent awe among the sheet-and-scaffolding stalls as it crunched and splashed its ghostly way through the potholes between them, its single wiper polishing a slow, wide rainbow through the droplets of acidic rain that stood like mercury on the black mirror of its windscreen.

The car stopped and a uniformed driver, well over six feet tall, got out, strode around and opened the back door.

After a pause, the man in the back stretched a black wool-clad leg out into the rain, allowing his long black sock and shining black shoe to be seen for a moment in all their clearly western glory. Then he planted his foot demonstratively in the middle of the deep puddle before which, inevitably, his door had ended up. He followed with the other foot and raised his seventeen stone slowly but without effort into the rain. He looked up at the flat sky without expression, and then turned back to the car, in order to talk to a woman who had half slid herself out after him.

She was dressed in black like he, but was much younger; she wore her black in such a way that you could not tell if she was dressed to mourn or to kill. He nodded, and she remained where she was, in the car.

He looked round again and fixed the mourners with slow blue eyes. Without waiting for his driver to close the door, without looking back at the woman, he stumped over alone to the open coffin, splashing through the mud in splendid carelessness. The girl and the driver watched.

He looked at the dead man's face, nodded quietly, genuflected, and then began to count fifty-dollar bills out, one by one, into a pile on Stefan Szymanski's cold, crossed hands.

Gradually, the market-traders could not help themselves: their gazes slipped from the dead man's face to the heap of bills that was growing slowly, rhythmically, and with no apparent sign of ever stopping. In their minds, the old, old weighing-scales were starting to materialise: A Just Scale is the Lord's Delight. Without wanting to, they were starting to think about Stefan Szymanski's market value, starting to set the price.

The big man seemed to see nothing, he just kept on peeling the notes off, already three times he had renewed the wad in his hand from the unseen, unguessable stock inside his black cashmere overcoat. Imperceptibly, the crowd of stallholders leaned forward, craned over each other, some of them even took a tiny, shuffling step forward.

Dollars, dollars, dollars. They knew what dollars looked like all right, dollars were the only thing they took except deutschmarks. Deutschmarks were OK, just, but even deutschmarks can come and go: who knows when they will become reichsmarks again, or east-marks, or be two million to the dollar like in grandad's youth? Germany is big and rich, but Germany is a real place, and real things happen to it: within living memory, Germany had gone rabid and devoured nations, then been smashed to rubble and carved apart.

But dollars!

America is not real, it is a dream. It is the place ancestors disappear for ever; the place that now and then, so the story goes, delivers back some gum-chewing demigod of suntanned wealth claiming to be a great-nephew, longing to have his gifts accepted. A dream is impervious to hurt, and the dollar never changes: and now they saw Stefan Szymanski's cheap coffin being turned, slowly and unstoppably, into a shrine to Mr Washington of America, Patron Saint of the Pursuit of Happiness.

Without looking up or pausing, the man with the money said at last (his Ukrainian had a strong Baltic accent):

—Where is the widow?

The small woman in black shawls was ushered through the men. She looked fifty-odd, though she was probably not much over thirty in reality. But then this *was* reality, it was just a different reality from first-world, centrally-heated, well-nourished reality: thirty years of cold, damp, winterbeaten, husband-battered, childbearing, stall-holding, spirit-drinking, tooth-rotting reality count nearly double.

Her eyes stayed locked onto the man as if looking at him were the only thing that would save her from looking at the money. She kept on not looking down at the coffin, but by now none of the men were even bothering to pretend they were not counting. The heap of fifties was spreading out over the chest of Stefan Szymanski, his hands were no longer visible at all. Still the payer counted on.

At last the pile of bills shifted under its own weight and half of it slid down into the side of the coffin. The man stopped counting, as if obeying a mysterious but exact signal. He looked down into the coffin for a moment, then added one more note and crossed himself again. He looked up into the widow's eyes. For a moment she held his gaze, and then she burst into tears of rage and ran into his arms. He patted her back in distant, paternal care.

Then he let her go and looked around at the men. He flicked his eyes from one face to the next.

—This is bad business. Now we do good business. I cannot promise that there will be reductions in the rents. I have my expenses, as you have seen. But there will be no rise over inflation for six months, you have my word. This week is a holiday. No rent this week. My associates will return next week. I know that you will treat them with respect even in my temporary absence. I wish you good business.

Then he crossed himself again and walked back to the black Mercedes, looking all the time at his feet sloshing through the mud and water. As he approached, the girl slid herself supermodel-style, arsewise back into the shadows of the car's interior; he climbed in after her and the driver closed the door. All the locks whizzed softly shut, the starter-motor sighed briefly, and the car wafted off through the mud and water.

From behind the church, the red-and-white police Lada snouted cautiously out, then rattled forward to occupy the place where the black Mercedes had been. The policemen kicked the doors open and sat smoking without embarrassment as they listened to a Polish radio station: it was Elvis singing Love Me Tender.

Inside the now-distant Mercedes, the man and the girl looked at each other. She produced three glasses of chilled vodka from the fridge, and handed one to him, one to the other passenger. This second man was tall and thin, dressed in a memorably yellow suit of softest tweed. His face was a deeper brown than even Seville can bake; his black hair swept back in short curls from his long temples, where it was just starting to grey, and his jet moustache curved grandly up around his massive, proud nose, almost to the corners of his dark eyes: he looked like a Sikh prince crossed with a Brahmin scholar, in a yellow suit.

He observed the ice-blue vodka with a mixture of unveiled distaste and fatalistic acceptance. Mr Kant raised his glass at them both, and they all tossed the vodka back. She coughed, the dark man grimaced and shook his head, and Mr Kant laughed like a bear.

—You were brilliant, she said.

—It was Dr Jones's idea. Your health, Dr Jones! (Dr Jones, understanding the gesture, if not the language, raised his glass and smiled without opening his lips.) Well, my princess, perhaps you really can learn something at the London Business University. The Englishman is right: business is mostly, what is called, ah yes, 'P-R'.

—Did he say 'PR'? asked Dr Jones, since this was the only word Mr Kant had spoken in English.

—He did, nodded the girl, speaking perfect Boston English. – I think we have persuaded him. And then, with an ease and appreciation which seemed curiously at odds with this intonation, she poured another shot each before Dr Jones could stop her, and raised her glass again:

—Well then, to PR, she said.

—PR, said Dr Jones.

—P-R, Mr Kant agreed, laughing at his own English. But before the glass reached his lips he halted, raised a forefinger and wagged it gently at Dr Jones as he searched for the only two other English words he had as yet felt the need to learn. At last he hit them:

—PR and firepower!

1. Chernobyl on the M25

At the end, at 6 a.m. that last Sunday morning, I was crouched down behind my filing-cabinet because here, whoever it was I was waiting for (logically, it could be any of them) could not put one in my back through the window; and here, I could see through the little wire-meshed window of the office door, to watch the lift-cables hanging like black creepers in the caged shaft.

I had to lay the gun down for a sec to half-raise myself and pull these stupid sodding leather trousers about, to stop them crunching my balls; as I picked it back up and settled down again, I was thinking: I am just an ordinary crap Brit for Christ's sake, I was born to mow my lawn and wash my car. Just how the hell did it come to this?

But if the how was a mystery, the when was clear enough. It was etched in my head, the exact second when the invisible clockwork kicked in and started hauling me towards my date with the black stretch Lada. I could remember it the way you remember the first time you heard of Chernobyl (remember?), when someone came rushing up, saying that Kiev had been fried and this glowing black cloud was rolling across the world. And you looked up at the sky and waited for the high, silent vapour-trails ...

*

I was stuck in my crap Volvo in the jam between junctions 12 and 13 of the dark, wet M25, flossing my teeth and watching a mangy dog crossing a rusty bridge.

Crap is unfair. My Volvo does about everything a car

could possibly do, and I still hate it. Maybe *hate* is too strong. OK I do not hate it; it just depresses me. Thing is, I only bought (well, leased) a shagging Volvo because Gerry Shepperd has got one (the sincerest form of flattery is copying your neighbour's car); and when I ordered it (two years ago), I naturally went and bloody specified (like Gerry) the built-in child seat.

Sarah was against this: she pointed out that Gerry and Melissa got the kids first, *then* the car with the built-in child seat. I just laughed.

Two years ago, I laughed.

Today, I was due for a sperm-test.

As I flossed and watched the dog, I was wondering vaguely how I was going to find a window to *deliver the sample* (i.e. toss off into a test tube and get it to University College Hospital within fifteen minutes) so they could decide whether I was a fertile extension of Life On Earth, or just a crap write-off of evolutionary time who might as well trade in his big, barren Volvo for a sexy little two-seater.

I was also surreptitiously half-thinking of cheating on Sarah anyway, with Charmaine, fertile or not.

Busy, busy day.

As a backing-tape to all this, I was listening to SouthEast FM telling me to avoid getting stuck between junctions 12 and 13 of the M25.

I hate SouthEast sodding FM.

Hate is exactly the right word. I hate the way even the weather report has to be read out by some audibly grinning, strength-through-joy coke-head. Usually, I only ever listen to SouthEast FM for the traffic news when things get really bad, when I start to doubt if the jam will ever actually end. Crazy, I know, but sometimes it happens. Especially this time of year.

It is cold, and it is wet. The grotesque, meaningless

consumption-binge of another thirtysomething, child-less Christmas is still echoing on, after nearly two months, in your head, your bank-balance and your waistline. You are *still* leaving home before dawn and coming back after sunset for Christ's sake, like some extra from *Revenge of the Mole People*. Your eyes are sick from the oily-rainbow starbursts of the headlamps crawling past the other way like trundling lighthouses; your head is numbed by the thumping wipers. You look at all the lights ahead and behind and around you, all these people queuing up bumper-to-bumper, as if we were all desperate to get to somewhere wonderful. Whereas in fact, all we are doing is going off again to work. And in fact, the only reason we do this is: so we can afford the crap little off-the-peg treats which we need so that we can bear doing this.

If only they ran a decent train service.

Well, and so sometimes, on this kind of morning, I find myself sneaking looks at my fellow jammers and starting to get the nutty idea that everyone stuck between junctions 12 and 13 of the M25 actually died last night. Our stress-mangled bodies are actually cooling off already on our safe marital beds; the arsetight, home-counties mourning of the unbelieving bereaved is taking stone-cold sober, infertile possession of the unloved houses where we spent our wasted half-lives.

And here we are now, here we sit like birds in the wilderness: lost souls still crawling to nowhere for no good reason; undead-locked into a car-culture limbo beyond all human contact, doomed endlessly to avert our eyes from each other through our half-tinted windows and stare ahead through a wet, sodium-lit eternity at the closed-off exit marked *Life*, and the big yellow signs that say

13

DELAYS POSSIBLE UNTIL: FOREVER.

Which is when I turn in desperation to SouthEast FM for the traffic update. I tap the pre-set and it at least confirms yappingly that sometime, somewhere, this jam really does come to an end, and the people in it, we, start living, however uselessly.

Apart from the traffic-news, all SouthEast FM does is let you know what kind of stuff twenty-year-olds only half-over their acne and their virginity, in whatever horrible fashion-victim crap they have to wear now to be individuals like everyone else, are listening to these days. And since I was now thirty-five, half-way to thirty-six indeed, why the hell would I want to know that?

I sniffed and looked for a disc to kill the jabbering voice of SouthEast FM. A bit of the old music would do me good.

You know, the old music: the stuff they played on the radio and at parties, back then. The stuff you might have heard, out of someone's window across the way, when you were smoking an after-sex cig at five in the morning, looking at the ceiling, feeling sleep wafting over you like a cool breeze, hearing this other, half-known person breathing beside you, with the sound of the air coming out of their nostrils already turning into a dream of big waves rolling onto a beach, and feeling the indestructible, physical certainty of a long, happy, unknown life spreading out in front of you.

The stuff you were into when you were twenty and just getting over your acne and your virginity, and wearing whatever horrible fashion-victim crap you had to wear in those days to be individual like everyone else. The stuff ad-men use now to play memory-games with your brain and your wallet. The stuff you are stuck with for as long as you have.

14

I was stuck outside Memory Lane.

I mean outside the factory. The Memory Lane cake-factory.

There it was, to the left, under the bridge, beyond the wire: the low industrial unit with those ridiculous eighties false red gables stuck on it. I knew it well, I bloody ought to, I saw it every day for Christ's sake. It crawled slowly backwards past my window every morning as I sat, turned off, tuned out, listening to the old music bleakly, sitting in my traffic-jam aimlessly, bumping up my blood-pressure pointlessly, smelling into my shirt inexorably, wrecking my spine inescapably, growing piles helplessly, annihilating any fertility I might have left. And breathing the cancerous, partially-burnt-hydrocarbon, particulated, traffic-jam air through my open window (if I opened it) or my ventilation ducts (if I turned them on) or just from the fumes that seep and creep into every car anyway, be it X-reg Ford or multi-airbagged Volvo. And just thinking, in a vague sort of way: *you breathe shit, or breathe shit, or breathe shit.*

No, not cakes: biscuits.

Memory Lane is an upmarket, packaging-driven, niche-market biscuit factory: you see their product in twee little specialist shoppes in places like Henley. A good pitch. Nice biscuits, actually. And well: at least whoever runs Memory Lane knows that bolt-on heritage knick-knacks is all UK PLC can do these days. The stores where the real stuff gets piled up and shifted to the C1's are all run by Japs and Germans and Malaysians and Koreans. We Brits can only tend the crap little tart's-parlour units that angle for the bored rich. Or stack shelves in the superstores.

Memory Lane. Every morning, I had to laugh a bitter little laugh as I clutched-and-rolled past it. Because beyond the fence, you could see a factory gate on the side-road, and some Transport Manager, either very witty, very thick, or maybe just a C&W fan, had put up this sign that said:

NO ENTRANCE TO MEMORY LANE.

I could never go by it without laughing that tight laugh and hearing the twanging Country guitars and two high, lonesome voices singing thirds in slow 4/4 time,
> (2,3 . . .)
> (Cos there) Ain't no entrance (twang)
>   to Memory Lane (twang twang twaang-ang-ang)
> (And) You're never really going to get
>   Charmaine.

Or whatever else I thought up that morning.

Too right.

No entrance. No point trying to get down memory lane, to that time – Christ, was it only three years ago?! – when everything was booming. When the money was rolling in, the partners queuing up, the bank shelling out and the contracts raining down. Christ, even my sex-life with Sarah had been great then, before we started worrying ourselves stupid, first about dough and then, more recently, about fertility and stuff. You know: whether I had to give up booze for at least two weeks (two weeks!) before she got the Prime Time White Flows, and whether she had to give up booze for two weeks afterwards in case she had actually got pregnant, and all that.

Memory Lane: When the old music had still been the new music.

I paused in my flossing and thought of Charmaine.

Fuck the old music.

Last Friday (today was Thursday), we were all in the

Spice of Life at Cambridge Circus, having the quick after-work Friday Night pint to debrief on the week and avoid the rush-hour. And it had (as usual) turned into a quick three pints.

Irons and Jobson, my Partners, the bastards, were naturally there too. We make business-training videos aimed at sixth-form colleges and the crapper so-called New Universities. They do the actual producing and marketing, I pinch the ideas from the Executive Books Summaries (most recently, for example, from some book by this weird-looking guru in a yellow suit). I also fiddle the books with Deeny, our slimy accountant. Irons and Jobson think the books are boring; they just want to hang out with Soho filmies, so they don't bother me. Big mistake. Our books are actually very interesting. The tax-man, for example, would find them fascinating.

So anyway, last Friday, there they were: Irons was leaning against a pillar near the juke-box, with wafts of deodorant billowing out from under his stupid bloody leather jacket. It was a horsehide job, like medieval armour, with epaulettes and god knows how many little zips and belts, the kind of gear you usually see only on blokes with big bikes or big moustaches; Jobson had dumped himself on a high stool and was wallowing up against the bar, browsing on the tired peanuts and slurping his lager, his eyes zipping this way and that under his mop of straight, black hair, like some gargoyle designed to portray deceit; behind Irons, I could see this pink-faced, balding bloke with a definite pot swelling his shirt forward above his belt as he leaned over to chat to some secretaries.

Then I realised that the pillar Irons was leaning on was a mirror, and it was me. It seemed impossible, since *I* was me, but there you are.

Pathetic: I mean, what did we think we were doing? What is the good of having three pints and stopping at six-thirty on a Friday night? You could be drinking with Uma Thurman, and having three pints and then stopping at six-thirty on a Friday night would still be the surest way of making absolutely certain that you felt like shit by seven.

Yet none of us had been able (of course) to resist the illusion of change that comes with booze. We could not give up on the fantasy that *in the Friday-night pub, anything can happen.* The evening was fired by lying memories that called to us as if they were still possibilities. We were pretending to talk to one another, but each of us was drinking alone, in the same crap, pint-fuelled dream: that he might, just for one night, be allowed to take the field again in Bachelor Heaven. You know: those halcyon twentysomething years when you have long since forgotten your spots and nervous laughter, but have not yet had to become conscious of your hairline and waist. When you can out-yarn, out-earn, out-drink and, if need be, outpunch any teenager and still laugh at the poor old tossers over thirty. When you radiate unknown experience to nineteen-year-old girls and unlined enthusiasm to thirty-year-old women.

Like I said: pathetic. Or rather (as Charmaine would say, and as we have all started saying recently): sad.

Back in Real Time, back on the M25, I stopped flossing. I took my fingers and thumbs out of my mouth and looked at the little grainy black lumps and the yellow gunge on my dental tape and I was thinking: Sad? *Saaaad?* So just when exactly, and why the hell, did a word meaning *emotionally down* suddenly come to mean *socially inadequate?* Goebbels would have liked that.

Anyway, last Friday night we quickly hit the fatal three-pint mark and were now aching to reach Escape Velocity. The defences were down: all round the warm, loud pub I saw people twitching as they looked to check their watches, hoping vainly that it was earlier than they knew it was. You could see their eyes wanting moremoremore. The new music was getting into our old heads: the pints had taken the pain out of the treble and the bass-beat was almost at home in our guts now. I could even feel the old, mad, saaad temptation to sing along. None of us wanted to admit that it was time to go home. To drive home slightly, uselessly, pathetically over the limit.

Drunk enough to lose our licences but not drunk enough not to care; late enough to have messed up any big dinner-with-pals plans Sarah might have had, but too early to call it an evening; tired enough not to care that much, too awake to do nothing.

You try for the best of both worlds and you end up, you can only ever end up, with a double helping of shit.

Q: Why is it that men start getting fat when they hit thirty-something?

A: Because they stop drinking so much.

When you are young and full of that speedy, puppydog desperation that does not count as desperation because you are still young, you drink ten pints then carry on till the morning comes, and you end up getting it away, fighting it out, dancing it off or chucking it up. Hence staying thin. Whereas I, with my coronary-inducing position to lose and my fondly imagined dignity to defend, have three or four pints and then sag home, guilty about nothing I did anything about, in my Volvo, to my understandably pissed-off wife and my married friends (if any of them have managed to find a baby-sitter) and nothing can happen so it doesn't. So I have a couple at home and sleep them off. And the booze metabolises into fat.

I am not bloated by excess, but by defeat: the hated love-handles whose presence I can no longer realistically dispute are just the tell-tales of the flab in my soul.

Charmaine, Charmaine! Our Lady of the straining Lycra!

So last Friday, I made sure I was the first to finish my third pint unsaaadly, like I had somewhere to go apart from to the bar to get the fourth pint. I stood up half in time to the music and checked my watch and lied straight through my eyes that I had to meet My Wife's Gang in an hour (like My Wife was some kind of bouncing supermodel and our weekend lives were just toooo full), and said *See you girls* to Charmaine and co., who were kind of jiggling about on their seats to the music.

Charmaine jumped up and hopped over to me in that funny way girls have to run when they are wearing high-heels and tight skirts: her ankles were going almost in circles. She came close and shouted (she had to come close and shout, because of the P.A. and the Friday-night revelries): *Here Pete* (actually, she shouted *Eya Pate*, because she is from Birmingham) *what music you fancy for the do?* and I looked at her all amused-like, as taught in Mills & Boon books, and shouted: *Hey, whatever you want, Charlie. Have whatever you want. You do it.* And she shouted: *You like this kind of stuff Pete?* and I shrugged and shouted *Dunno sounds ok to me* and she goggled and shouted *Ain't you never heard 'Partyline' before?*, so I looked her right in the eyes and smiled and shouted *Charlie, I'm a married man, you know* and she looked back at me and shouted *Don't mean to say you can't like the music*, and before either of us meant to, we were looking at each other in that very particular way when the conversation can do either of two things: it can be about harmless things but said with wicked smiles, or about wicked things but said with harmless smiles. The music suddenly went muffled: we were homing in. So I shouted (choosing the harmless things/ wicked smiles option, which is far easier to carry off): *I like this alright* and she shouted *You listen to SouthEast FM, like?* and I shouted *Na, only for the traffic*, and she shouted *Try it next week, it's the biz*, and I shouted *OK I will*, and then I winked at her and went.

I laughed all the way home, except when my arse starting cooking because I had accidentally turned the heated bloody seats on while fumbling to put the belt in. So much for my sperm count.

Naturally, I did not say anything to Sarah about what had happened, because of course, nothing had. It was just a little brush with possibility. Nice, in a way. Flattering, in a manner of speaking. One of the secretaries had asked me to choose the music for the party, that was all. To some extent it was just another part of the job. It was surely important for someone in my position to be able to relate to junior staff. Definitely. No doubt about it. Any of our own management training videos would confirm it. Teamfeeling. Yep.

Charmaine is nineteen or something, yeah, nineteen, of course, we had her birthday booze-up in the pub just before Xmas. She came and sat on my lap, playfully. She has about two years of lager-and-lime time left before getting fully hitched to Trevor, a tubby young Brummie greaser who is our usual agency bike-messenger. She has those kind of plump-armed, round-shouldered, big-breasted looks that nothing can make last

21

beyond twenty-five tops; her nose slopes up and her cheeks are round; her mouth is set in that look of surprised thickness that goes naturally with her accent; when she wears a longish skirt (which is admittedly not often) the material hangs tight to the swell of her until it reaches the apex of her buttocks, then it tumbles straight down, dancing and juddering at every step with the hidden motion of what will one day be a very considerable arse.

At sixteen, I would have thought her an unattainable sex goddess; at twenty-five, I would not have given her a second look.

At thirty-five, I started listening to SouthEast FM.

Saaaad but true.

All week, I had been striding youthfully into the office, gut held in and shoulders back, humming SouthEast FM stuff and just blithely saying, as I drifted past, closer each morning, *Here what's that band again Charlie, you know the one that goes da da da da dadada* so she would start singing and twirling about on her gas-strut chair and nodding her head and doing that kind of half flamenco, half noodle-spinning stuff with her arms.

Yesterday (Wednesday) she said: *You all set for the party, Pete?* and I said *Yep, looking forward Charlie* and she said *Me too* and then she said *You bringing your wife, like?* and I said *Shouldn't think so, you bringing that Trevor?* and she said *Naaaaa*, and I said *Be there or be square*, and trotted off.

Now, I could tell the sound of her heels among all the sounds of the office, at fifty paces.

I did not lie to Sarah about the party. I do not mean I told her, I mean I did not lie: I invited her straight out.

I suppose she is used to me being shifty and sulky about the business, and about the Breeding Thing, and about how I wished we made love more often and more surprisingly, like in the old days, and, well, you know: just generally being kind of dumbly, pathetically dissatisfied in that crap way that is strong enough to mess up your life, and the life of anyone around you, and yet not strong enough to force you into doing something about it. She is used to seeing me half-alive. And so now I was telling her the absolute truth and she could see I was for real. I was saying *Why not come?*: not like I wanted her to come for some shifty reason, and not like I didn't want her to come for some shifty reason.

I had the ersatz freedom and false honesty that come from totally giving up on responsibility. I had decided to let whatever wanted to happen, happen: to Sarah it looked like the truth. Maybe it was.

Maybe the truth was that I was just so tired I no longer gave a toss, and maybe that was what she saw.

Maybe giving up is a kind of liberation (twang twang).

So anyway, Sarah was not coming to the party and that meant something would happen with Charmaine.

Something or other.

Back in the middle lane of the M25, a wild idea came to me. I could flirt with Charmaine today, in the safe and secure knowledge that I was morally allowed a wank. We could go for a drink at lunchtime, say, and if things got out of hand, I could take them in hand and give the sample in the pub lav., thus killing two birds with one toss. I mean, I had not had a wank for ages. Naturally, I sometimes feel like a quick pull-through, everyone does. But I am married man; you cannot be a live-in married man and wank, that would be just too saaad. But today it was my marital duty, no less, to have a quick Sherman, a crafty J. Arthur, at some stage. It could even be argued that by messing about with Charmaine a bit, I would more accurately be imitating the actual reality of making love to Sarah; I mean, the foreplay and stuff. So the sample would be more realistic, wouldn't it? Definitely.

Good eh? It makes you wonder why anyone bothers with arguing about facts when we are all so able to see anything the way we want to. Take, for example, the pre-booked Serious Conversation in our kitchen some four days before, when Sarah and I decided (i.e. Sarah decided) that I should have this sodding sperm-test in the first place:

SCENE: THE KITCHEN IN No. 22 HUNTER'S RISE, AN EXCLUSIVE COMMUNITY OF JUST 26 SUPREMELY APPOINTED DETACHED CRAP EXEC-UTIVE DWELLINGS WITH GRGS & LXRY FTTD KTCHNs, MST CNVNNT FR M's 3, 4, 25, MNY STLL WTH NGTV EQTY.

ME: A sperm test? Me?
SHE: Well, you are the one with the sperms.
ME: Sexist bastard.
SHE: Seriously. Look, we agreed at Christmas, remember? Two more periods. It would just be a check, you know, to see . . .
ME: Just to see if I'm a mutant.
SHE: It's a simple test.
ME: Yeah, yeah. I suppose . . .
SHE: Let's just test and check, yeah?
ME: You think that's what it is, don't you?
SHE: I just think we should check.
ME: We?
SHE: OK, you. You might as well check.

ME: OK, OK, fine, so I'll check. What about you?

SHE: What?

ME: I will get my sperm checked, what about you?

SHE: I don't have any sperm, Peter.

ME: Ha ha ha.

SHE: More's the pity.

ME: What?

SHE: Sorry.

ME: Me too, I'm sorry. Sorry. I just mean, you know, maybe you could have something else checked.

SHE: Such as?

ME: Such as? Such as how do I know? Tubes, or something?

SHE: Tubes or something. Uh-huh?

ME: Look, Christ, I don't know, I'm not a gynaecologist.

SHE: Oh, and of course, you're a man, and no man understands what goes on down here in a woman because it's all so weird and complicated and *female*, right?

ME: I didn't say that.

SHE: Well you should have.

ME: Should I?

SHE: Because it is, yeah, that's right, all you've got is two boiled eggs in a sack, I've got all these, yeah *tubes*, tubes and caves and cavities and passages and repositories and membranes and entrances, yeah, damn right, it *is* more complicated than a couple of ping-pong balls in hairy clingfilm.

ME: I never thought of them that way before.

SHE: No, you probably thought of them as God.

ME: Christ it must be tough being a heterosexual woman what with all men being sooooo hideous and pathetic.

SHE: No, most other men are just hideous. Sorry. Peter,

Peter. Oh God. Look, all I'm saying is, we seem to have a problem, yeah?

ME: Seem.

SHE: OK, OK, um, let's say: if we don't do something pretty soon we will have a problem.

ME: Is it suddenly *soon*? Jesus, I didn't know the calendar suddenly speeded up.

SHE: We have been trying for two years, Peter.

ME: Well, we stopped *not* trying . . .

SHE: We did. It was exciting, wasn't it? it was like, wow, so *this* is sex, all over again.

ME: Yeah.

SHE: Well, I'm glad you remember it.

ME: How could I forget.

SHE: You waiting on the bed wearing nothing but brand-new Levis and a smile.

ME: Mmmmmm. (we kiss)

SHE: (suddenly) But it hasn't worked! It's so unfair!

And she cried like a child, her chest heaving like she would choke.

Not *fair*. That little meaningless word even little children know the meaning of, as if instinctively. Fair: the first thought that says: *the world is not how it should be*. Christ, think how easy life would be if we could all just sit and say, Well, that's the way the world is, bad luck. But we stopped saying that sometime about two thousand years ago, and started saying: it's not fair. Now we all have a big picture in our heads, vague maybe, but wide and bright, of how things should be, and it is not how things are. Now we all shout at heaven, now we are not sure any more about the difference between *could be* and *should be*, we all want to play God and make worlds. No wonder so many of us end up doing the Gravity Waltz off high buildings or forgetting to open the garage door one morning. Fair it isn't.

No wonder Sarah was crying. And maybe I should have joined in, but I didn't. Like I said, I am a Brit. I was brought up on *Biggles* and *Roy of the Rovers* and *The Victor*, they were still almost openly preparing us for the next Somme or Arnhem. And now I am supposed to cry *just because my life is utterly fucked up?* Oh no. I should have curled up in a ball with Sarah and howled, but instead, I held her Daddy-ish and talked like some bloody Dickie Attenborough clone: *Look, I mean, absolutely, you're absolutely right darling, I'll take a test, I'll do it, right away, I'll see the doctor tomorrow, we'll get it all sorted out, you'll see . . .*

And soon she stopped crying. Daddy mend. And so I had managed to keep it all bottled up and screwed down again. Thus, no doubt, adding a few more rebellious little cells to the big, rollover cancer-or-cardiac jackpot.

But it did mean that I could now permit myself a little fun with Charmaine, followed safely by a nifty piece of wrist-work. Sometimes it's tough to be a man (twang twang).

I let go the floss with my left hand and dangled it carefully away from my shoulder with the right and heaved myself over against the seat-belt, so I could flip open the glove-box and root about in all the crap in there, until I got hold of the little, white-capped plastic specimen-tube in its handy sealable pouch. I looked at it, and the mere thought of how I could now mess about with Charmaine, but be insured, started to give me an erection. So I shook my head to rattle my brain back into gear: I stuck the bottle in my pocket, feeling just the tiniest pre-echo of fate as I did so, and made myself concentrate on my flossing again.

I was having trouble getting my fingers in the right place and the right way up: I had both my index-fingers and both my thumbs stuck inside my mouth again now, with the waxy flossing-string wound around the right-hand finger. I had to keep hold of the end of the tape with my left-hand finger and thumb and get it right up in between my teeth and up into my gums, like I had just been taught by my dentist's buxom hygienist.

Maybe I had not paid full attention to the way she showed me on the plaster tooth-model: all I could remember was the warmth coming up out of her starched uniform and her big, serious eyes telling me what I should be doing, and how bad I had been, and how, if I got my act together and did the right thing, I could still just about save myself. I just sat and nodded.

I do not want any more fillings because I read somewhere that dental amalgam maybe gives you Alzheimer's. My grandmother got that: she ended up on an orange armchair in a room full of other old ladies and not quite enough air-freshener, with Queen (for Christ's sake!) playing on some local radio-station. Now, whenever I hear Queen, it is like a memory-tag for: Death In An Old People's Home. I see the sights and smell the smells. I feel that feeling again, the feeling of nothing: like waiting for a late plane to somewhere you didn't want to go anyway, just half-holding your breath, just half-looking up at the announcements board every now and then, without hope or great annoyance.

Whenever I hear Queen, I want to run out and buy one of those little printing-stamps. I would stamp it in bright red ink on every page of my filofax and on little yellow sticky notes: I would plaster these notes all over my office and on the screen of my VDU; I would put them on the milk-bottles in my fridge and the remote-control of my telly and all the mirrors in my house; and especially I would stamp it on Sarah's forehead, so that wherever I go, and especially whenever I look at Sarah and find myself not listening to her, or hear myself droning on to her, I will always read:

this is not a rehearsal
this is not a rehearsal
this is not a rehearsal.

But then, I only think like that (of course) when I can't do anything about it, like at 3 a.m. in bed, the time (they say) when the old die, or now, i.e. at 8.10 a.m. stuck on the M25, the time (they say) that the not-so-old get their heart-attacks. So I just try to do something half-useful instead, something that makes me feel I am at least trying.

I thought for a while about joining a sports club to get fit. But then I thought seriously about it. In a pub, I can hold my own even if I have to hold my gut in; at work, I am the Senior Partner never mind my love-handles. But if I joined a sports club I would be relegating myself voluntarily, suicidally, to the new underclass of fat, bald tossers.

FAT BALD MAN IN GYM: Please, please, all I ask is a body like a Greek God! (*His arms, nose and dick drop off*)

So I just decided to start flossing my teeth instead.

I removed the floss and looked again at the result, like someone who has just squeezed a blackhead. Nas-ty. Think of all the years all this stuff had been lying

29

around unflossed, twixt gum and tooth, rotting away. Lumps of the stuff. I sniffed the floss. I sniffed my fingers and thumbs: the smell of whatever it is that lurks in those warm, dark little gaps had got onto my fingers and thumbs too by now. It was a hard, metal smell that went so far up the back of my nose it was almost a taste, not a smell. There was something of the sour-sweet whiff of a brewery about it, and something of the poison hit of burning diesel. But mainly it reminded me of something it could not, logically, remind me of, because I had never known it, and how can anything remind you of something you never knew? But all I know is that it smelled of rancid aluminium.

I looked up into my mirror without meaning to, and clocked my face like it was someone else's face. It was the sort of face you might see on a six-year-old kid busy prodding a dead rabbit that is saggy with maggots, or a half-awake building labourer scratching his arse through his dusty jeans and sniffing his hand without thinking. A mixture of abstract interest, dark satisfaction and instinctive disgust.

Not entirely unlike when you look in a mirror and see this lardy, unshaved, overnight face, a face already starting to get dragged down at the corners, not so much by time as just by gravity, and realise it is you.

I shower every morning, and shave twice a day, and wash my hair, what is left of it, every other day. Because I long ago realised: some lucky bastards have the secret (or the gene, or whatever) that makes them look good the morning after. Even into their forties, the more rumpled and crumpled and tangled they look, the more it makes everyone think: *Christ, the lucky bastard must have had a great time with the wild dancing gypsies last night, shit, if only I didn't have the house and the mortgage and the kids, I could be like that too.*

Not me.

Nope.

The most I could hope for, the most I had ever been able to hope for, even when I had all my hair, was to look roughly fit for human consumption. When I am shat, shaved and showered, I don't look toooo saaaad, in a boring English way. But the morning after, or even the afternoon after a long lunch, one day too long without washing the hair, one morning without shaving, and I know I look like I have just decanted myself out of some women-free-zone bedsit. I feel myself shambling about like some warning to younger men: *look out look out, this could be you, get your pension now and settle down, apply now or end up like this.*

I was going to floss my teeth every day now.

So I was flossing them this morning.

And as I flossed, I was, for no reason, half-watching this dog crossing the pedestrian bridge above and in front of me.

It was the kind of bridge that goes from nowhere to nowhere you want to go, sitting there, grey, cold, hard and rusting in the steam and the fumes and the February rain. And this dog, a big, old, mangy, wet, brown dog, lolloping arthritically across on its own. I sniffed the string again.

Then I noticed her watching me.

A moment ago there had been a horrible old Transit in the lane on my right (someone had written in the grease and shit: *please do not clean this is a stealth van*) but suddenly it had changed into this Golf cabriolet with a pretty woman in it, and the pretty woman was watching me as I flossed my teeth and sniffed my fingers.

31

She did not like what she saw; it was like I was something with too many legs and eyes to be socially acceptable. But it was so disgusting she was fascinated. It was as if she was sure something truly appalling was going to happen to me any minute now, and she didn't want to miss it.

Then she caught my gaze, mouthed *Jesus*, and shook her head and stared ahead at the queue before her. Then she thought what she could do and picked up her car-phone. It was so clear that she was doing it just to avoid thinking about me that she even blushed.

I woke up and stopped gawping at her, and took the string away from my nose and refocused my primate eyes on the interior of the car. I felt myself getting hot under the armpits already. A whole day of smelling ahead. It was horrible, I was stuck for God knew how long about seven feet away from an attractive person of the opposite sex who had objectively valid reasons for thinking I was a piece of slime.

I would have given five hundred right then and there for tinted windows. Now I could even smell that smell off my fingers when I had them resting on the steering wheel. I couldn't rest them in my lap or the stink would get into my clothes. But the woman would know why I had my hands on the wheel in the middle of a three-mile jam. If I tried to wipe them on the seat-bottom, like a kid wiping off snot, she would see that too. If I tried to dry the smell away by putting on the fan and holding my fingers in front of it, she would know just what was going on.

Which was (sorry it took so long) that moment in question. The moment it all started, remember? Chernobyl-time. The moment Deeny, my smarmy Irish accountant, called me up on the mobile.

Shocked? I even forgot to hold the earpiece a few inches away from my ear, to save my brain from frying. Never mind my brain, this was my whole *life* going up in smoke:

—What do you mean they want the lot?

—What do I mean? I mean the lot as in the lot. I mean cash books, ledgers, banking records, invoices, asset fucking statements. The whole shebang, Pete.

—You said it would be OK!

—I said it *should*.

—You said they never question annual summaries!

—I said they only examine 3 per cent. I have taken A1 care on this, Pete, I swear to God: our books are watertight consistent year on year. I'm not fucking stupid, I broke it all down, sound as a trout, there is no change this year, nothing that looks dodgy, I tell you they have no fucking reason at all to call us in. Unless.

—Unless?

—Ah no, it's too bizarre.

—Sean, are you telling me someone's shopped us?

—How the fuck could they, no-one knows, do they? Have you told anyone?

—Of course I bloody haven't.

—Not even Sarah?

—Sarah? No, what's the point, it would only upset her.

—Well look, Pete, I don't know what happened, but in the heel of the hunt we have two options: we present the full accounts, the real books, as they are . . .

—We can't do that! . . .

—. . . and we go for the Hansard Procedure.

—Hansard? As in Parliament?

—As in a legal cute-ery. They drag us into the Special Compliance Office and read us the Hansard Extract, and I mean read as in *read* out fucking loud.

—Lovely.

—As in not fucking very. They read; we crawl; we cough up; they settle. Legalised fucking bribery of the State, in other words. They only had twelve criminal prosecutions last year, all told: they don't want bods slammed up, they want the dough. If we're unlucky we get hit with a penalty, maybe up to double, but we'll get mitigation for full co-operation: maybe 40 per cent discount on the penalty. Job done, case closed, the revenue can't talk to the cops because of the old Official Secrets Act, so you just fold the business and no-one goes to the nice open prison.

—Sean, there's just one problem. We haven't got the money.

—So I do a runner back to the ould country, the County Officers kick your door in and the Collector distrains upon your goods and fucking chattels. I jest, Pete, I jest.

—Look, can't you say you just messed it up?

—Oh sure. Tell them that and we're into Fraudulent Accountsville.

—Shit. Can't I transfer everything to Sarah?

—Too late. Would've had to be when it still looked at least half-kosher. Try it now, and all we get is Sarah in the frame for conspiring to cheat and fucking defraud. We have to buy the bollixes off, Pete.

—How? I mean how much is it anyway? Shit, we must have siphoned off a hundred grand this year and last year.

—Um, more like three-fifty K over three years, Pete.

—Oh, is it? Oh shit. Plus a penalty? Oh. Oh well, that's it then. Christ almighty:- Irons and Jobson!

—What about them?

—Sean, it must have been them that shopped us!

—Slow down now, Pete. What good would it do

them, Pete? They're your partners, they're jointly and severally liable. Mind you, mind you. There's this new stuff on partners' liabilities just come out. Now, I wonder could they have cut their own deal with HM fucking Inspectors in Kensington 1 district? If they got wind, and got scared, and said it was just you doing the old defrauding? Yeah, yeah: I'd say if they shopped you they could get immunity all right. Then you get it in the neck personally and they could keep on.

—But they don't know about us.

—Says you.

—Well go and ask the Revenue. I mean, shit, we must have a right to know our bloody accuser.

—You jest. This is the fucking Revenue, Pete. They'll just snuggle their arses into their chairs and polish up their specs and grin and say: *'We have been made aware.'* Irons and Jobson, is it? Well, you'll just have to watch that brace of cunts yourself.

—Don't worry, I will. Shit, they never bloody asked too much when it came to payday. I'll kill the bastards.

—Don't go doing anything fucking stupid yet.

—Sean: when did I last do anything fucking stupid? Oh yes, I remember, it was about thirty-five years ago and I thought *hey, I know, how about trying being born?* Give me one good reason not to do something fucking stupid.

—Hey, Pete, I'm an accountant, not a fucking Jesuit. I jest. OK, OK, look, Pete, we need to meet, we need to take a position, look at the angles . . .

—We may as well take a position with our arses at a high angle in the air, because we are buggered anyway. Oh well. Bye, Sean.

—Pete! Hold on, Jesus, we have to fucking talk!

—Another time, Sean, another time.

And I put down the phone and turned it off.

I looked around the world again. Objectively, I knew I should have prepared for this moment. I mean, I could have worked out this was coming. I had known for years that anyone who looked at Deeny's annual estimates for more than thirty seconds would be liable to start looking very carefully indeed.

Cash-flow. It all started with cash-flow, late-paying invoices, that kind of thing. You know: you have a kosher working business that gets into trouble because you are doing *well*. The stuff is shifting fast, times are good on ye olde whelk-stall, so naturally you keep pumping in the cash up-front to make more of it to flog. And then some bastard gang of creditors says they want paying *right now*, and you show them your lovely full order-books and the blind sods still say *right now*. And then they start talking about applying to have you liquidated. So suddenly you are in the shit through no fault of your own. So what do you do? Take out interest-free loans from the Revenue is what you do. By which I mean: you just kind of not bother to tell the whole story to the big bad taxman. You kind of start overstating expenses, then claiming fictitious payments to suppliers, say for second-unit filming and audio re-dubs we never had to do, you know. Very habit-forming. Who doesn't want to give unto Caesar as little as bloody possible? Next thing you know, you have got so good at it that it stops becoming a temporary fiddle and starts becoming the actual meat of the day-job. And soon you start thinking that since it is *you* who is keeping the whole sodding shop afloat, you deserve the odd, unofficial, stress-related bonus without drawing undue attention to it in the accounts you present to your Partners.

And that was in the good days. When the bad days came, it was just a question of survival: I mean, why the hell should Sarah and me suffer just because some bastard mismanaged the economy?

But like I said, I suppose I always knew it couldn't last. There again, I know that smoking and boozing are shortening my life, but the fact that I know these things does not mean I do anything about them. Sometimes, the Truth is so big you can only live by blanking it out. Until one day it goes critical and whacks you in the gob and guts you clean.

I sat on the M25, filleted.

There was now a space of thirty feet ahead of me and the Granada behind had been sounding its horn for twenty seconds. A man's face looked out of its window and roared something generally incomprehensible but clearly including the words *dozy fucker*, addressed to yours truly. I returned to earth, zapped down my own window and roared back: OH, TRAGEDY! MR WANK-STAIN IS GOING TO BE THIRTY FOOT LATE FOR WORK. WELL JUST FUCK YOU, MR FUCKING WANKSTAIN!

Talk about the feelgood factor. But then, having rolled forward the thirty feet, I found myself next to the woman in the cabriolet again, and caught her eye again. So much for feeling good.

I felt an overwhelming desire for a drink, which shocked me, because I never drink in the morning. I hardly ever even drink at lunchtime. My little sop to morality: well, you have to do *something*. Not that I will ever be a candidate for Alcoholics Anonymous. I mean what's the point? People don't despair because of drink, it's the other way around. Despair Anonymous: now *that* would be something I could join. But then, who couldn't?

LONELY?
DESPERATE?
SUICIDAL?
Welcome to the Third Millennium.

At which point a big fist whacked through the still-open window and into my right ear.

—You calling me a wank-strain, mate?

The bloke from the car behind. The pot-bellied, stink-breathed man from the car behind.

He had thought about it carefully and let his blood cook slowly, and now here he was at last. This was no unthinking teenage reaction: this was an adult bull-male who positively wanted a fight.

—Right, I shouted, and snapped my seatbelt off. But as I got out of the car (I wilted slightly as the windblown drizzle hit me, like a slug nosing into salt), I was thinking that this was impossible, this did not happen to me any more.

Bizarrely, I found myself blipping the car shut without thinking about it; I already had the key-ring out: I saw my own hand fire the signal, as if it was a hand controlled by some distant autopilot; I heard the car bleep and the door-locks whizz and clunk smoothly, in their oiled, Volvo way.

Oiled locks.

From somewhere way down Memory Lane a voice floated into my ears, a high tenor voice, so high it was not just unmanly but almost inhuman; not only the pitch was artificial, but the pronunciation too, a high tenor singing in music-lesson English, on just one floating note:

Turn the key softly in the oiled wards
And close the shuttered casket of my soul

I was so busy wondering where the hell this memory had escaped from, that I turned without thinking, and Mr Wankstain hit me again before I was halfway ready.

—Right then, I shouted again.

How long since I had been hit? Christ, I was a grown man, I was thirty-five and married and balding and fattening and flossing and piling up symptoms of inevitable physical decay. I had a Volvo, a reproachfully virgin built-in child-seat, a bankrupt firm and a house I had never liked. And I was taking sperm tests to see if I was now officially a biological dead end. It was years, ten years, twelve, since anyone had actually hit me, I had completely forgotten what it was like to be hit.

It stung, that is what it was like.

It made my eyes water.

So I hit him back.

It was years since I did that, too. It was pathetic, like when you try to serve at tennis with your left hand. I got no power in it at all; the wafting notes of the unearthly tenor were still flowing round my muscles. Surprising, how hard even a fat red face actually is.

Even so, Mr Wankstain took a step back. It had got real now. Even that useless pad at his gob had made it an authentic, two-way fight. He had to take stock a moment, calculate damage and odds. And I was doing the same, of course: I realised that though he was taller than me and no older, he was fatter, and maybe more red in the face, and he was wearing a shirt and tie too. His trousers were suit-trousers, like mine. There were none of the tell-tale signs of hardness about him: no tattoos creeping out from his collar, no heavy rings, no anecdotes of closing-time violence written in scars or absent teeth. A virgin nose and a plump, soft jawline.

No reason, in short, that I could not beat him no sweat. Except I didn't want a fight and he did.

Why? Maybe he was fucking his secretary and his wife had just found out? Maybe he had just been told he was bust? Maybe he had just failed a sperm-test? Or maybe he had just turned round once too often and seen how fast Memory Lane was fading away.

He watched me, then jabbed with his left, twice, three times, harder each time. The first was no more than a ranger, the second a test on my readiness, but the third one was halfway to being a real, kosher, straight-arm punch; there was even some shoulder behind it. It snapped my head back a fraction and bust my mouth slightly. I could see the sadistic joy coming up in his eyes and drawing back his lips. This was ideal: I had hit back, so this was not just bullying, this was just what he had ordered, the fight he had probably been dreaming of for years, a genuine scrap with someone about his own size and age – but one where he was booked to win. Where he knew for certain he was going to hit me harder and more often than I was going to hit him. I could taste the sweet, salty blood building up in my mouth and welling out over my bottom lip; I could see his high-gravity body winding up, slowly but surely, for a real, big, right-hand punch at last; I could see in his eyes that Christmas had come early for Mr Wank-stain.

Except that then, without meaning to, I found my brain reset and rebooted at nineteen or thereabouts, on some terrace somewhere. The world cleared, I felt the hair rise on the back of my neck and my busted lip draw back, showing teeth. Suddenly, it was all there again: long-forgotten nerve-endings snaked out like explosive harpoons on steel cables, they impacted in volleys into lost muscles and strange, dark folds of my brain. I was dancing again in a hard, loud, post-match club: it was Fuck Or Fight time, Saturday night, 1980 or thereabouts; Oliver's Army were on their way again and the memory-tag video showed uncollected rubbish piling high somewhere in pre-yuppie Islington. White riot time again.

So I did what I used to do, my party trick when necessity required one in those days. I took a step back and spread my arms, like an Italian full-back who has just poleaxed someone and been given the red card: I looked up at the sky and shouted: REFEREE! WHAT DID I DO? BIG REF, ARE YOU BLIND? and, just like they always used to do in the old days, Mr Wankstain naturally paused for that vital half-blink, wondering if he had accidentally picked on a psycho axeman in civvies.

And then it was just physical memory that drove me, that amazing, engraved, embedded knowledge that lets pianists hit the notes faster than neurons can travel and tennis-players make returns no chip could calculate. I arched my spine and clenched my arse and dropped my pelvis a bit so the strength was coming up from my thighs; I radar-locked on to the inside of the back of his skull for total follow-through; and I bounced up strutting and loafed Mr Wankstain right between the eyes.

As he went down, I was already cooling off and thinking *Fuck, that's me up in court*, so I turned to the woman who had seen me flossing and sniffing and shouted at her, through her window:

—You saw that, he started it! You are my witness. Three times he hit me before I hit him back, yeah? OK? If it comes to court I'll need you.

I was about to grin at her, like a van-driver.

And then Mr Wankstain tackled me round the waist.

41

This was serious. We were not nineteen any more, for Christ's sake. And when you are not nineteen any more and you enter GBH city by introducing loafing into the discussion and then the other bloke comes back at you despite, it is time for you both to check the small print on your health insurance.

So I grabbed his left leg with my right hand and half-lifted it while he tried to charge me down. He battered away at my ribs, but at close range and hence without any real leverage; I pummelled him wastefully on his fat-padded back with my hopeless left. Blood was pouring out of his face and splashing around on my shirt: Christ, I hope the bastard hasn't got AIDS, we never had to worry about that in the old days when fucking or fighting. I started to lose my balance.

Shit a brick! The sperm-test flask was still in my pocket!

If it got bust, bang went my guilt-free Merchant Bank; and with no safety-net and no excuse, I would have to do without my little fix of fun with Charlie, in case it became more than fun. No way. No fucking way, mate.

The thought injected me with such fury it almost scared me; now I knew what a cheated junky must feel like. Suddenly, this fight was for real. I felt my blood go dark. I let go his leg deliberately and fell back quicker than he was going; I jerked us round at the last possible moment, almost too late. Great timing. I felt a wave of pride in my old body as he impacted under me and I landed smack on top of him.

He blinked, his stuffing well knocked out, and I saw fear in his eyes. For just a second, it was my turn to show my death-teeth; I drew my fist back to smash him right in the gob. But then I used my free right to pat my pocket instead: the relief that the test-tube was still intact slackened my muscles, and he almost managed to wriggle free. I hastily retrieved the position, and pushed him back down flat on the wet tarmac; I grabbed his collar with my left, and his left wrist with my right and just held on tight to keep him as close in as possible, so that he couldn't do any real damage, unless the bastard was your actual lump-hammer job, a nose-biting ex-prop forward or something.

We wallowed there, sweating, panting in each other's ears; too fat, too deskbound and far too near to forty for this kind of thing. Neither of us had it any more, the explosive power to wrench free or finish the job, or maybe just not the unconditional willpower. We were a big blob of harmless flab flailing about on a wet M-way. Any minute now, I knew I was going to start laughing.

But soon enough, a brave crowd of lads in suits had hopped out of their cars. They were delighted to have something else to do except sit in the jam flossing their teeth or thinking about wanking or whatever it was they did to kill the gridlocked time that was killing them. Me and Mr Wankstain were picked up and pulled heroically apart. We checked ourselves and found that despite the impressive blood from his nose and my lip, nothing hospitalisable had happened to either of us.

We scraped our credit-cards and car-keys off the road. Our eyes met for a second as we both saw the half-dozen pound coins lying around, but we both sniffed contemptuously, as if by mental arrangement, and left them there. We shook off our saviours roughly, as the script demanded, and got back into our cars, leaving this section of the M25 a far happier place than we had found it.

I knew Mr Wankstain knew I would tell everyone at work about this guy who I had loafed and *still came back for more*, and I knew he knew I knew that he would tell everyone at work how he had hit this bloke three times and all that happened was *he just stood and loafed me so that was when it really started.*

I had the insane desire to invite Mr Wankstain for a drink.

Why was I suddenly thinking about drink for Christ's sake? After all, like I said, I never ever drink until lunchtime. And hardly even then.

I got back into my car and the locks whizzed shut. I remembered that the last time I heard that sound I had thought of some poem; I tried to recall it, but it flitted away from me, like a fish in dark water. I laughed because of that stuff about the Big Ref: I had not thought about that for years and years.

I saw the old dog hobbling arthritically down the last steps of the grey bridge above me and disappearing into the brown, damp grass. I rubbed my face where Mr Wankstain had hit me and smelled my fingers by accident, and that reminded me about fuckface Deeny and the bastard taxman.

As I turned the ignition on, the old music started up again together with the engine, because the player was still switched on. I caught sight of the sign again, NO ENTRANCE TO MEMORY LANE, and wondered how the hell I going to tell Sarah it was all over.

(cos there) Ain't no entrance (twang)
to Memory Lane
(and) There ain't no roof can stop
That burning rain.

I felt a dark, mad, inexplicable wave of delight at the thought of telling her it was all finished, that our days of being well-off were done; that the statistics had just swallowed us up.

And then I remembered that we had just agreed that

44

if Sarah did not get pregnant by Easter, we were going for IVF or whatever. At £3,000 a no-guarantee shot.

So that was gone too. Finished. All gone.

Daddy can't mend.

Daddy will not be a Daddy.

Unbelievably, tears were coming into my eyes. It was not right, not fair, how had it come to this? How had I become this? Christ, where were the sweet dreams gone?

I grabbed my own face and made myself stop. I made myself say: *No Entry*. I ordered the central locks on my mind to whizz shut. I made myself see:

> Memory Lane is lined in lead, it is where we
> bury our dreams thirty feet down in concrete
> tombs. Turn the key softly in the oiled wards.
> Memory Lane is Chernobyl: the place you
> cannot enter, and live.

They were hooting behind me again now. I went to move off. For one terrifying, sickening half-second I could not remember how to put a car into gear. I looked down and saw my own hand hovering feebly over the gearstick. It seemed an awfully long way from my body.

I don't usually smoke until lunchtime, either.

2. In and Out

Gerry Shepperd was just kissing his wife Melissa and his three children goodbye on the steps of his house in Hunter's Rise when he heard the phone ring inside, in the living room, and he knew it would be them calling. Melissa half-turned to get it, but Gerry held her back:

—If it's work, tell them to call on the mobile, honey, I'm already on my way. Bye now you guys. Be good!

—Bye! all four chorused as they waved, in those English accents which Gerry could never hear without a curious mixture of emotions: love; a pride which he knew to be absurdly typecast; and the frisson of distance which any parent must feel when his children do not speak as he does, a sort of pre-echo of the time that will one day come, the day he would have to admit they were not his at all, but their own, with lives that would be unknown to him long before the day of the real, final parting.

But chiefly just love.

A protective love too, the kind of love that made him mutter to himself, as he strode quickly to the car:

—And tell them never to call me at home.

Them.

He even screeched the Volvo's tyres slightly as he bumped out of the little drive. He grimaced in embarrassment as he waved his goodbye in the mirror: he wanted to be right out of sight of the house before *they* called his mobile, as if the mere digital signals could somehow infect the place.

Gerry Shepperd did not like some of what he did.

Not being moneyed, he had had to take out vertigo-inducing loans to cover the fees for law-school at Fordham. As a result, he had long ago got involved in certain activities (as he called them even to himself) which were not entirely to his natural taste. He was no longer directly obliged to do these things, because the loans had finally been paid off some three years ago (oh day of days!), but the temptation to make really quite substantial sums of money, in addition to his already handsome day-job salary, for very little work, was still constantly being placed in his way. The justification of having to provide for his wife and three kids was more than enough to help him give in.

He was determined, however, that no shadow of his Other Life (a life which was not entirely without real and present dangers) should ever come home to knock at his family's door. He guarded his home life as if it were a small patch of virgin innocence.

Not that Melissa was innocent in the accepted sense: she was no more innocent about sex, for example, than any woman can be who religiously takes in the articles in *Elle* and *Cosmo* and, indeed, pursues The Perfect Orgasm conscientiously in practice as well as theory. Three kids had been unable to make an impact on Melissa's heavily worked-out Pelvic Floor Muscles, and Gerry looked forward immensely to each new demonstration of their unimpeached condition. Melissa was not innocent about her family's health, either: each of the kids had been stuffed full of organic baby foods from the earliest possible age, and she hunted down any possibility of vitamin deficiency in the family diet. As far as agribusiness, food additives, water companies, nitrous oxide levels, nuclear lobbies and the chemical industry went, she was anything but innocent.

47

She considered them capable of all and any evils; she was practically a Maoist where they were concerned.

Not innocent, but hopeful: Gerry Shepperd, London City lawyer (specialisation: European Trade Laws) modelled himself partly on The Summer of 68 (which he was too young by some ten years to have experienced) and partly on the Battling Bastards of Bastogne (one of whom had been his grandfather). He was a Militant Liberal, who was liable to react to any anti-liberal proposal with the same answer his grandfather's C.O. had given the surrounding S.S. when called upon to surrender.

And yet, and yet.

The trouble was, he was losing his faith.

Hence his protective love for Melissa: Melissa still believed. Gerry wanted to believe in certain things: decency, honesty, fair play, plain dealing and, well, shit, life, liberty and the pursuit of happiness. Whereas Melissa did believe in them. Melissa still believed, like she believed Monday comes before Tuesday, that in the end the world is built to take into account the needs of mankind, that somehow, it is all working out for the best.

Which was why, when they called him on the car-phone, Gerry almost snapped:

—I asked you never to call me at home.

—OK, OK, sorry Gerry. But there is a reason.

—A good one?

—Are there any others? You better come to the In-and-Out tonight.

—Tonight?

—Yeah. Hey: I thought you'd be dying to see Swedish Eve's tits again.

—Ha ha, sighed Gerry, and put the mobile back

down behind his gear-stick (it still gave him a ridiculous kick of exotic pride to know that he was driving with a clutch and gear-stick).

But he knew damn well that his sigh was only half-real. Because the temptations of his Other Life were not merely financial: Gerry was more and more having to admit that he actually looked forward to these brief excursions into a world far removed from Hunter's Rise.

Maybe it was just because he needed just the occasional break from his offspring? Doesn't any man need, now and then, a decent evening among his fellow men? Or maybe he was actually changing, maybe (he confessed the possibility) his objections to *them* were actually growing less. Was it old age and loss of purity, the death of his youthful dreams? Or was it a coming to his senses? When we claim to be objective, is it just tiredness, really, just us sighing with relief at finding something to hook ourselves on to? Or is what we call passionate commitment just the overheated need of youth to find, and give, unconditional devotion?

Maybe, when all was said and done, it was simply because Gerry Shepperd did particularly like the In-and-Out club.

3. The Morality of Wanking

At about 3 a.m. on that last Sunday, as I creaked and stumped in the leathers around the empty office, just checking that behind the filing cabinet really was the best place to wait, I was thinking: if only we had clearer vision, if only we could look at all the little things that happen to us, as they happen, and see which of them carry the seeds of our future. And since our future is always made by our collisions with other people, I suppose that means: if only we could see other people more clearly.

Sometimes you get a quick flash of insight: the first time I met Masha, when she looked round at me from the front of the big black Merc, I felt the wires of my fate being pulled; and I have this silent shot in my head of the first time I ever saw Sarah, though nothing happened between us for years afterwards. But mostly we just veer about in a short-sighted fog, with the strange, big shapes of our possible lives looming suddenly up unseen, greeting briefly and then fading away again. And before we know it, we are out in the middle of a river that seems as big as a sea, a thousand miles from any star we recognise. Like blindfolded prisoners of ourselves, we struggle to get our bearings by recounting the movements that got us here.

Like me telling Charmaine that morning.

*

Well, trying to.

I have never been very good with secrets. Secrets that only *I* know remind me of when I lived in crappy bedsits. No matter how small the room was, I did not seem able to fill it. I would like to be different: I would like to be able to fill a big old house with just me and my secrets; I would love to be able to stuff a mansion with nothing but me and the aura of my quiet, strong life. In my dreams I see myself sitting at a pub-table and laying down the law with slow-talking strength, lit up with the internal power of my own portable conviction and my big, secret story.

In other words, I would like to be a Movie Hero (twang twang). Very original.

Anyway, me being me and things being what they are, I ended up entering BIZVID (my firm), having nipped up Charing Cross Road to get a new blood-free shirt and tie, with the sensation that my head was going to explode unless I could tell someone what Deeny had said.

I shoved in the street-door past the heaps of junk mail and immediately everything had that funny look about it, you know, like when you have decided to leave a house and the For Sale sign is up outside what was once your home: a sudden cold distance that verges on hostility.

Funny. I had devoted seven years to BIZVID. No, eight. Over a tenth of my rationed breathing-time. More like a sixth of my actual time in play (as a male, you don't get your first real kick of the ball till about twenty-one). I never meant to. It was just that Sarah is a teacher, you see, and back when we were a new number and I was looking for a new job, I was listening to all her friends moaning about this then-new crapology called Business Studies that was suddenly everywhere. They all knew that in twenty years it would sound as naff as sociology does now, but they had no choice. Well, when I heard them, I had to stop mid-pint and rush to the pub lav, because I got this big adrenalin

51

hit that whispered: *alert alert market opportunity!* If I made Business Studies videos, they would all get their Heads to buy them, because the school could look sexy and modern without having to pay someone to actually *teach* this shit. It looked like money for old rope. And it was, in a way. I mean, getting businessmen and suchlike to appear free on BIZVID videos was easy because no-one can resist the thought that their lives are so important they are worth filming. (This is the photo-age: no-one really believes anything until they see the prints. Weddings are just photo-opportunities nowadays; births are going the same way: at the moments we should feel most alive, we are half-thinking *Hey, these'll be nice pics!* Funerals are the last video-free zone, the last-ditch fortress of unfilmed emotion. The day we start videoing our funerals will be the day the Big Ref should blow the whistle.) So yeah, it was easy money. A great way to tide us over until the Real Thing started. Except you kind of forget exactly where this great tide was supposed to be taking you. You take your eyes off the sails for just a month or three, and suddenly you are somewhere you never meant to get; this vessel, that was supposed to be ferrying you into your big new world, has become a wallowing hulk that takes your whole life just to keep it afloat. Seven sodding years. Eight. Funny, in a way.

This weird sense of distance from what had been my own life for so long got stronger as I climbed the linoed stairs that wound around the old-fashioned see-through caged lift (step aerobics for free), up to the fourth floor. I found myself looking round each corner as I got to it, as if someone or something might be waiting for me with a lead pipe. Well, after all, it was true: *someone here was stitching me up!*

I passed our little kitchen on my right and nipped

quickly past the door to the editing suite, in case young Harold grabbed me and made me watch six TVs all pumping out some crap interview with a businessman. I now stood in front of the once-trendy BIZVID logo that adorns our main office door. It is late-eighties estate-agent's purple and seriously in need of a respray. I eyed the office through the wire mesh of the little window, then kicked open the door and stepped quickly through, as if I might somehow catch whoever it was red-handed.

No-one did any more than look up, except Charmaine, who waved hello with both her hands, like someone guiding a plane in to land. I did a miniature version of the same greeting back before wondering how ridiculous it must look. I said hello to Irons, who was poring over his shooting-schedules at his desk (much good it would do him); I waved good morning to Jobson, who was shouting at some actor's agent down the phone (waste of air, Jobbo). They looked, in some weird way, just a little bit smaller than usual.

I watched their faces very carefully for any sign of guilt or hidden, embedded file-commands, but all I saw in their eyes was a vague resentment at me being late yet again and playing the Senior Partner publicly. I thought of ordering them both outside into the corridor and telling them everything: maybe one of them would let slip a body-language giveaway, or just break down. Then perhaps I could unite with the other one and sort them out. But what if it was both of them? Maybe they really had found out about the books and had cut a deal with the Revenue? Or might they have some secret customer up their sleeves? Were they trying to coup me out of my own firm so they could take over? Or have me done for evasion and then sue me personally to try and claw back their collapsed investments?

All the more reason to act normal: sit tight, watch for enemy action, take up a position, be the one to jump first. So I turned, as normal, to look at the wipe-clean board on which is permanently printed: ORDERS TODAY and ORDERS THIS WEEK. Today was £1,905, this week was £4,309. About average.

I pondered the board while trying to send out my feelers into the office behind me to work out what was going on. I felt everything, never mind everyone, was a potential enemy: maybe the heaps of cardboard boxes and black plastic bins that clutter the office were creeping up behind me right now? The office seemed thick with mysteries. I needed to talk to someone to get back my control; I needed to make the secret unsecret to stop it growing and splitting my head like a flowerpot; I needed an ally, for Christ's sake. I did not know who my foe was, all the more reason to start lining up my friends.

And so since half my available brain-RAM was already dedicated to pondering Charmaine anyway, it was only natural to tell her.

Well, try to.

Big mistake.

I grabbed a file from off the desk in front of Charmaine and told her quietly that she had to come out into the corridor with me, right now. I went out ahead of her and, again bouncing past the door to the editing suite, sneaked through the kitchen door. I stood there and waved her over to me when she appeared in the little mesh window, behind the door, beyond the lift-cage.

She looked across at me through all the wires and cables.

I could see that I had played it badly. I had let the atmosphere of secrets and betrayals in my brain colour my voice. But Charmaine had no idea what was going on in my head, so she jumped to the natural conclusion. She thought I was going to do something very saaad and uncool. She probably thought I was going to tell her all about how I loved my wife. Or maybe she thought I was just going to grab her clumsily, or start quivering at her pathetically. I waved again, as she stood undecided in the office door.

I won: she looked quickly back into the office, then she bit her lip, opened the door, slipped out and shut the door behind her, all without taking her eyes off mine once. She hesitated one last second, her hand still on the door-handle, but then she gave in visibly: she focused on the ground about five feet in front of her, folded her arms and came towards me. She walked head-down past the editing suite and stood in front of me, in the door to the kitchen, weight balanced on one hip, not making proper eye-contact. She looked side-ways, sort of accusingly at me, like I had broken the rules of the game, not played fair.

I dragged her into the kitchen by the arm. She actually looked round openly now, as if she would have liked someone to appear and see us and save her. But there was no-one there, so she came anyway, looking past me as she did so. I let her squeeze past me in the door; I shrank myself back and pulled in my belly, but her right hip still brushed strongly against my thigh. For a moment I nearly forgot what I was doing here. I shut the door and turned inside to look at her.

She was drawing patterns with the slop-water on the sink draining-board, looking very pissed off. No, not pissed off. Disappointed, more like.

—Charlie, I said unpantingly, without moving any closer, and held up my hands like I was surrendering.

She looked up at me, with maybe the light just coming back in her eyes.

I said *Look Charlie*, and she frowned and said *What?* and I said *Look, I have to tell you something.* And she said *Oh yeah?* and I said *Look* (again) *Don't say a word to anyone OK?* and she said *OK* and frowned again. Her frown was very nice, the way it often is on people not used to frowning. I looked around and said *OK: look we're in big trouble, Charlie.* She breathed a sigh of relief and changed her weight over to the hand that had been drawing waterworld maps on the worktop. She leaned over on it and frown disappeared. It disappeared completely, leaving no lines.

She shook her hair out and grinned and said *So we're in trouble are we Pete?* I nodded: *Big trouble,* I said. *Whew,* she said, *Does Sarah, like, suspect?*

—Suspect what? I asked, blankly.

Believe it or not, it was an honest mistake. For a second. For less. And then, of course, I clocked what was going on, being soooo very sharp. Except I let it keep going on. You know, in that way you just let something happen when, sneakily, it is maybe just what you wanted to happen anyway.

—Right, she said, – I mean, like, nothing's happened, has it? Not really.

She put her head on one side and checked the door over my left shoulder, then took a step up and stood in front of me, her hands held together behind her back, her weight now equally balanced on both feet: *So how come we're in trouble, then, Pete? Am I trouble?* I could smell her hairspray and her toothpaste. She had flecks of brown in her blue eyes, I had never noticed before.

I was not sure any more if I was trying to tell her my

big true secret or a lying little story; I could no longer work out whether anything was really wrong with my life, apart from wanting Charmaine desperately. I looked down at her lips and the need to kiss her was like a strong, fast undertow. Somewhere in the cellars of my head the New Music started up softly. I raised my eyes from her lips and looked into her eyes and said *Well, depends what you call trouble, Charlie* and she said *Like, say, someone caught us doing this?* and she leaned forward, rose up on her toes and flicked her tongue round my lip quickly before settling back on her heels.

Her face stayed about five inches from mine. *That would be one kind of trouble* I said, and I gently put out my right hand and pressed it slowly onto her left breast, looking at her eyes all the time. *No trouble*, she said, and she grabbed my dick through my trousers with her left and kept on looking me back in the eye. I swallowed and said *What about Trevor?* and she said *You're the one that's married*, and I said, I just managed to say, *I don't care*, and she said *So why should I, like?*

Then she suddenly french-kissed me for exactly two seconds and took my hand off her breast and just pressed it for half that long up between her legs, so I could feel her mound through her skirt and knickers. Then she laughed, said *Earth calling Peter Thompson come in please*, and whipped out of the room before I hardly knew she was going.

I looked round out of the door and saw her going round the landing, laughing silently and shaking her head to herself so her big hair flapped. Just as she was almost through the door into the main office, she looked back at me through the lift-cage and just kind of raised her eyebrows. Then the lift-cables dropped down between us like uncoiling snakes; the car slid down, blacking her out, and when it had gone, the door to the office was shut again and she was inside. And I was left standing in the door of the little office kitchen, watching the taut metal cables shivering and wondering what the hell I was doing.

I leaned against the wall: it felt cool and hard on the back of my head.

So much for the truth.

So now I knew damn well I was going to cheat on Sarah, it was now just a question of when, not if. And after all that, I still had my secret flying about inside me, banging on the walls of my head, trying to get out of my mouth and share itself around a bit before it blew me apart.

I also had an erection, naturally.

—Um, Peter, would you come and check out this footage of Jonathan Aitken?
—Busy, Harold, busy.
—Oh, rightyo.
And his head zipped back into the editing suite.

I stood for a second with one hand in my pocket to hold my erection down and the other hand on my forehead to hold my head together. I fled to the shared lavs on the floor below; there, I splashed H-2-0 coolant onto my face and temples, before my control-rods gave out, while avoiding looking in the mirror.

I decided I had better do my anti-stress relaxations. So I locked myself in the cubicle, noisily raised the lid and messed about with my trousers, like I was taking them down, in case anyone was about, and then silently shut the lid again (turn the key softly) so I could sit on it and just relax a minute, two, three, four, five six, that's better, deep breaths, two three four, shake out those shoulders Petey Baby.

Ok, so I was talking to myself, which is crackers. But it was not like it was me talking to me. I am too clever for that: when I am relaxing, I summon up my in-house Lifestyle Advisor (who has a Californian accent, or at any rate what I think is a Californian accent) and who is thus obviously not me (since I have an ordinary English accent, or at least what I think is one).

My Lifestyle Advisor materialised on command, in my virtual world, in his virtual tracksuit and ridiculous baseball cap:

> OK Pete, let's try that Re-lax Program again: In two three four and hold two and out two three four. Good. That's it Pete. Let those little synapses loosen up there, feel them going! Ping ping ping! And let your back go, let it go Pete! Feel all your spines loosen up

(my Lifestyle Advisor thinks vertebrae are called spines)

> and hang down there, elbows on your knees, Pete, and head hanging low, heh heh, like you were trying to suck your own dick, rest that poor old heart, Pete, and bounce, and bounce, hang down, hang out! And in two three four. Feel the blood run to the head! Red blood! Oxygen, Pete! Gol-den Energy! Let-that-big-old-primate-brain-breathe! Energy going to the brain, to the head. To those hair-roots, Pete! Let them breathe. Think: growth. And in two three four. And now straighten up slowly. Slowly, Pete: spine by spine by spine ... Ease that shattered casket, turn that key

slowly, oil those wards (twang twang twang)
spine by spine by spine (2, 3, . . .)

(Cos there) Ain't no entrance (twang)
　To Memory Lane (twang twang twang-ang-ang)
(And) Stress is simply lack
　Of Oxygane

So now I was relaxed.

Except the trouble with having an erection – especially one caused not by some safely insulated fantasy
but by an unsafe, real woman having just really
grabbed your dick and stuffed your hand between her
real unsafe legs – is that as soon as you relax, the
erection takes over automatically. The erection is now
your default setting. It is the low, growling note you
hear when the white noise and the fuzz and all the high
jangling trebles of everyday life are edited out by your
relaxation programme. In the quiet dark of your
steadied eyes, the little silvery rainbows start to appear
at the edges of things, and the world goes 3-D, like it
looks in the flat green light underneath black storm-
clouds. Your eyes narrow and your throat goes dry and
all those nerves that you know so well, but can never
really prepare for, start to fire their tiny lasers about in
your brain.

I stood up bravely to go, but a strange, fateful weight
in my suit-pocket suddenly reminded me that I still had
the sample-bottle in there.

I mean, shit, why not?

Surely this was the time, before I saw Charlie again.
A marriage-saver, if ever there was one. Hey, but no
need to hurry things. OK, so let's say that business in
the kitchen has got things going a bit. Good so far. But
why not take my time and enjoy it. It would be far more

like real sex, wouldn't it? I mean, when Sarah and I have sex it is not just wham bam thank-you ma'am, though of course, I would sometimes like it to be. It is Making Love. So if I have a super-speed, just-for-duty wrist-job, that could very well not *genuinely* imitate the *kind* of, or the *amount* of, sperms that come out when I am making love with Sarah. So the test result could be all to cock (ha ha) and a waste of time, wouldn't it? I mean, who knows? So really, in order to simulate the *reality*, in order to give the lab a *truly representative* sperm-sample, I should enjoy myself.

Yes, I really *ought* to enjoy it.

So what will it be: Fantasy or Memory?

There are (as there are for everything) two opposing schools of thought (I thought, as I sprang my dick out, gobbed on my palm, and began to stroke) concerning the morality of wanking.

School one says: it is morally preferable to toss yourself off to *fantasies* since this means you are drawing a clear and sane line between the real world (where you are nice and normal and tip your soup-plate away from you) and the virtual world (where you wank).

School two says: it is morally better to polish your flute to your *memories* since at least you did really do those things once, even if you are not able (for whatever reason) to do them right now, so you still have your feet on the ground, even when your trousers are round your ankles.

The first school says that self-abuse is merely a biologically inevitable piece of physical business, which should be best carried out without connection to your normal life. The second school says that onanism leaks into your whole life, and should therefore be tied down to reality in case you start to confuse the virtual and the real.

The first school says that people who wank to memories are sad, broken individuals.

The second replies that people who wank to fantasies always were.

Both schools of thought agree on one thing only: that wanking is saaad.

The only animals that wank are almost any animals that are kept locked in zoo-cages: the physical contortions are (I gather) strange to behold except in apes, our cousins in this aspect too. Lions, for example, use their hind legs. Bizarre. But that is the point: being in a cage is bizarre. Like being in an office in the twentieth century. Or, worse: maybe like being a human full stop. If there is one thing you can say with certainty about the world it is: show me a man, and I will show you a man who has wanked, and will wank. A useful thing to recall when watching a bouffant demagogue reading from his autocue.

Of course it would be better if Homo sapiens as a species spent their whole time chasing each other about, proposing, flirting, rejecting, hinting, wooing, accepting and at last shagging happily, instead of bloody wanking. Both schools of thought agree that wanking is best not done at all. Then again, the same goes for getting old, boring, fat, bald and dead: best not. But it happens, and it happens to everybody, and all we are left with is longing and remembrance.

Anyway, today memory won out: the big oiled gates rolled slowly backwards, the screen flickered its countdown and I positioned the sperm-sample bottle carefully upon the end of my dick, closed my eyes and leaned back dutifully to enjoy:

MEMORY LANE FILMED ENTERTAINMENT presents:
Last Tube from Harrow Weald (18 and then some)
We travel through a deserted, rattling tube train, it is pitch-dark outside, with wind and rain. We go through empty carriage after empty carriage. Just when it looks like the train is going to go on for ever, we pass something just in shot on the right. Something colourful. Someone. We reverse and look back: It is SARAH THOMPSON (neé, and at this time still, HASTINGS) herself, with her black jeans down round her calf-high, string-up goatskin boots, hips shoved forward onto the edge of the seat, arms back and spread out along the top of the backrest. And in between her legs half-kneels, half-lies, half on the floor and half on the seat in what, under any other circumstances, would be a distinctly uncomfortable position, none other than YOUNG PETE. He looks around quickly and then tweaks her knickers aside so he can get properly at her redhead muff, so he can lick in long strokes that start half inside her and push up and bump nicely over her clitoris, or what he thinks (not being a medical student) is probably her clitoris, but she says: *No, No.* With irritation.

Irritation?

Young Pete's erection fades ever so slightly, he blinks and looks up, away from the short, hard, red hairs (rather a relief, actually, he is going cross-eyed and his jaw is aching slightly) and up to her eyes. And she says *Not like that*. And her eyes say: *Well then?* so he

63

scrambles to his knees as elegantly as possible, manfully drags her knickers right down to join her jeans (she helpfully lifts her arse while unbuttoning his jeans) and then lets her roughly tug his mouth onto hers, to sustain the illusion of ravishment. She takes his dick in one hand, shifts her buttocks even further forward, her weight is on the small of her back now and on her strong legs, she slides him easily into herself and he comes almost immediately; but then so does she, it is him coming that makes her come, the actual proof she is doing this.

Two minutes later they sit back next to each other, gasping and grinning, like people just back from the verge of death by tickling, holding hands.

Leaving me, in saaad reality, holding nothing but my deflating prick, sitting on the closed lav seat and thinking, with that spacewalk coldness that comes after you do:

What does it mean when you find you can no longer believe that it really was like that once? When memories sound like fantasies to the person that did them? Jesus, how did it come to this?

and

Shite and onions, I have somehow created a vacuum that has stuck the tube to the end of my dick! Omigod, what if . . . ? Would they have to . . . ? A vacuum can be pretty strong, can't it? Could I fit the lot down my trousers and stagger to the out-patients? Ah, thank God . . .

and

Hey, good shot, Petey Baby, right up the spout and into the

64

bottle. Not a splash on the outside of the glass! Hmmm. Looks a good few cubic cm to me. Must be millions of the little things in that. Millions of me.

THE BIG REF: And thy seed shall be numberless as the stars of the desert.
ME: OK Ref, so how about *just one* makes it to the egg next time?

Then I pocketed the bloodwarm flask, bounced down the stairs, battered my way through the doors, and scuttled up to the Seven Dials, hoping not to get squashed while crossing the road with this thing in my pocket, I mean, what would people think? That I had come at the moment of impact? I drove hooting away through the traffic up towards University College Hospital.

It was not traffic, it was a plot. Everything in my way was either a taxi picking up a fare, or the kind of cretin who *deliberately* stops on orange. Or a bloody one-man bus, I mean: what maniac ever thought about putting one-man buses in London? They should have an extra thousand Routemasters with conductors on the roads, tomorrow, today, everyone knows that. They should just *make* London Transport do it, whatever the cost, they should just ... Come on, come on!

I could feel it. Millions of me were drying up. The genetic potential to populate whole galaxies in a few generations was screaming in tiny, ancient voices. Entire milky ways of my DNA were being wiped out. In my M&S suit-pocket, Death was triumphant: the stored-up experience of four hundred million years of Life was being annihilated. And all because they don't dare impose a rational bloody transport policy.

I must be nuts! I should have bloody hoofed it! Ten minutes!

As I hit Tottenham Court Road, the last straw floated gently down: Deeny called me up on the mobile, which I had instinctively but foolishly switched back on on leaving BIZVID. He demanded that we meet tomorrow, today, soon, now, tonight. I could hardly hear him over the traffic because I was holding the phone away from my ear: I was buggered if I was going to microwave my head just to listen to Deeny's useless patter. At the same time as all this, I was trying to look around the big red backside of a one-man bus, to see if I could whip past it somewhere. Eventually, my stress-levels reached critical and I just yelled:

SEAN, WOULD YOU JUST . . . FUCK OFF? WE ARE FUCKED SIDEWAYS, ALRIGHT? SO WE MAY AS WELL JUST TAKE IT. AND I AM *TRYING* TO GET A SPERM-SAMPLE TO THE CLINIC, AND IT HAS TO BE THERE IN FIVE MINUTES OR IT'LL DRY UP, UNDERSTAND? BYEEEE!

I slammed the mobile down and then I looked around in Brit-like shame and saw (of course) that my windows were down again. And then I saw that four feet away, a convertible Beetleful of female student-types, likewise gridlocked on the other side of the road, were pissing themselves laughing at me, over the strains of SouthEast FM.

Christ, it is so unfair! (See: the F-word again.) Just five years ago, well, six or seven tops, I would have had a fighting chance, given the right circs and half-decent footwork, of making these girls think of me as belonging to roughly the same species as themselves and therefore as someone at least theoretically shaggable. And now I was just another old tosser in a Volvo. Jesus, what kind of unfeeling bastard invented Time anyway?

Then I had to crash-stop at a zebra-crossing. These two fat little sixteen-year-olds, wearing sagging grey leggings and pushing double-barrelled prams, came waddling out straight into the road, mouthing and fagging away.

Referee! So how come *they* can have kids? Is that fair, Ref? If I have a kid, will I batter it about? No. Booze myself up and smash Sarah around in front of it? No. Abuse it? No. Feed it PriceRite Mechanically Recovered Burgers and smoke 40 a day in its bedroom? No. Desert it? NO NO NO. And will it get a good education and domestic stimulation and Winnie-the-Pooh stories told to it and CD ROM interactive educational games and grow up into a nice, normal, decent, responsible, resourceful, self-aware citizen, unlikely to fall for demagogues and tabloid hysteria? YES YES YES. So how come *I* can't have one, Ref? You blind or what, Ref?

These girls will probably be grandparents by Sarah's age; their boyfriends will be grandfathers by my age.

Ah, but I have my compensation: I will probably die a few years later, and richer.

Come on, come on, you stupid bloody . . . Excuse me, are you actually *waiting* to catch the red light? For Christ's sake, mate, have you got a paralysed right foot or something? Come on!

The sperm-test technician at the clinic was called Mr Cox. I kid you not.

Mr Cox the spunk-expert, 'Spunky' Cox to his mates maybe, did not (as I had expected) snap on a pair of little latex gloves. He just took the bottle with, I thought, a remarkable lack of distaste, shook it, glanced at the resultant cloudy mix and asked how old the sample was.

—How old? Oh, um, twelve minutes, I said: – I'm only out of breath because I had to run to get here, ha ha. So, er . . . Is it ok?

Mr Cox nodded and turned away, a man who had seen it all; the recipient of more wanks than the Czech Women's Beach-Volleyball Team Calendar. This was the little man in his stained white coat, not even a Doctor, who was going to tell me if it had been worth bothering when the first newt crawled out of the primeval swamp on its way to becoming me (unlucky choice, newty). This was the man who was going to decide whether I was booked for the lead in PETER THOMPSON'S NICE LIFE ('A superficial feelgood movie') or PETER THOMPSON: A FILM BY INGMAR BERGMAN ('A stately meditation on futility and despair'). I watched him shiftily, like you watch the examiner writing up his notes at the end of your driving-test.

—Do they, I mean, *die* after fifteen minutes, or what?

Mr Cox looked up, surprised to find me still there:

—Oh, we say fifteen minutes to concentrate people's minds. It is very hard, practically impossible, to tell exactly how old the little fellows are. Their condition depends largely on the temperature and environment. Then, there are such large natural variations in motility anyway. For all I could prove, this could be from your home bathroom this morning, or from just down the corridor. These chaps can last six or seven hours. Seventy-two hours in the fallopian tubes, indeed. After all, they have taken three months to grow inside you, and they have been hanging around in your scrotum for . . . well, for only *you* know how long.

—Right. Um . . .

—It takes three days, he said, suddenly tired, – The results get sent to your GP, you know.

68

—Oh, of course. Ha, yes, absolutely. Sorry. Three days. Right. Um, could I take another test-tube now, in case, you know, the results are, well, inconclusive, and . . .

—Yes yes, he said, and waved me toward a pile of test-tubes in little bags with pre-stamped labels. I took one.

—Right, well, thanks, um . . .

So then I went to the pub to talk my troubles over, having no-one else to talk them over with, with my old friend Mr Talisker. I patched my brain into his peaty, seaweedy depths. Now I could gently download, unload and offload all my problems: my tax-meltdown, my backstabbing partners, my crap accountant, my sperm-count, my marriage and my sex-life. My being bald and mortal. That sort of thing. You know.

Together, Mr Talisker and I shook our heads in quiet disbelief at the whole, monumental cock-up: we agreed that my crippled granny could run the game better than the Big Referee.

4. A Walking Ad for Ralph Lauren

Chernenin sat in his office and looked down through the thick, ballistic glass, onto the foyer of the House of Progress in Samara, on the river Volga. The office had belonged to his father as the local Communist Party chairman: by some mysterious process of inherited legitimacy, it had descended to Chernenin as Mayor on the National Liberal Salvation Front ticket.

In the foyer, some of the photographs of Heroes of Labour had gone: you could see the brighter, scarlet patches where the big black-and-white prints had kept the light off the faded velvet display-stands until the spite of their enemies, the shame of their families, or simple vandalism had removed them. But most of the prints remained curling and brittle in their places; most of the glaze-eyed faces still stared out, self-consciously resplendent in fat tie-knots, wide lapels and long sideburns, proudly flanking the twelve-foot statue of V. I. Lenin that still stands inside the heavy bronzed doors in the foyer of the House of Progress.

Chernenin grunted with contentment and pride at the thought of Mr Kant's girl. God, what a woman! She had made him feel like a Cossack hero. And he reckoned he had given her a good time too, at that. Chernenin fondled his dick absently, in pleasant remembrance. There was no doubt about it: it was time for Kant to move over, in bed and in business.

Though he had not thought it would all fall into place so quickly. Smart girl, she knew which way the wind was blowing all right. Perhaps he should not have confirmed her guesses, but then what the hell: she knew so she knew, and anyway, he had been a bit drunk – more with lust and his own daring than with vodka – and she had told him that story, how did it go? Something about a house with black windows and bats.

And in any case, she could hardly run to Kant and tell him! What, tell him that she had fucked Chernenin stupid and that was how she knew? No way. She was not just any old girl to Kant, everyone knew that. She had been everywhere with him for years. He was sweet on her. And Kant did not take betrayal lightly, everyone knew that too.

If only he could remember her story about the house on the river.

Chernenin shook his head to clear away the rags of the unremembered tale and answered the phone that had been ringing for some moments on his desk.

It was good news: the four transporters of Ladas from Essex, England had arrived in Minsk without having to pay quite as many bribes as they had expected to the Poles and Byelorussians. Those boys knew repeat business when they saw it.

Dr Jones could have explained the reason for Chernenin's market existing. Dr Jones would have said that the lunatic price of Ladas in Russia was a result of the way state borders deform the free market. Probably, Dr Jones would have used the following example: if you take a Citroen to some peasant garage just twenty miles across the Italian border, they look at it like it is the Car From Mars, because all they know about is Fiats. In Russia, the State decided that people should only know about Ladas. Practicality and the human predisposition to stick with the devil (or the car, or the politics) one knows combine to inflate the price of Ladas in Russia, Dr Jones would have said.

Chernenin did not need Dr Jones to tell him this. He did not like Dr Jones. He thought Dr Jones was just a slimy zhid in a lemon suit. No, Chernenin just knew that at the moment he could buy a half-knackered Lada for $1,000 in Essex, England and sell it for $3,000 here, and that was good enough for him.

—Mr Kant's black car outside for you, Boss, buzzed the armed guard at the door.

Chernenin strode whistling down the stairs. As he went, he admired the figure he cut in the fine, deep-dyed western tracksuit which appeared to have been designed mainly as a walking ad for Ralph Lauren. He always looked forward to his rides in the black Mercedes, secretly relishing the time when it (and the girl) would be publicly his.

But today, when he saw the black paint, he stopped, and felt a strange taste come up into his mouth.

The car outside was not the Mercedes. It was a black stretch Lada with extra chrome.

Chernenin looked halfway round, at the guard on the door who had buzzed him. He already guessed what was coming when, instead of the usual respectful nod from his underling, he got the grin that comes help-lessly when the little people watch the mighty fall. He heard a noise behind him and turned fully.

Mr Kant and his tall driver and the girl were standing there. She had her arm tucked into Mr Kant's. Cherne-nin looked at Mr Kant:

—She was in it too, he said, in a half-hearted attempt to take her with him: – She fucked me. Ask her.

Mr Kant nodded:

—She will never betray me.

72

Behind Chernenin, his own doorman softly cocked his gun.

As Chernenin shrugged and looked around to take the bullet, he was trying to work out what the taste in his mouth reminded him of. Just before the shot, past his killer's shoulder, he saw a man outside walking up and opening the big back door of the black stretch Lada.

5. A Berni-ing We Go

As I parked the motorbike in Neal's Yard that final Sunday (it was 2.30 a.m. now), a black cab trundled round the corner in front of me, and I jumped.

Partly, I was afraid of the driver remembering me being here, at this unusual time, but I soon calmed myself: I was in black leather head-to-toe, and wearing a helmet; the plates on the bike were deliberately greased up and mucky, almost impossible to read; and anyway, it was logically odds-on that I would be dead tomorrow anyway. Funny.

But mainly, I jumped because that square, black cab reminded me for just a second of another car, far away. As I watched it rattle off, I was thinking: the world is much more fragile than we imagine. You don't even have to do anything, you just take the first step, you just think about taking the first little step; and somewhere halfway round the world, the black stretch Lada starts up and sets off to meet you.

*

—Sean, I am not going to bloody Russia.

—Why not, sure? Lovely place. The lads name a street after you one day and chase you down it the next. I jest: Pete, did I *say* you had to go there? *He's here,* I'm telling you. And he's our man. Loves England. Can't think fucking why, heh heh. Millions, I'm telling you, *millions* to invest. And he wants to dig it into England. Stupid bollix probably thinks they'll make him a Duke. On the other hand (*Awn de ooder haawnd,* he actually said) if I was a millionaire I'd settle in good old England myself so. I would too. I'd get me a nice Big

74

House and a few acres. Now, where else would you find such a load of big, brainless, Tory-voting, arselicking, forelock-tugging gobshites as in good old rural England? Paradise for a millionaire, I'd say. Anyways, there I was so, shooting with Lord Southampton last weekend, deadly crack. And this Mr Kant was there. No better man with the old twelve-bore too, fair bollix to him. Big fellow. So we got chatting, you know how it is.

Paddy-on-the-make.

We were sitting in the horrible Berni Inn round in Shaftesbury Avenue. I kept on wanting to laugh because the other day Deeny said it was about time we took Charmaine and the other girls out again, he said *Yeah, we could go berni-ing with the ladies, Pete,* and all I could think of was that me and Deeny were among the first people in the history of the English language to be sitting here berni-ing.

Deeny was trying his best to save our skins, to be fair: he reckoned this Russian was a possible White Knight, and he had shown me conclusively that it was not his fault, that someone *must* have put the boot in with the Revenue. All well and good, but who are you supposed to blame when you go bust if not your accountant? If there is one thing worse than a bent accountant it is a crap bent accountant.

I didn't know why I was bothering listening to the bastard at all any more, really. Maybe it was down to his horrible, slimy, Bob Geldof soundalike accent and all that smiling, back-slapping, have-another-we'll-be-dead-long-enough stuff they are all so bloody good at, which is no doubt why every other bloody PR type or ad-man you meet in London is Irish.

—Berni-ing! I thought.—OK OK, I said: – So he loves England. But why the hell should this Mr Rasputin invest in me?

—Kant, his name's Mr Kant. Well, why the fuck does anyone decide to do anything? You're telling me businessmen take their decisions on a rational basis, are you? Do they bollix. Nice girl, that Charmaine. Lovely tits.

—What the hell do you mean?

—I jest, I jest.

And he half nodded and half shook his head and half winked, all at once.

Deeny had strode into my office that morning like he owned the bloody place, and he had seen me chatting to Charmaine.

I say chatting.

I was almost grateful when Deeny walked in, because I could feel myself losing control: I had no idea what Charlie and I were saying any more, it was just our eyes and lips moving and saying *yes yes yes* in a dozen different, wordless ways. The WP screen that Charlie was allegedly talking me through was just a jumble of meaningless hieroglyphs to me: when I looked at it – when I *had* to look at it now and again to keep the pretence up – all I could see was her hand, pointing. I wanted to kiss it. I wanted to bite her knuckles.

With my final reserves of rational thought, I was trying to work out if I was a raving sex maniac or just a man.

Once, in those far-off happy days when everyone assumed that *our* Volvo, too, would soon be making proper use of its built-in child-seat, Melissa started going on about how You Men could never understand what it was like to be pregnant and in the grip of Raw Hormonal Impulses. Maybe so. But perhaps it is the other way around. OK, pregnant women may chew coal or suddenly decide to bin all the coffee in the house or whatever for a few weeks; but men spend their *whole bloody lives*, from teenage den to mansize study to pensionable shed, doing bizarre crap. By day, we found Model Plane clubs and run Fantasy Football Leagues; when the evening falls we pore sneakily, with feverish, ravenous eyes, over glossy spreads and inset close-ups of impossibly clean cars with five (not six, mate, *five!*) spoke wheels and (wow!) chrome nuts around the filler caps. Or built-in child-seats. We drag our loved ones around a dozen travel agents to compare the exact prices of two weeks in Portugal; as we emerge with our piles of brochures, we catch sight of another woman's leg, and it is like walking into a lamp-post. We spend half our time manically creating databases with no earthly use, and the other half actually running our lives on fetishistic whims. Like I said: maybe it is the other way around; maybe the Hormone Rage of pregnancy could give women an insight into the control-freaky yet cage-rattling, literally and figuratively wankridden world of the y-chromosome?

Or maybe it was not because I was a man, but because I was infertile? I had this ancient auntie who was almost well-off and used to breed beagles: when I was quite young, I was with her and her favourite beagle in some nobby restaurant, and the beagle started trying to shag the chair; Aunt Jane bellowed at him across the room, with her mad lisp:

—Oh Toby, really! It'th awful, you thee poor Toby only hath one tethticle, tho of courth all he thinkth about ith thex.

Maybe being infertile has the same effect? Or maybe I was just human, and maybe Charlie really did feel that way too? Was it possible? About me? Despite the balding, despite the flab?

I wanted to bury my face in her big hair, at the back of her neck. Like an asthmatic gasping for his inhaler, I longed for just one deep, deep breath of her warm skin.

So anyway, all in all, Deeny did not have to be sodding Einstein to work out just what kind of spell he had broken when he strode in, like I said, like he owned the bloody place. But his wink was just another little sign that added to an unnerving feeling I get now and then: that Deeny knows far more about me than he lets on. More about me than I do, maybe.

I suppose this is just the way everyone who has a bent accountant feels: when some arsehole has been fiddling your books for you year in, year out, you might as well wear a see-through plastic suit in front of him. I sometimes think Deeny knows which lump of gunk came out from between which tooth when I flossed this morning. Sometimes, I really wish he would get sent off by the Big Ref, just get hit by a falling 747 or something. Anything. But please, Ref, let him sort my accounts out first, because I no longer know my input from my output or my credits from my debits, and all I can see in the books is the Red Sea lapping higher and higher, about to break the dykes.

—I'm telling you, Pete, I really think you should meet this Mr Kant. I tell you what I think: I think it's the film bit he likes. Maybe he wants an ould JV. Joint Venture. It's the big news eastwards: their side sorts the legal and security angle, our side provide the dough and the know-how. *Gno-ghow*, they call it, the eejits. Video is massive over there, the copyright laws are even more of a fucking joke than the rest of the laws. Maybe he wants a legit crowd here to cover dodgy stuff there. Maybe he wants you to turn out hard-core porn for him. I jest. But what I mean is: who the fuck knows? All I know is, he's into it and his dough's burning a hole in his pocket. Which, given the state of play, should be worth a look.

—I can see him now, don't tell me: some little spoilt-brat ex-apparatchik's son with a quiff and some ripyouoff business-school fantasy about the glorious West. Some bastard who has never been near a real business in his life, huh?

—Well, I wouldn't exactly say that was Mr Kant, Pete.

—Alright, alright. Let's meet him. Christ, and let's have a brandy for God's sake.

—Are you not due to pick up that sperm test now? he said, looking at his Rolex. See? The bastard knows more about me than I do. So I agreed to let him fix up a meeting, and then snuck off to the Doc to get the verdict.

The Doc had to look the results up in a book, which was not encouraging. His face was trying to look grave, like he was just checking, but I could see he was actually scanning desperately through the pages to find out something about this subject he knew nothing about. Tough, being a Doc: we come begging for salvation, and all they can do is look up the maths.

—Mmmmm, he said, halting at last, as if the information on the page merely confirmed what he had long suspected, the lying bastard, – Yessss. Let's just, um, double-check.

And he looked again at the results from the clinic and at his book and nodded sagely again.

79

—Normal, he said, firmly but with his eyes still flicking over the page to check.

—NORMAL?

—Yes. On the low side of normal.

—Low?

—Low but normal.

—So . . . normal?

—Normal. Just a bit lower than average, perhaps.

—Perhaps?

—Definitely.

—Definitely which? Normal or below average?

—Both.

—I see. Look, so can I have kids?

—Oh yes. In principle. You might just have to try a bit longer.

—OK, a bit longer. Or . . . more often?

—Or more often, yes, possibly.

—So if my wife and I want to get pregnant, her pregnant, I mean, the best thing to do is to . . . make love more often? More often than the average couple, I mean?

—That would be one way.

Thank you, Ref!

I checked several questionnaires in the Women's Mags section of the hospital newsagent on the way out, to see how often the Average Couple supposedly shag. I was encouraged. It looked as though we were in for a good time.

But Sarah was not impressed. She was depressed. I could not work out why until she told me, by which time it was too late, of course, and I had another huge black mark in her book as a Selfish Unfeeling Bastard:

—Peter! It means it might be me.

—Oh, sorry, is that so much worse than it being me?

—Of course it is.

—That's nice.

—I'm more bloody complicated than you down there, you selfish bastard. I'm talking about *us* not *me*, and all *you* can think of is *you*. If *we* want a baby, it's better for *us* if it's *you* that's wonky, not *me*.

True, of course. I realised that straight away. Sarah was (as usual) absolutely right. If I was really and truly dedicating my life and feelings to *us*, not to *me*, then logically I should have been really depressed to find out I was not infertile.

But of course, I was thinking nothing of the sort. I was thinking: goodee, I'm fertile, I can have kids, I am normal, I am not one of the Big Ref's merry little jokes, I am like everyone else. Near enough. It was true: I was not totally dedicating my existence to *us*. I know I should in theory, but there it is. Does anyone? I mean, anyone who was not just looking out anyway for *anything* they can dedicate their lives to?

—Anyway, said Sarah, – You're on the low side of normal, so it still might be you. And I've always known you were a selfish git so I forgive without forgetting. So long as you try now.

—Try what?

Guess what she did then?

She ran a cold bath.

I'm serious. She dragged me in to look at it, she was in a good mood again now, she is great when she laughs and I only wish I could make her do it more. Trouble is, she is usually in a good mood when she thinks of me suffering comically, which makes it hard. I looked down at the full bathtub. I could feel the blue cold radiating out from it:

SHE: Get in, I'll go and lie on the sofa and think of that bloke in the jeans ad.

ME: I thought only poofs liked him.

SHE: Don't kid yourself. Come on.

ME: OK OK. Is it *all* cold?

SHE: Yep.

ME: I really don't think this is necessary.

SHE: It might help.

ME: Says who?

SHE: Says . . .

ME: 'Says Melissa'?

SHE: It's only a cold tub. It could be fun. Are you man or mouse?

ME: Gimme the cheese, gimme the cheese. You get in then.

SHE: Me? Why.

ME: For fun.

SHE: I didn't say it was for fun.

ME: Yes you did.

SHE: I said if you've *got* to do something you might as well make it fun.

ME: Got to? Oh, so it's now an order, it is now a necessity of life that I have to sit in a tub of freezing water?

SHE: No, but . . .

ME: But?

SHE: But Melissa says it might help.

ME: Did Melissa try it?

SHE: No, Gerry did.

ME: Oh, *Gerry* did. Brave Melissa.

SHE: Melissa has not got testicles.

ME: Oh, so she *does* let Gerry keep something. Melissa selects the houses and chooses the cars and checks the credit-cards and plans the holidays and gives Gerry his pocket money, and makes him drink health-food muck that tastes like panda's piss, *but* lucky old Gerry gets to keep his monopoly on testicles, he . . .

SHE: Thresholds, darling.

ME: Yes, well . . .

SHE: Finished?

ME: OK.

SHE: Sure?

ME: OK, OK.

SHE: Right. Before they had Nicky, they had been trying for two years. Gerry tried cold tubs for a month and his count went up from density 50 to density 60. And then they had Nicky. And Ben. And Laurie. OK?

ME: Ha! But I'm 60 already.

SHE: So maybe you'll go up to 70.

ME: 60 is normal. The doctor said I was normal.

SHE: Yes. On the low side of normal. You told me.

ME: But normal!

SHE: Borderline normal.

ME: Normal! Low-ish, yes, but normal. Borderline-ish, maybe. But normal.

SHE: Seventy would be much more normal. Get in.

ME: *More* normal? (feet touch water) Oh shit, that's so cold. Ugh! You cannot be *more* normal. Agh! Normal means, like the norm, norm-al. You are, or you aren't. Christ this is going to give me a heart attack. Seriously. Ow! Do you know what this is doing to my arteries? You can't be *more* normal, it's like being alive. You are, or you aren't. You can't be *more alive*. I'm not sitting down in this.

SHE: I think we could, you know.

ME: What?

SHE: Nothing. Sit down. I'm going to lie on my sofa and think about stroking a young man's hard, downy buttocks. Don't you dare come in till you're warm and dry. (exit) (re-enter) And you've got to sit with them

fully immersed for at least two minutes (exit) (re-enter) Sit! (exit, laughing horridly).
ME: (shouting after her) It's not fair! Bugger Melissa and Gerry, the lucky bastards, I'm normal. I am not a mutant, I am not a write-off, my sperm count may not be off the scale, but it is *on* the scale. Maybe I do not sprout fertility at every pore, OK, maybe women can stand next to me in the office kitchen without immediately conceiving, but *I-am-normal!* (balls enter water) Aaaaaahhh!!!

I don't know if this really helped the sperm-count, but I have to admit it felt great afterwards. Like all my nerve-endings had had a de-coke. Physically great, that is. But as we lay there, Sarah chatted happily and (I suspect) tactfully away about how we did not have to get worried because, after all: there was always IVF to fall back on. And all I could think was *oh no there isn't. Not on the NHS there isn't, and the NHS is all we have from now on.* I could think of no good reason not to tell her, except that I just couldn't.

On the edge of my mind, down that little-trodden and overgrown path called Honesty Road, a thought was lying in wait: that if I told her, she would leave me; that I was only letting her live in false hope because I was afraid for me. That I was, in short, a classic bottle-job. But who admits that kind of thing for long? So I shut that rusty little gate again quickly, and as I settled to try to sleep, all that had escaped from the dark lane was the vague, unfocused feeling that I could really not complain if the Big Ref chose tonight to send me off for bringing the human race into disrepute.

6. To Fuck With It

Sean Deeny emerged almost unpanting from the tube station at Russell Square, despite having jogged up the three hundred and fifty-seven steps. He shot the sleeves of his heavy, dark, heather-tweed jacket and slapped the stomach of his Every Englishman country-check shirt with approval:

—A grand old flat gut, bejasus, you'd nearly feel the backbone through that belly, said he, unconsciously slipping into a generic culchie accent, Mullingar-cum-Galway.

Like many from his heavily anglicised background in South Dublin, he was prone to express himself thus when addressing himself; as if somehow the words of his less urbanised countrymen were at the same time an object of gentle derision and a source of timeless wisdom. Deeny was, that is to say, what is called in Ireland a West Brit; one of those types who even in his deepest unconscious is not entirely sure of his allegiances.

Deeny looked around, in case anyone had heard him talking like that, and settled himself to think. The choice was simple. He could turn left and into Russell Square itself, cross the square to the School of Slavonic Studies and visit Dr Jones at Dr Jones's new CEEBI think-tank (the Centre for East European Business Information) as he had half-promised to do. Or he could go straight across the street, hang a righter, then left alongside that hideous Aztec pyramid lookalike block of council flats and up to the red brick, school-like building beyond them in Handel Street, and get pleasantly twisted with the lads.

Deeny was not greatly excited by either prospect. Really, he would have liked to be going to the In-and-Out, that was what he called a club, but he could not think of anyone, right now, who would take him there. Cunts.

—To fuck with it, said he, and crossed the road.

As he approached the red-brick building (the brass plaque saying LINGUISTS' SOCIETY was now visible beside the door) he saw the lights on in the big second floor room. From here he could not see the men – it would be all men, for sure – but as he got closer he could hear the stupid fuckers singing inside, banging out the old Soviet National Anthem. Deeny shook his head. Why? he asked himself for the thousandth time. Why is it that people who speak French or German, say, maintain a decent critical distance from France or Germany, whereas almost every fucker who speaks fluent Russian seems to fall hook line and sinker for the whole works? Mother Russia, cornfields and ballet in the evenings, for fuck's sake.

As he came up past the Aztec flats, Deeny looked up and measured the distance from the last balcony over to the big, brightly lit window. A hundred and twenty feet, maybe. Christ, all anyone would have to do would be to get a half-together man into one of those flats, wait for the room across the way to fill, like tonight, and one RPG would do the trick.

Deeny imagined it shooting across the gap, blasting through the window, and detonating inside the room. He shook his head:

—Half the officers of the T.A. Intelligence fucking Corps with one shot!

As he buzzed the intercom, he wondered if any of the

lads from 12 Company in Coleraine would be there
tonight.

7. Break-Out of the Shit-Soaked Pampers

At about 1.30 a.m. that last Sunday, I was cruising very carefully off the M3 and through Sunbury, towards town, on the horrible old Kawasaki. Carefully, because I did not want to get stopped tonight, and also because it was a long time since I rode a bike, and I had been twenty-three then, and still indestructible. Now, at thirty-five, I could not help looking down every now and then at the front wheel and thinking: Shit, a little piece of glass, a pint of sump-oil in the wrong place, and all they would find would be thirteen stone six of Pedigree Chum in a leather sack.

As I cruised, I was scanning round at the twilit immensity of London, all these millions of people sleeping happily in the light-polluted semi-day we call night, never dreaming of the flares across the black steppes. And I was thinking: Yes, but it is all so easy to believe. Like me believing it was me pulling the strings on the night we met Mr Kant.

*

I wouldn't have bothered going to this bloody dinner Deeny had arranged in the first place, except it was at the Manoir Aux Terrains du Midi. Now, this happened to be one of the local joints I had always *really* wanted to go non-Berni-ing in, on someone else's expenses, while I still had my teeth, a full-length colon and a body that did not look *too* saaad and stupid when displayed unaccustomedly in Daks jacket, newest Levis and Chelsea boots.

I know, I know, it sounds crass. But that's the sort of

place the Manoir O'Terr (as we would-be habitués gather it is called) is: one of the ones you find in all the guide books in the section entitled *arm and a leg jobs for folks paying a lot of 40 per cent tax with cute accountants.* Barnes people, record producers, the odd Rolling Stone on a day-pass from the dialysis clinic, you know. So if some Russian git wants to waste his money, let him: maybe this is our last chance to Dress To Impress before BIZVID finally goes belly up and starts to honk.

For one thing, it would give Sarah a chance to wear her flashest silk number. Ladies at the M.O'T. (as I understand it is known to *real* insiders) always dress up. This is because they are usually much younger than the record producers and are (of course) only with the record producers precisely because they want the chance to dress up and be seen in this Big World far away from Mum'n'Dad's naff gas-effect hearth. Meanwhile the record producers and guitarists insist on the inalienable right to wear denim below the waist: without denim, a ponytailed forty-five-year-old walking in with a quasi-anorexic sweetykin babe in red silk minidress and DMs is just another sad old tosser in a Versace suit; with his Levis in place he is a lucky sod defying time.

Not that Sarah and I are dressing-up freaks or anything, it's just that, for once, I was praying to the Big Ref that Melissa might be right. The thing is, Melissa reckons that what couples having Fertility Troubles need is just a total change. She says that our problem is not unlike the seven-year itch. The theory is this: if a girl doesn't get pregnant with one particular man in eighteen months, Nature (which is Melissa-speak for God) decides that This Man Is No Good For Breeding (Nature not knowing about Durex and the like) and so gives up until you get another man who may have better-grade sperm. So what you have to do is Change Your Life completely, especially your patterns of sex'n'emoting, thus fooling Nature into thinking that you have gone boldly off and selected a new mate from the gene-poolside.

I just nodded and looked impressed when Melissa told us all this, because the practical implication was clear: she was telling Sarah that she should feel good and get horny with me in some unlikely, new and turn-on filled way. A holiday of sun, sea and sex, in other words. Sounded OK to me. And since we could not do that right now (– *Ah!* said Melissa, – *There's always some excuse, isn't there? You need to prioritize the life-change, Peter*) I thought that maybe an evening without worrying about the tab, a paid-for, posh-nosh fest with silk dress and all, might be a reasonable substitute in the feelgood stakes.

I mean, Deeny said the guy was even sending this black Merc to pick us up, so who knew? Maybe on the way back, Sarah would feel so good and so relaxed that her hormones would forget she was just with crappo Pete yet again, and mistake me for some gold-tanned tennis-coach?

This was partly why I had still not yet told Sarah that BIZVID was done for. Not likely to help relax the hormones. But only partly. Really, I just simply did not dare to. Not with the horrible pack-ice that had been forming invisibly between us over the last year or so; I had not noticed it until it had us almost surrounded, and was starting to growl around close by in the night. It was not that we *never* got through to each other any more: just that we were never entirely off guard. There was always the sense that one word out of place could open up the big steel doors and let all the built-up disappointments come roaring out. We looked forward to the next meeting with friends, the next expedition to some flick or someone's barbie, with a relief that was getting uncomfortably close to desperation: each evening out was a stepping-stone in the cold water; we were stumbling and hopping from one distraction to the next.

When we were alone, we picked our way towards each other like barefoot lovers on a carpet sown with broken glass.

I was hoping almost beyond hope that tonight might ice-break a clear way through for our lives to start running again. Then I could tell her about BIZVID, because then saying *us*, saying *we* are in big trouble, might have some meaning again.

So anyway, there I was, standing in front of the mirror, shaving. I was nice and relaxed because I had not yet crammed my lower body into my corsets (i.e. my 34 inch Levis). I was looking at my balding head and my face. Funny. I mean, it's not that when you're twenty-one you don't *know* you're going to get bald and fat. Of course you do, you're not stupid. It's just that you don't know that when you are bald and fat *you will still be you*. That double chin will be *your* double chin. No, come on, let's not exaggerate, that's not a double chin. I mean, you've got to have *something* between your chin and your collarbone, haven't you? And what are you supposed to have there if not ... flesh? Flesh. *Fleshy* flesh. But not flabby! Can't flex *fat*, can you?

I looked in the mirror and flexed my neck muscles. I held in my stomach and glared at myself. Totally saaaaad. What would Charmaine think if she could see ...

Charlie?

Who said anything about her?

For a moment my knees nearly went as I found myself back in the office the other night. Or rather, back in the lift, going up to the office, after the pub, allegedly to get something we had forgotten, never actually making it beyond the landing. Charlie's strong arms held me again for a second; her light-brown pubes zipped across my mind; I smelt the dust in the landing carpet again; I saw her Tintin ear-ring, and the little scars from where her old ear-rings had been, in cross-eyed close-up.

It had had to happen, so it had.

I locked Charlie softly away back down Memory Lane and washed the foam from my face. I watched the warm water drain away: it left a pinky film of dark specks, like coarse-ground pepper, on the avocado basin. I looked down to check that a gout of foam had fallen, as always, onto a spot of the carpet where a dark stain had already built up. Interesting. Perhaps, if I shaved here for another thirty years, it would build up into a stalagmite of soap and bristles. And the sixty-five-year-old man shaving here would still be me.

There must be some consolation, some recompense for getting old. If there isn't, I might as well have an accident while shaving right now. Although it would be hard to make it convincing with a twin-bladed, independently-sprung Gillette. The insurers would be suspicious. As I looked down at the stain of shaving foam, I imagined myself, slicing desperately and gro-tesquely away with my crap little razor, and had to laugh out loud. Then I sighed, splashed my face in cold water, and looked up into the mirror again.

Behind me, the Interview Panel had appeared.

I don't think I've told you about the Interview Panel. I may have been hesitating, because it is arguably a couple of stops the wrong side of Fruitcake Halt. But OK: the thing is, about six months ago I saw a job ad for Personnel Executives for one of the Big Players, and for about three days I wandered around twitching, thinking about how I could apply for it and maybe even stand a chance of getting it.

Imagine! A job with a big firm: Corporate Heaven.

No more Deeny and his dodgy accounts. No more VATmen. No more shuffling the papers that will decide my fate, like some ancient granny playing tarot. No more having to look out, even when you don't want to, for some deal, some opportunity, some quick few bob. No more of that horrible, slippery vagueness of where friends stop and contacts start. A job you can start at nine and leave at five! Holidays that begin when you hit the plane and don't stop until your arse touches your free, company-supplied, gas-suspended swivel seat again! A pension fund sussed out for you! A pay-cheque rain or snow! The odd freebie now and then, the company car ... Jesus! What cretin would go self-employed?

Anyway, so this job was on offer, and it so happened that I had just read, in some article in one of Sarah's *Elle* mags, that you could prepare yourself by imagining an interview panel and thinking what they might ask. So I did. However, in the end, I decided it was not worth the trouble humiliating myself when I had bugger-all real chance of getting the job, and I never went for the interview. I just stayed where I was; where I am.

But somehow, my Interview Panel stayed on too.

My personal Interview Panel is made up (God knows why) of a tweedy lady with an Edinburgh accent and two less well-defined elderly men. These days, it is not interviewing me for some crap job in KPMG Personnel (which was what the real one was) but for The Job.

Don't ask me what The Job is, because I don't know. All I know is: I will never have to go on the M25 in the rush-hour again. People I know, or once knew, acquaintances in the BBC, in the City, at the Bar, will look respectful and even envious when I casually mention The Job. I will swan into town late, having had my morning whack at the health-club, from somewhere genuinely rural yet not too far off (not far in a big smooth Merc anyway), long after the rush-hour. It will be a big job in Corporate Heaven, of course, copper-bottomed and competitively packaged, and yet, and yet: I will be to a certain extent my own boss, I will be so senior I do not have to wear a suit.

No more mortgage repayments. No more stuffy pubs and red-faced, beery laughter. No more fags, no lunches of Single Malt and mornings of grinding tiredness. No more hopeless half-thoughts of Other Women. My sperm-count will recover, or Sarah's tubes will untwist, or whatever is wrong with us, and we will rediscover that laughing, open lust that used to get us doing mad things, like fucking up against her green Mini in a country layby by a river, in pure daylight, just because neither of us could wait. Soon, we will have three or four kids, each with the correct number of arms, legs and chromosomes. The presents will pile up under the Christmas tree with its real wax candles; on Boxing Day all of us will go for long, crunching walks across fields where the grass cracks with the frost; afterwards, we will stand and warm our arses on the rail of our Aga as our troops of friends start to arrive and . . . And everything will be alright, always, for ever!

When I get The Job.

I licked my teeth and got the start of a strange, bad

taste I half-remembered from somewhere. It was the taste of a wet, cold motorway going nowhere.

I looked down from the mirror, and slowly reached for the toothpaste as the Interview Panel settled down around the bathroom. Not Colgate. I buy any old toothpaste except Colgate. I will not have Colgate in the house. I lived in Spain once, and in Spanish *colgate* means *go hang yourself*. Call me a control-freak if you will, but I have no desire to get existential hints from the contents of my bathroom cabinet, thanks very much, however wise the advice might be.

As I brushed my teeth, I could see the Interview Panel in the mirror, whispering and nodding to each other as they prepared to start today's grilling. As always, it was the Tweedy Edinburgh Lady who did the talking:

—Mr Thompson, is your desire for The Job in any way connected with, shall we say, a certain tiredness? A certain lack of what I believe you call *bottle*? Have you *bottled* it from your own business, Mr Thompson? Do you simply want this Executive Position in Mega-corp because you have *copped out*? Do you think a wanked-out, bankrupted small businessman has anything of value to contribute to a large multinational organisation? Or to anything else, indeed?

Careful! I had to answer the truth. There is no point in lying to the Interview Panel. The Interview Panel is no scabby little tax-inspector, to be fobbed off by Deeny's bullshit. It is not some potential customer you can butter up or stonewall. The Interview Panel knows everything. *Everything*. It has access to every job application, every tax-return, every diary and letter you ever wrote; it has recorded your secret phone-calls and your little, lost whispers in the night. You can only answer the truth, and not just the undisprovable truth, but the true Truth. I saw the two male members of the Interview Panel watching me as she spoke, not hostile, not friendly, just watching. I prepared to speak.

—Move it, called Sarah, – They'll be here any minute.

So I stuck my head in the basin of cold water to cool down my brain, and shook it like a dog shaking off water, as if I could shake the useless thoughts away too. I stood there, head down, and felt my brain settling back like a snowstorm toy.

And so, ten minutes later, Sarah and I were standing on our little drive waiting for Mr Kant's car, chatting to Gerry and Melissa.

Gerry and Melissa were coming too. About two hours before, Gerry had called to check what time were *we* expecting *them* for dinner that evening. This date was news to me, though our domestic and social arrangements quite often are. Sarah couldn't remember it either, but Gerry and Melissa had already booked and paid for the fully-qualified ACME babysitter. Anyway, I called Deeny and explained the double-booking and asked if we could slip them in too: he could tell this Mr Kant that Gerry was my lawyer, since that is what Gerry is. And Deeny said *Yeah, that might impress. So what's this Melissa like, is she any crack?* and I described Melissa, and he said *Sure bring them along, Mr Kant likes giving out to Yanks and I never heard of a fine big sporty girl turning up at the wrong party.*

Actually, I was really chuffed at getting Gerry and Melissa in on the dinner, because there is nothing to oil the wheels of a maybe-friendship like a really top-notch freebie.

Gerry and Melissa live at the other end of Hunter's

Rise. It is really nice, the way this came about, a sort of village-style happening in this big world.

About two years ago, Sarah and me were just rattling out of the local Safeway, our trolley stuffed with the kind of image-led, comfort-food crap that childless thirtysomethings blow their useless Freedom Tokens on, when we saw this couple with two kids and a baby in their Volvo, broken down next to our VW. The bloke asked if I knew anything about carburettors, and, being a man, I naturally had to pretend I did. So we got chatting, and suddenly it turned out that Gerry (for he it was) had actually been using a BIZVID video while training his underlings at his law firm. Meanwhile Sarah had started going nesty about Melissa's sprogs, so that was that. We ended up having dinner the week after. And then it turned out that Gerry and Melissa liked the area and needed a new house, and one way or another they ended up moving into Hunter's Rise, just up the road from us. Nice.

I was glad. I really like Gerry. Gerry is a Yank lawyer, he is a liberal, even a lefty, which is a rare thing among any lawyers, let alone Yank ones, and he even takes the occasional cigar after a heavy meal, which is amazing and heartwarming, considering. I not only like Gerry, I am really jealous of him. Maybe that is *why* I like him, who knows, and who knows if that would be a good thing or a bad thing? I mean, as a male, I know that what I fondly call my *personality* is not much more than the sum of what I have borrowed from my male friends: when we are hardly more than toddlers, we are made to realise we are not like our mothers, who we love: and so we spend the rest of our lives making ourselves up, usually on a just-in-time basis. Well, and so maybe the most important thing, maybe the only real choice we actually have, is to make sure we hang about with good people, not shits. People who are better than we are. And how do you tell if someone is better than you except by the fact that you are jealous of them? I don't mean of what they've got; I mean of them *being them*.

I am partly jealous of Gerry just because he is a Yank. His family made the right decision two hundred years ago or whenever. I mean, look what they missed out on: the Somme, Auschwitz, the Gulags, the Blitzkrieg, the Warsaw Pact and Bosnia and all. Good move, Gerry's grand-grandad. When he and Melissa take off every now and then to see the folks back home, it is like they are riding Virgin Atlantic (Gerry is into trust-busting, so he never flies BA) into the last sunset frames where we poor sods cannot follow. I mean, America may no longer be the Promised Land, the Great Destination, but at least it is an important interchange with a grand central station. Whereas Britland is just a crap, vandalised bus-stop somewhere off the coast of the Greater German Economic Zone, where the only people who get off are the ones looking for tax breaks, cheap labour, easy pollution laws or fibreglass Heritage Experiences.

I am also jealous of Gerry because he has the kind of hair that is going to go silver, not away. But mainly I am jealous because of the kids. On the other hand, Gerry is married to Melissa, so there is some justice in the world.

Melissa is a tall, tennis-playing English rose, with that unusual and fanciable combination of square shoulders, big tits and small arse. This turns me on, as it does everyone. But she also has a rather thin little mouth and her top lip never moves as she speaks in one of those tightknickered just-made-it accents that I personally find the world's greatest contraceptive. Each to their own: Gerry clearly loves it, and apparently it knocks them dead in Yankland.

Melissa believes that by a careful study of *Country Living* she has transformed their Executive Unit into a hop-hung, dried-flower-strewn Country House. She also believes that if only we understood Nature's Voice Within Us, everything would be fine for ever.

It hard to argue with Melissa, not because her arguments are good; they are not. The thing that makes it so difficult to argue with Melissa is the same thing that makes it impossible to have any kind of sane discussion with religious people. You know: you immediately get down to the point of no contact, the point where it becomes clear that you might as well exist on two different planets. I mean, what am I supposed to say to Melissa when she gets off on her nutcase ideas? All that can happen is what happened the first time we had a meal at their place:

MELISSA: Do you like the potatoes, Peter?

ME: (cautiously) Yes, yes, very good.

SARAH: They're delicious.

ME: I said, yes, very good. Delicious, in fact.

MELISSA: (triumphant) They're organic.

ME: So was the Black Death.

GERRY: But Melissa is right, Pete. You Are What You Eat!

ME: (reaching for the wine unconsciously) That makes Melissa a nut-cutlet, right?

SARAH: Peter.

ME: (pouring) OK, so you are what you eat, well, what would you rather be? A nutroast or a pig? Either you sit in the Linda McCartney section of the freezer in a wholefood shop for a few months and then get scoffed by some hippy, or else you root about for a bit in the mud before they blow your head off. Choose now.

SARAH: Well, we can see which one you've chosen.

MELISSA: Most pigs don't get to root about, Peter, only Happy Pigs are kept in the open, and ...

ME: (pouring again) That's me, that's my reincarnation, I chose first: A Happy Pig! That sounds like the life for me, a ...

SARAH: Thresholds, darling.

So I gave up ages ago. Now, when we are with Gerry'n'Melissa I do all the right things, like telling stories to the kids, playing Babyboomer Trivial Pursuit and doing her questionnaires out of sub-Miriam Stoppard books. I know Sarah likes her, so I try.

I also try because I like Gerry. In fact, I have to admit (though it is not easy) that I would like him to be a best pal of mine. Trouble is, it looks like the feeling isn't mutual: sometimes, just when we are doing fine, this funny kind of curtain comes down over his eyes, and you know you are being shut out. There is something sort of very old, and very simple, and almost unbearably hard about the idea that you can just happen to like someone more than they like you. It seems so unfair.

Just to be clear: the fact that I want Gerry to be my friend does not mean I want to bugger him or suck his dick. These days, you are not allowed to want to get closer to some male semi-friend without some loony telling you that actually you want to shag him. Please! The whole point of every crap bloody buddy-buddy film is that it is *not* about shagging, it is about a relationship *without* shagging: a crippled, hobbling attempt to show some kind of human thing that is not reducible to shagability or lack of it. There are very few things I would like less than to shag or be shagged by Gerry, and few things I would like more than to go drinking and hill-walking for a long weekend with Gerry so we can have a good chat about things.

I even floated the idea very carefully one time. But I had to haul it back in sharpish. Like I said: Gerry does not seem to want us to be friends as much as I do. Jesus, even saying it again hurts. I suppose he is just happier and less screwed up than me at present, due to having the hair, the kids and the passport, as described. So I got on with it, and we kept talking about what is in the papers or on *Panorama*. We had to do without the other great crap male chat-crutch, because of course we mean entirely different things when we say football.

However, we have recently started to talk sperm-counts, too.

When I first hinted at this topic, in their garden one night, while I was having a fag outside and one drink more than usual with Gerry, he simply did not believe me. He spilt his scotch. He looked at me like it was impossible, almost like he was scared. Then he questioned me closely: when he realised I was telling the truth, he told me, as if this was the most secret revelation he had ever made, that *he too* had been there and done that, and succeeded. He actually shook my hand and swore, several times, that he was not lying. It was somewhat overwhelming, actually. I mean, why should I think he was lying? Anyway, he soon calmed down again.

But in that moment, this sperm-count business had broached the locker-room-unfriendly subjects of mortality and life-on-earth. We had got beyond cars, cultural gossip and news. For the last few months, I had been feeling that we were on the verge of a break-through, I could feel us getting closer each time. It was like Gerry had something to say to me, and that when he did, we might actually become real friends. Like I said, I have to admit that I want this.

And so now, I was hoping that a slightly unusual evening, with a mad Russian providing the ante, might be a bit of fun to chivvy things along the tricky road to friendship.

And so here we were, on our drive, in the cool, fresh evening air, waiting for Mr Kant's allegedly fabulous car. Deeny had said it was a *massive yoke*.

I was already disappointed, though. Gerry was in one of his cold, distant moods again. He was telling me how the entire Federal Deficit would be wiped out if only some prez had the balls to hike gas-tax to just half the European rate. Melissa and Sarah were discussing whether Sean Connery was still the best-looking man in the world. I nodded politely and smoked gloomily, with cavalier disregard for their accusing looks, thinking about bankruptcy and my Memory Lane rhymes (*When your hair retreats, it don't regroup again, twang twang twang*).

—Is this the car now? asked Sarah.

It was not.

It was our bastard neighbours, the Johnsons, barrister or something he is, coming back with their two spoilt-brat kids from some child-friendly nouvelle cuisine place in Henley or somewhere, doubtless, in their spit-new Beamer.

Wankers. I mean, they actually said to us once, about the only thing they ever said to us, when Mrs J. was coming back from the privatised dolphin-filled birthing-suite or wherever with Tancred or whatever he is called, baby number two (we were out on the drive as they came back in triumph, I could feel Sarah trying not to reveal her deep hatred and jealousy): Johnson actually *said* that two was enough. Otherwise they would *have* to get a people-carrier because after all, there just *wasn't* room for three *really* safe kiddie-seats in a BMW.

Hell is other people's children.

I mean, Christ, Ref! How come the Johnsons get to breed and I don't? Do you actually *prefer* titbrained yuppies who want to bring their kids up in some security-guarded whites-only heaven under the guise of necessity? Do you *desire* more kids called Tarquin and Tamsin who will kill themselves out of sheer teenage pique if they don't get the little white cabriolet on their seventeenth birthday? Does it not occur to you, when you look down and observe these over-bank-rolled eighteen-year-olds, these luckiest people in the history of mankind, these ludicrously privileged inheritors of the earth, and you gaze (as you can) into their dreams and see (as you do) nothing but sweet careers in advertising and as much surfing as they can get in, that you should maybe whistle up and call the whole game off? Are you never, ever tempted to unleash a nice little limited H-bomb war in the Northern Hemisphere, just to give these little shits a lesson and the rest of the world a chance? Not ever?

Am I really worse than that? Is it not possible that my children, if I had them, might be decent, concerned, even occasionally violently outraged young people who would see their incredible good fortune in being born here and now as containing something like a duty as well?

Well, Ref?

And so it was with a knee-jerk of howling delight that I saw Mr Kant's black top-of-the-top-of-the-range Merc stretch limo come hushing along Hunter's Rise looking for us, at just the very moment the Johnsons were reversing into their driveway.

—Wow, said Melissa and Sarah.

—Stretcheroony, said Gerry.

I saw Johnson's face etched white in the glare of the limo's colossal headlamps as his own lights swung round onto his drive. Perfect. He did a useful Cary Grant double-take, did Johnson.

I waved to Johnson, lordly-like, very cool, like this was strictly an everyday occurrence for we secretly powerplaying Thompsons. Ah, a chauffeur too. Of course. Hear those soft-whizzing locks. Very tasty. Oh, look, what a shame, darling: that absolute crapfaced wankbucket Johnson has just driven into his own privatised wheelie-bin due to eyeballing Mr Kant's, ours-for-tonight, Merc'n'Chauffeur so hard. There go last week's shit-soaked pampers, spilling all over their drive, dearie me. Had to stick the anchors on sharpish there, Johnners! And the cleaner isn't around, is she? No she is not. So you will just have to scrape the shitey pads up yourself, won't you? Yes you will. Thank you Ref! Oh joy and bliss!

—I only hope the poor children aren't traumatised, said Melissa.

—Yeah, maybe poor little Tancred has submarined under the belts of his kiddie-seat. Maybe he's half choked himself, right now he's throwing up his creole-chicken-and-mango-paste dinner up over her Kookai dress, maybe they . . .

—Thresholds, darling.

—Sorry.

I was starting to like this Mr Kant. I nodded in a warm and friendly manner to his chauffeur – my warm friendliness only tempered by the fact that the bastard was about 6 foot 7 and could make an alternative career as a B-movie S.S. man any day he got pissed off with chauffeuring.

He opened the door quite un-nazi-like, though, and we all ducked into the living-room-sized back of the car. There was warm yellow light inside, and a cocktail cabinet opened up on its own as we sat down, revealing an iced bottle and glasses.

—Oh! gasped Melissa.

—Vodka, I gloated.

—I never actually *saw* a remote-activated one, said Gerry.

I picked up the bottle and poured.

—Not for me, said Melissa.

—Thresholds, darling, said Sarah, not looking at me.

—Just one, I said.

Then I noticed she was not looking at me. She is not normally shy about eye-contact when ordering me about, so I looked up to where she was looking, and saw that

> the most beautiful girl in the world was looking round at us from the front passenger-seat, through a glass partition that had mirac-ulously turned from black to clear.

Her eyes were brown and her hair jet black, it started low down on her forehead. Her eyebrows were unplucked, natural, thick and dark; her nose was not one of those Hollywood non-noses, those snubby little nothings that disappear with a bit of make-up and light: it was a proud, powerful nose. Her mouth was big; not one of those stupid little South English overbite-mouths, almost a Habsburg underbite, but just this side of too much; when she smiled she showed big white teeth behind dark-red lipstick. Everything about her was almost too much but not quite, she looked like a princess out of the Old Testament or something. She must have been about twenty-five. She was beautiful now, and yet you knew: the best is still to come. When she is thirty, powerful men will wreck their lives for her; when she is forty, worked-out thirtysomethings will stitch each other up for her favours. And you could also tell that she knew all this too, and was looking forward to it. She had that far-off air of someone who carries their own big story around within themselves and will always be essentially happy in their own skin, whatever shit hits them.

—Good evening, said she via some very high-quality intercom system that spread her voice out unnervingly from behind our heads, – I am Mr Kant's secretary.

For a second I wondered if she was American, or what. But then the tone underneath the accent hit home: in her mouth, and her eyes, the word *secretary* was suddenly stripped of all the rubbish and restored to what it really means: *secret*-ary. The one who knows secrets.

—Mr Kant will meet us at the restaurant. Please relax and enjoy the journey.

The partition turned black again and the locks whizzed softly shut all around us.

8. The Unfussy Gods

Dr Jones was taking his evening stroll around the leafy streets of Ealing, in order to marshal the thoughts he would later put down that night, in the peace of his study, after his five children had been put to sleep for the night. He was pretty well certain that he had found another two companies for Mr Kant.

Sean Deeny was actually rather good at his job, Dr Jones had to admit, though he did not like the man personally: Deeny certainly played the part well, and seemed to know his clients. Dr Jones laughed at the thought of BIZVID being among them. He was rather looking forward to meeting this Peter Thompson. Yes, Thompson might well be just right: they would very soon have reached their target, and it would be time to select the unwitting victim.

—Milk for the god, milk for the god! cried an ancient man in his face, and Dr Jones returned to his body.

He looked around. A queue of people was filing into the re-used Presbyterian Church that (he had never previously noticed) now evidently served as the local Hindu Temple. Their mood and dress was festive, but tinged with an anxious expectation that set Dr Jones's whiskers twitching, easily unnerved as he was by demonstrations of popular fervour.

He was not a friend of the Big State, but whenever, for example, he found himself in a part of London where there had recently been, or was soon to be, a soccer match, he found himself noting any Police presence with undeniable feelings of gratitude.

Dr Jones did not enjoy soccer matches. Yielding to the fashion, he had recently allowed himself to be enticed to see Arsenal play Manchester United in the company of several male colleagues from the University and their journalistic-cum-literary friends. Dr Jones had noted a curious phenomenon: highly educated and personally rather diffident young men *first* taking off their glasses very quickly and *then* leaping into the arms of their tough, unknown neighbours to celebrate a goal.

Dr Jones had said, after the absurd delirium subsided, that he found the self-conscious embracing of unthinkingness by the educated highly dubious, particularly where it clearly involved an element of spurious, tribal unity. When intellectuals fawn on pectorals, the next Nuremberg Rally cannot be far away. The young male intelligentsia was very heavily over-represented in the early Nazi party, Dr Jones reminded them.

He had not been invited again.

And yet, and yet: this was different. As he watched the crowds pressing into the temple (he could see the bright light from within through the big doors, and hear the music and cymbals) Dr Jones could not help admitting a strange, distant tug on his heart-strings. He remembered his mother and father, his own childhood in Uganda, all the long-lost ceremonies of innocence; and his eyes filled with tears with a speed which would have astonished his colleagues.

He himself found it hard to account for them. Account?

Curious, thought Dr Jones, even as he sniffed his tears back. We account for our decisions. As in much religious imagery we account for our sins. Is the God of monotheism not simply The Great Accountant?

—Milk for the god! cried a small child in front of him,

in Gujarati, waving a box of milk. Dr Jones smiled at her proud father in some embarrassment. If only he had been buying milk to take home! He would have been able to wave his milk vaguely about, and smile back happily at these people, and say the right meaningless things. It did not, he noted, appear to matter much to the God whether the milk was skimmed, semi-skimmed or full-cream: the God is unfussy, he accepts our milk for what it is, it is not the creaminess that counts, but the will to sacrifice.

Dr Jones blew his nose and turned and walked away from the temple, aware of the family's eyes on his back, knowing that these people knew very well he was an apostate, which is always worse than a stranger: strangers unite the tribe against them, apostates are splitters. That is why we take our enemies prisoner but kill traitors.

Dr Jones half-wished he were dressed in a white robe and skullcap instead of one of his yellow suits. He half-wished he could be one with this particular crowd. For a moment, the desire to belong, to chime in with these half-remembered rites, hit him with a force which almost deprived him of the power to walk. To belong. To accept. To believe. To come home.

No, thought Dr Jones to himself, fiercely. *That* would be treason.

And as he walked swiftly on past the next little shop that was selling its milk to a long queue of happy, chattering people, his mind dwelt on an endless, oil-sodden wasteland dotted with petroleum flares.

9. **Dreck and Gherkins**

*As I stood in the trees and watched Trevor drive off down the
M3 in my Volvo that Sunday morning at 12.45 a.m., I
wished I was going with him. I longed to see Masha. I ached
to see her, just to see her, you know? To be in the same place
as her. But I knew I could not, and so I was thinking: well, I
have time to kill now. Before the killing time. If I took exit 3
and headed north, I could be there in half an hour, on a bike,
at this time on a Sunday night. I could do a little tour down
Memory Lane before it maybe closes for good. I could go to
Mr Kant's house, and look and see if I can tell which is the
window where . . . No, no, I would go to the Manoir Aux
Terrains du Midi first, because that was where it all started.
That was where I got lost in her eyes.*

*

You know the M.O'T? You know the way you turn off
the old A40 (why are A-roads always old?) and take the
fork indicated by the thirties jewelled fingerpost onto
that little (and, I suppose, old) B-road? You remember
the sharp right you have to make, so easy to miss as
you take the long swing of the bend, through the big
gates and up the short drive to the semicircular lawn in
front of the Edwardian house?

No?

Nor me.

Well, not till tonight. I mean, you and I are not
supposed to know. Ex-Genesis drummers and stuff do
not pay top book to go to some eatery everyone knows
about. This is not where the likes of us go a-Berni-ing,

this is the real business, one of the places you come to in order to be crawled to by other high-order primates as you are hand-stuffed with rare little chunks of the biomass.

Now, of course, if you are a Brit you will say: but the *true* rich don't like to be crawled to, the *real* aristos talk to their gardeners like old friends, and all that stuff. To which I reply: you poor, suckered Ealing-Comedy-and-PG-Wodehouse victim, you. Have you ever actually met any of your actual, genuine, kosher (*not* a word they would use) aristos? Well, as a small but formerly successful businessman who once did so (in the course of filming *From Big House to Big Business: the country house hotel in the 21st century*, for the National Cert. in Hotel and Tourism Studies) let me clear things up: your Good Old English aristo, as far as I can tell, is a bread-headed, anti-Semitic, racist, sexually fucked-up milita-rist, pathologically aware of his own rank and everyone else's, the world's most vicious snob if ever he feels someone has spoken out of turn, and perfectly happy with the idea of funding death-squads if his private income was ever seriously threatened.

And what the younger ones really like doing, when the cameras are off, is going to the M.O'T. and hobnobbing with the Stones.

Which means that no matter how few public schools you have been to, you have nothing to fear from the place. Providing, that is, that you arrive in a sodding great black Merc ghostmobile with an obersturmbann-führer chauffeur to open the door for you. On the brief journey from climate-controlled limo to airconditioned lobby, you quickly realise that the doormen and hostesses have already put you down as a party liable to tip above its weight: no-one calculates disposable wealth as accurately, or reacts to it as speedily, as your hotel'n'restaurant-sector worker. I was liking Mr Kant more and more.

We strode through the black-and-white floortiled, mahogany-and-mirrors, neo-jacobethan vestibule (mmm! beeswax, the authentic air-freshener of Old Money). We shed our coats into eager, pimping hands that conspired irresistibly in the fantasy that we did this every evening. We tracked insouciantly past half-a-dozen grovelling faces in the hall and on into the sitting-room-cum-boozery, where we found this giant Russian waiting for us in a huge armchair, before a table groaning with drink. Deeny was already tucking into it.

Now, as an experienced expense-account freeloader lately rather down on his luck, I have often felt that moment of disillusion when you suddenly realise that, after all the fuss and hustling, all you are actually on for is rationed House Wine and a tarted-up Berni Set Menu. Well, as soon as I saw that table, with a good gallon of various spirits laid out and ready, my heart gave thanks to the Big Ref. This was the business all right. From the kick-off, the whole atmosphere said: *welcome to the trough.*

Not that I am a boozer. I know too many actual boozers to confuse the issue. But I am not scared of a drink. My mother put me on the right track many years ago, when I was maybe fifteen. We were watching some prog on the telly about the Evils of Drink, and this harridan blonde gym-teacher type was talking about livers. She held up this horrible blackened liver and told us how much the guy drank, then:

STRINGBEAN GYM MISTRESS: (holding up second liver) And here we have the liver of a healthy man.

MY MOTHER: (pouring sherry) If he's so bloody healthy, what's his liver doing on the telly?

My motto for life. None the less, I am often aware that I drink more than other people: at almost every dinner party, I am aware of Sarah half-counting my drinks, which is very unfair since I never do anything bad. I have never in my adult life got sick without making it to a lav in time; I have never ever pissed the bed or tried publicly to grope someone who didn't want me to, or told a host and hostess to Fuck Off or anything like that. I just like getting nicely pissed. I love the slow rising hit of booze, the warm, cheap illusion of spiritual change that it never fails to provide; and the only embarrassing thing I ever do (indeed, always do) is sing.

I can't help it. We all have the secret passwords, or pass-sights, or pass-smells or pass-sounds or whatever that can suddenly shoot the explosive bolts off our security doors and send us spinning backwards down Memory Lane, into our own lost years. For me, it is singing that does the job. For me, there is no point in boozing without singing. I don't care what. I'll join in rugger-bugger drinking-songs or Gregorian bloody chants, if that is all that is going. Even SouthEast FM, if I am desperate. I just don't care. I have no taste where singing is concerned. Not bad taste, just no taste. In my heart of hearts I do not believe anyone can be totally evil *if they can sing harmony when they can no longer talk.* Saaad maybe, but there you are: you have to know what it is that gives you unconditional pleasure, and with me it is harmonies. When I am pissed but still holding my close thirds right on in there, every second is for ever, twang twang twang.

In short, I am happy when I am three-quarters twisted and just letting it all out, which is to say: I am like 95 per cent of the human race. Ever since Homo saps appeared (archaeologists tell us) every culture has had some way or other, usually booze, of getting off its head. There are even some (I read) who say that the main reason we gave up hunting and took to farming was to grow more wheat to make more booze. The Big Ref must be pissing himself laughing: a whole civilisation based upon the desire of its creator-species to get bombed out of their collective skulls on a regular basis.

But there we are: who the hell can expect us to turn down the quick little hits, the short-attention stories of pleasure and remorse when we have forgotten all the long epics? I mean, can you imagine anyone approaching Salisbury Council today and proposing to build this huge community-centre type of thing that would take three hundred years to build? Of course not. They can't even plan the economy beyond the next budget. So the young wipe their unused brains out on Temazapam and E and the 1,000-decibel Repetitive Beat New Music; and we balding oldies stretch across the table of supposed civility to grab the NZ Shiraz while we may, and sing the old songs:

(Cos there) Ain't no entrance (twang)
        To Memory Lane
    (And) Society's contracted
        Spongybrain.

Anyway, the first thing Mr Kant did, almost before his sex-bomb sec had introduced us, almost before we had shaken hands manfully and looked each other in the eyes good-fellowishly, was stick a glass of this chilled vodka in my paw, raise his own, say

—Business! (*Beeizniss!*, he said) and toss it back. Since he clearly expected me to follow suit, I did. And even as it was going down, liquid icebergs with pepper, he started filling the glass up again. My whole body/mind nexus relaxed and prepared to make room for major scoff and uncapped boozing.

Melissa and Sarah started studying the menu so Melissa could decide what I could eat to boost my sperm-count; Gerry and Deeny had already discovered a common interest in guns and were discussing the various dead fauna and other shooting-fetishist gear hanging about on the walls; and since Mr Kant's secretary stuck close by Mr Kant, and since I very much wanted to be face-on to her with a good excuse, I launched straight in at Mr Kant:

—Mr Deeny tells me you like England, I said.

—Mr Kant does not speak English, said his secretary, – I will translate.

She did, and Mr Kant watched her closely as she did so. He then simply nodded. She turned back:

—Mr Kant adores England, she said.

I was somewhat wrongfooted by the lack of take-off this reply offered, and by the sight of expectation in those wonderful eyes.

—Has Mr Kant been to, er, Windsor Castle? It's quite near here.

—Mr Kant has not been to Windsor Castle, replied his secretary, without even bothering to ask him. Mr Kant simply shook his head and grunted the word *Weeindsor!* as if it were a bad joke. – Mr Kant has been to Weymouth.

—Ah, Weymouth, um, yes . . .

—Mr Kant has a considerable interest in several factory-ships which are currently anchored off Weymouth. Scottish fishermen from Fraserburgh are helping him in his businesses there. There are also many Ladas on Portland for Mr Kant to repatriate.

The eyes had it. They had me pinned. I could not

115

speak. The conversation around me seemed unnecessarily loud:

—Of course, darling, with oysters it's a balance between the zinc, which is good, and the probable trace PCBs, which are dreadful.

—Myself now, I would never use the old no. 4 for anything less than ducks, I mean, Jesus, you'd want to have *something* left for the dog to fetch!

—Mr Kant suggests you try this chilli vodka. It is Russian.

—And carrots, of course, to mop up the free radicals.

—Um, Bath is, certainly worth a visit.

—You know, I've always wanted to be one of those.

—A carrot, darling?

—No, a free radical.

—Nope, you just do not see a side-by-side gun at home. Well, maybe in Virginia.

—Has Mr Kant seen, um . . . the Houses of Parliament? They look really good now.

Mr Kant actually laughed when his secretary translated that, waving his big hand in a wide semi-circle above the cluster of spirit-bottles, as if he were sweeping Big Ben clean into the river.

—Jesus, said Deeny, – For a man who likes England you don't like England much.

She translated. Mr Kant roared with approval and thumped Deeny in the ribs so he coughed out cigar-smoke. You could see Deeny hated this, but he still smiled. Slimy git.

—Mr Kant says you have a Russian sense of humour, Mr Deeny, said she.

—I wonder is that a compliment? joked Deeny to Gerry. Mr Kant's face darkened when his secretary repeated this to him, and he said one word back to her.

—Naturally, she translated.

—Oh, right, said Deeny, and looked at his drink.

Then Sarah saved the day:

—Maybe he'd prefer Stratford. Shakespeare.

This time Mr Kant did not need translation.

—Szhekspir! he cried, and banged on the table, setting off a crystal peal, then launched into a long speech. Whatever he was saying, he was saying it with feeling: deep-brown gravy and throaty notes. His words were accompanied by frowns, grins, arms flung this way and that, chest-beatings, ferocious chopping-gestures and fist-shakings. The climax came about halfway: he looked up and raised both hands to the sky (for a mad moment I thought he was talking to the Big Ref too) and twice shouted out

—Dreck and gherkins!

I half-thought the bastard was going to take off his shoes and start banging them on the table like Khrushchev. I supposed *dreck and gherkins* was some kind of Polish-Yiddish curse or something, you know, like *shite and onions* or whatever.

When he had finished, Mr Kant's secretary looked at him. He nodded: she composed herself, coughed tunefully, and then translated his entire speech without stopping once.

She was the greatest translator I had ever seen.

She did not just give us his words, but the emotions, the exact gestures even, that had gone with them. The communication was so perfect that Mr Kant kept on nodding vigorously and repeating his own gestures as she re-used them for us, he obviously sensed that she was telling us exactly what he had said; it was as if he could tell from the rhythm of her speech exactly which point she had reached in the speech he had just given her. She was not a translator, she was a superconductor for his ideas and emotions.

What Mr Kant had said (it appeared) was this, and so (like me) you will have to imagine it is him saying it, not her, because it sounded pretty spacy coming from a drop-dead twenty-five-year old in beautifully-accented though somewhat weird American, despite Mr Kant's impressive physical accompaniment beside her:

—Shakespeare, yes! Shakespeare is of the true England. You think Mr Kant loves Windsor Castle? Big Ben? Balliol College? Nineteenth-century Disneyland! False medieval trash for Victorian faggots! You call this England? Mr Kant calls it a decadent ass-fucker's paradise, a bank-clerk's dream of an Empire filled with nine-to-five jobs in administration. That was the end of England, not the climax. No, give Mr Kant Shakespeare and give him Hakluyt. If you have not read *The Voyages and Discoveries of the English* you should have your testicles crushed between two large stones, assuming you have any. That was England: The England of Drake and Hawkins!

(she raised her arms and eyes up to the Big Ref or the Big Commissar, or whoever)

Drake and Hawkins! These are the English Mr Kant adores, men who set sail with an 80 per cent chance of dying and 10,000 per cent profit if they came home. Those were the business-men he admires, men who dealt with cannibal Chiefs as local Kings and Lords; men who had never heard of Nationalism or Racism; men

118

who saw other men as trading partners, no more, no less.

(She banged her small fist on the table; Mr Kant banged his big fist down beside hers; their joint eyes blazed four-square at me)

Men of hard Enlightenment!

(Yes, yes, that's me! I nodded, lost in her eyes)

These were Englishmen. And everything good about England became what? America. England and America at the end of the eighteenth century, when the true revolution, the revolution of freedom, spanned the Atlantic Oceans. This was greatness! You think Mr Kant should love the Burlington Arcade? Huh? You think he must adore Stiff Upper Lips and Fair Play? Mr Kant scorns all that. These are things for neurasthenic faggots. The England Mr Kant adores is the England that came freebooting out of the Northern fogs and in two centuries opened up half the world to Free Trade. What infertile bureaucrat's crypto-Jesuit dreams of the Perfect State, what beer-sodden Hegelian drivellings of World-Historical Forces, what Stalinist mathematician's death-wish fantasy of a Plan to end History can match the grandeur of England's unplanned drive to freedom, to America? Long live the Free Market and Anglo-Saxon financial institutions! Drake and Hawkins!

We drank, and I goggled. I had just received a fix of

pure fuck-you emotion, the mindset of this crazed Russian millionaire giant, but from out of the mouth and (more importantly) straight out of the eyes of this beautiful woman. I suddenly felt like some deep wellspring, almost forgotten, had opened up in me again, after years.

In the midst of the arsetight home counties, where everyone knows what everyone thinks and nothing has actually happened since about 1066, we had just got a dose of someone who was neither riddled with car-coat banality nor just trying to complete some broken short-circuit in their own saaad head. Someone who sounded like they actually felt something.

I looked at her eyes for far too long, and was grateful when the management, unused to and unsettled by such displays, made haste to get us under starter's orders.

At the table, we were arranged as follows, anticlock-wise: Mr Kant; Mr Kant's secretary; me; Melissa; Deeny; Gerry; Sarah.

Now, in normal, crap, civilised circumstances, this arrangement would have filled me with instant despair, because it would have condemned me to an evening of horrendous bullshit, trying on my right hand to make conversation with Melissa about nutritional values and the evils of tight male underwear, while attempting leftwards not to make it too obvious that I was wild about Mr Kant's secretary, and generally reminding myself about thresholds boozewise.

Thanks to Mr Kant, things were rather different today.

Mr Kant led from the front in consumption and conversation. When the wine-waiter arrived, wheeling before him an impressive trolleyful of various wines,

Mr Kant just sniffed at each in turn, nodded to himself, grabbed the first bottle without even looking up and waved him away for good, henceforth dispensing wine himself to anyone who left any room for reasonable doubt in their glass.

Over the soup, Mr Kant described to us the state of the German Automobile Industry and the reasons for its superiority; with the fish, he dished out his chablis and explained the Nationalities Problem in the former Soviet Union; during the entrée, while he kept the Château Christknowswhat Grand Cru coming by the pint, we learned of America's Internal Disunion, which led seamlessly into pud and fat glasses of white burgundy, as he argued the need of every businessman to learn how to shoot straight, like his heroes Dreck and Gherkins.

All of which should have been stupendously, catatonically boring, except it wasn't.

Maybe this was just because everything Mr Kant said, his secretary had to translate, and that meant I got my fair share (more, I rather thought) of looking into her eyes with a perfect excuse. Maybe so: it was nice, and more than nice when, moved by some of Mr Kant's reflected or shared passion, she bounced about on her seat so much that her thigh rubbed up against mine once or twice. Maybe that was part of it. But you are not going to tell me that Melissa and Gerry and Deeny and Sarah fancied her too? And yet they were clearly as unbored as I was.

We all have friends who we let get away with the most boring crap because they are our friends and we love them. (If you are in any doubt as to who these friends might be among your wider pals, try out this infallible test: imagine what you would do if you had to bath in their unscrubbed bathtub, dry yourself in their unwashed towel, and sleep in their unchanged sheets. If you would scan the bath carefully for old pubes, sniff the towel nervously before putting it to your face, and only squeeze reluctantly between the sheets after checking for nameless stains, they are acquaintances; if you feel snug and nice doing it all, they are in your inner circle. Easy.) But why? What makes us feel that way about some people?

The point is that we only realise how much leeway we give our Best Friends when another, non-mutual, friend comes along, and we see very soon that pal #2 thinks pal #1 is full of shit. This is always worrying, and leads one to question one's judgement. And I would have been disturbed if I had been alone in not finding Mr Kant boring. But I was not, like I said: I honestly believe that we would all have sat there and listened quite happily if he had been chatting away in his native language without us understanding a word.

Mr Kant, in short, had it.

Maybe the endless free booze helped? Maybe, but booze can do the opposite, it could have helped put us all to sleep, or helped make us brave enough to just ignore this rich but boring git droning on in the corner. So it wasn't the booze.

I think it was the spectacle of Mr Kant's freedom, the way there was no gap between his desire and his actions; the sight, the sheer beautiful sight, of someone doing exactly what they wanted when they wanted.

We all love to hear about Van Gogh's ear, or Einstein losing his Y-fronts on a bus or whatever, because these stories tell us that there is a sort of democratic justice in the world, which is just what we want to hear. We know from our own lives that the more you think about things, the more you just realise that your life is not what you wanted it to be, and we nod and say wisely to ourselves *That's how it is, see: if you think about it too much you fuse your brain.* The talented fuck up, we say; the stars get caught having $60 blow-jobs while the starlets end up in drug-clinics; Mr Universes end up in wheelchairs; eggheads never shag and poets slash their wrists just as the postman is walking up the lane with the prime-time TV contract. It all comes out in the wash, we say: and we turn over gratefully and our clichés lead us sweetly back to sleep.

But what if you meet someone who is clever and *not* fucked up? What if you come across some seventeen-stone six-foot-four millionaire who just laughs and nods and clearly has a brain the size of the Albert Hall and yet, and yet, has clearly never felt the need to look into a mental mirror to see himself, because he has never been in a moment's doubt as to who he is. A man, in short, who does not give a toss.

What you do is you watch and wonder, and think: how much time, what gigantic proportion of our lives, we spend *not* doing what we want, in the simplest, stupidest ways. We do not sleep when we want to because the clock says we cannot; we do not shit when we want to because we are stuck in our traffic jams; we do not booze when we want to because of what people will think; we do not smoke when we want to because of cancer; we do not shag when we want to because of busting up our marriages and being left alone; we do not even piss when we want to for Jesus's sake because we are locked into some meeting, spouting the boss's crap back at him. And so we nod and fit in and hold on and keep it in and screw it down and dry it out and close it off and then we are surprised when one fine day the fuses blow, we grab our arm, grasp our chest, turn blue and drop dead.

Stress? Balls. Stress is just the polite word for low-grade, long-term fear. We live in semi-fear, almost all of us: fear of loneliness, death, cancer, old age, Annual Staff Reviews and rises in the mortgage rate. And so when we see someone who does not live in fear, someone who actually, really and truly enjoys being alive and on this planet and is really and truly in charge of his own life, what can we do? What chance have we got?

Mr Kant's radiant sense of freedom was made worse by the fact that I was feeling very unfree indeed because of sitting next to his secretary. As a result, I was trying desperately to hide from her – and from Sarah – the fact that I fancied her more than I dared admit to myself.

I just kept on looking her in the eyes. I had to. If I did not keep a fix on her eyes, how the hell could I help staring at the movements of her lips, or drinking in the rise and fall of her thick, black eyebrows?

What do you do you do if you suddenly find yourself placed face-to-face to a girl who is a living argument against democracy?

I always wondered how the Anorak People felt. I mean, I asked myself if they *realise* they are too unattractive to get someone better, and thus aim only at other Anorak Persons? I often doubted it. I mean: surely life would be unbearable like that, always knowing you had settled for far less than you wanted? And now I knew. Because here I was, sitting next to a girl in comparison to whom I might as well have been wearing a stained parka and a nylon shirt. And so now I knew how it felt: it felt *unfair unfair unfair!*

What happens to one of the Anorak People who has ideas above their station? They get shat on from orbit, is what.

Surely Sarah would notice? Or maybe Sarah would

just think I had drunk too much Vodka too early? And maybe I had? In vino veritas, or in vodka bullshit, who knows?

—Yes, I keep a handgun in our home in Philadelphia, said Gerry.
—Really? I asked, returning from Planet Navelgaze.
—Of course, said Gerry.
—Coo, I said, involuntarily jealous. Not of the gun, but of Gerry: I had just got this strange echo again, the echo of a big, Yank-style life which Gerry had, but which was unknown to me. I felt boring.
—Mr Kant says that is very good, said his secretary: – Mr Kant recommends the use of 9mm 147-gramme subsonic or .38 158-gramme ammunition. Mr Kant believes that any handgun firing a weight over 180 grammes or at a velocity of over 340 metres per second renders accuracy impossible to anyone but a trained marksman. For home security, penetration is not an issue. Mr Kant assumes that your weapon is for home security?
—Yup, said Gerry.
—I hate it, said Melissa, – I'm always terrified in case the children find it.
—I keep it safely locked away in a metal box under the bed, explained Gerry patiently, mainly to Sarah, – And the ammo is in the study in another locked box.
—Mr Kant wishes to know if Gerry expects the robbers to wait while he arms up.
—Oh no, said Gerry, without thinking, – We'd have plenty of warning.
—Plenty of warning of a robbery? asked Sarah. Gerry realised what he had said. Mr Kant and his secretary conferred as Gerry blushed himself to death:
—Mr Kant believes Gerry is referring to race war. Mr

Kant believes that this is what Americans always mean when they talk about crime. Mr Kant believes that America is decadent now, almost as decadent as England. America is the Cherry Orchard and Japan is the former serf who supplies them with loans and will soon move up into the Big House. The American dream was a dream of trade and work and melting-pots, now it is the American nightmare of luxury without purpose and ethnic ghettos. Mr Kant does not adore America today.

—Where *does* Mr Kant like, then? demanded Melissa, a home counties lioness defending her husband.

—Mr Kant has a certain sentimental fondness for the habits of Russia, the country of his birth, but he believes that every good businessman, which is to say every good man, should be a wandering Jew. Mr Kant believes the words of St Hugo of Villon: the man who loves his country is merely a beginner in life; the man who loves every country as his own is far along the road; but the man who is everywhere a stranger is perfect. Mr Kant has no homeland. People do not have roots, says Mr Kant, vegetables have roots. In his hours of weakness, Mr Kant admits, he dreams of a house beside a still river and a veranda among silver birch-trees, to sit on and rock through the endless summer evenings. But he knows these dreams are merely the tempting whispers of the grave.

Mr Kant nodded slowly when she had finished.

There was a long pause, while we assembled WASPo-Celts, trained lifelong to make small-talk at dinner, tried to digest Mr Kant's thoughts while avoiding the open, serious gazes which he and his secretary had levelled upon us.

Then Mr Kant plonked down his glass, folded his hands under his chin and looked straight at me for much longer than polite manners would dictate. His secretary looked at me too. Once again I got this extraordinary wave of understanding between them, it was like one person looking at me with four eyes and two brains, a great big bastard and the most beautiful girl in the world rolled into one. After a couple of eternal seconds it got too much, I tried to laugh and shrug, I said:

—What?

—Beeiznis, said Mr Kant.

I took a deep breath, and made my pitch.

What I wanted was to be saved, of course. But why the hell should anyone save anyone? You cannot go alone to a pub and let people see you want company: you have to try to look like you don't need to try. And if you need half a million to save your neck, the last thing you can say is *I need half a million to save my neck*. I knew what I had to say: with half a million BIZVID can destroy its chief competitor, TV CHOICE.

TV CHOICE is a good, tight show run by young people who are really into what they do, the bastards. (Which means they are in the right thing, because this is a match of one leg only, the result is the result is the result, so why waste it doing anything you are not into? When the Big Ref blows, we all end up in the same muddy bath, rich and poor. I have to tell myself this again and again, and I keep forgetting. Maybe forgetting is the big sin, I mean, forgetting the important things, getting led astray by the cheap bright lights and MSG-enhanced junk-snacks, forgetting the true league-table of things. If only we really and truly remembered. But we are like guard-dogs that keep forgetting what the hell they are supposed to be doing: we hear some far-off yapping and our ears start to flap and off we trot, forgetting the big story of our lives. And then we are surprised when one day we wake up and find that we are old and somehow we feel that we missed out on something somewhere along the way, way back. Twang twang twang.)

But anyway, even though TV CHOICE is run by nice people who deserve to succeed, bugger them, and do, and BIZVID is run by a shifty waster (me) who does not (and indeed has not), with half a million we could pay off my taxman and be left with a fat, big wad to mount a price war which would take their market-share clean from under them. You got no market-share, you got no cash-flow; you got no cash-flow, you are footoo unless you got big-time backers with long purses. Fair it is not.

That was how I had to pitch it. Easy to think about, not so easy to do when everything is riding on it. Not so easy not to let the desperation show through. I would not have been able to do it except for Mr Kant's secretary.

Thing was, I was saying it all to her, obviously, for translation. And I fancied her like mad, quite genuinely. So I just let all my lust come out as I talked her through the business. Like I was twenty-six again, with nothing in the bank and no prospects, and trying to get into the knickers and (more importantly) the Life Itself of a beautiful girl called Sarah who would quite rightly run a mile at the slightest out-of-tune flutter of needy wings.

Mr Kant's secretary translated it all into his right ear. We made up a strange triangle of communication: I was staring at her, she was whispering to him as she stared back at me, and I could see him staring at me as I stared at her. As I spoke, she repeated not only my words, but my intonations, inflections and gestures, like she had done with Mr Kant. I felt between her and me the incredible horniness of unexpected mutual comprehension.

But there was another player, too: out of the corner of my eye, I saw Sarah glaring at me as I stared at Mr Kant's secretary. I saw her mouth *thresholds*, and so I just once shot her a big glance that said *us us us*; and, unbelievably enough, I thought I saw the boredom that shrivels a soul turn in her eyes to the jealousy that lights a tired, workweary lust with the sudden rediscovery of distance and desire. When I looked back at Mr Kant's secretary, I caught her still looking at Sarah; Mr Kant was looking away from Deeny and back to me.

I could feel it all, never mind see it. My radar was back. I was fighting for my life, and alive again.

I also had an incipient erection.

I say again: incipient. It was not so much an erection as the buzz that goes through your body beforehand, the hormonal rush that can come over you for no reason, like: you can be sitting at your desk looking over some papers or whatever, you know, thinking hohum nothingverymuch, and then without warning your eyes start to unfocus and the colours change and this humming starts at the edge of whatever you can hear. Before you know it, you are like some tortured pasha who would happily throw half his kingdom away for a shag right now with the dancing-girl before him.

That was the way it was, that buzz.

I finished my play, I shrugged with a smile, and went off for a pee to let it all sink into them. As I got up from the table I was safe enough erectionwise, but I had to force myself to walk bogwards as if I had been on crutches for a month, my knees had forgotten what they were evolutionarily designed for. The emotional feelers between Mr Kant's secretary and me, and now between Sarah and me too, had gone straight through my brain and raced down my groin and from there had whacked back up into my central nervous system.

I looked at myself in the mirror of the airconditioned lav.

Behind me, the Interview Panel materialised in the mirror.

I was slightly surprised, since I had never seen them outside my own bathroom, but I had no time to wonder much about this, because the Tweedy Edinburgh Lady was already asking the question of the evening:

—Sex, Mr Thompson?

As always, I tried being honest with the Panel, since (as I said) there is no point doing anything else:

Of course it was about sex, I mean, yes, I wanted to fuck right there. There on the table would have suited me fine: I wanted to rip Mr Kant's secretary's dress off, or Sarah's dress off, over the table and shove my hand between *her* legs or *her* legs (Charmaine, Charmaine!) and fight her or her down onto the oak parquet all right. And yet and yet: it was nothing to do with the erection I got the other day when Charmaine grabbed my balls.

—A likely story, Mr Thompson.

Who knows why we are what we are? Maybe it is something pathetically simple like: we are really still in love with our mothers; or: we are really just life-support systems for our DNA. Or maybe we are not really built to be lonely go-getters, maybe we were designed to live in big gangs shagging more or less indiscriminately, taboos and siblings excepted, bringing up the tribal sprogs together like meerkats, and all we have done is let ourselves get tricked into a big game where sex is made so complicated that we confuse it with life.

—You appear to be somewhat *fuddled* tonight, Mr Thompson.

Then the Interview Panel disappeared from the mirror, to be replaced by Deeny:

—My fucking man, that was mighty stuff! I think we've got him! Infuckingcredible.

—You reckon?

—Hooked. Now we just have to play him nice and easy back at his place.

—His place?

—He just invited us all back.

—Right. We'll have to go.

—My man, I have already said our yesses. Hey, what about the young one, the sec? You fancy a crack at her, my man?

—In my dreams.

Deeny thumped me in the ribs, the git, and scuttled off to piss in the urinal, so I shouldered my way swayingly out of the bog, braced myself against the wall, straightened up, and set a course back to the table. A gull-like flock of waiters had already gathered, and Mr Kant was shoving piles of notes at everyone.

—We have to get back to the children, said Melissa.

—OK, said Gerry, feigning resignation but with that secret gratitude that you often see in married men's eyes when they are *forced* to leave a bachelor-style drinking-session a bit early. I mean, why the hell else do you think men get married? I looked at Sarah and spoke softly, expecting resistance:

—I really think we'll have to go along . . .

—Peter: is there something I should know?

Only one answer to that:

—Yeah. Yes there is. Can you wait till tomorrow?
She looked at me:

—One more night won't hurt. One.

But she was not saying it school-teacher-like. She had
her old eyes back again.

As we waved good bye to Gerry and Melissa and the
locks whizzed shut and Mr Kant's car scrunched away
over the fine gravel and away from the Manoir O'Terr, I
caught Sarah's look again and I was sure now: those
deserted tube-train eyes. I knew that if bastardface
Deeny had not been with us, we would possibly even
have shagged right here, in the back of the car.

I wondered whether, if we had done so, Mr Kant's
secretary would have been able to see us. I betted she
would. Mad. But even more madly, I felt that Sarah
knew too, and that it would not have stopped her. The
ground was slipping beneath my feet, and to my shock
I found I was loving it. I stared out of the window,
grinning at my own reflection in the black glass.

Out of the corner of my eye, I saw the Interview
Panel watching me from behind me, in the car.

—You appear to be enjoying yourself, Mr Thompson,
said the Tweedy Edinburgh Lady. – Is there anything
more you wish to say to the Panel?

—Yes, I said, – Twang twang twang.

10. **Waiting for the Cavalry**

The attractive French girls in the little porters' lodge were already waiting with their coats as the young American officer and General Oblomov of Bulgaria strode, resplendent in evening clothes and happy with fine wine, across the grand black-and-white tiled foyer of the Naval and Military Club in Piccadilly.

They paused only to admire the little statue of Napoleon, cast (as the plaque says) from guns captured at Waterloo, and the large painting of the Rally at Balaclava.

—This is great Art, said General Oblomov.

—It's certainly, er, highly competent Victorian genre-painting, said the American.

—The details of the uniforms are quite correct. That is what I call Art.

—Aha.

The American, who had been here on related Navy business, had found himself, as the most junior officer present, detailed to entertain this new ally after dinner. He had dutifully shown him the works. Earlier in the evening, they had strolled before the portraits of Sir Garnet Wolseley, Lord Roberts and all; they had read the framed copy of Sir John French's upbeat order of the day to the doomed B.E.F. of 1914; they had taken a turn around the fountain that sits in the middle of the little patio with its white cast-iron trellises, its tall chestnut tree and that pair of absurd soft-porn bronzes named Swedish Eve (the rather embarrassing donation of an eccentric but simply *too* well-connected Brigadier some twenty years before). They had noted with amusement the invisible line just beyond the large bust of Edward VII in the Members' and Guests' Lounge; that line beyond which no female may tread; they had even peeped into the pastel-shaded Ladies Bar upstairs, where the aviatrix Amy Johnson stares down from her frame above the fireplace, swathed in a curiously suggestive orange fur, halfway to a flying jacket, returning any overbold male gazes with her thwacking blue eyes.

The American regarded these surroundings half with Republican disdain and half with a wistful satisfaction he could never explain; but he found his Bulgarian guest not overly moved. Once again, he had to admit that the Officers' Corps of Eastern Europe unnerved him utterly even now, even in the New World Order. Two catastrophic World Wars and the Warsaw Pact's notion of tactics had instilled in the General Staffs of Eastern Europe a positively Haig-like attitude to casualty-rates that would have made a Colonel of Marines flinch. They expected their orders, their budgets, their demands for recruits and their status to be accepted without question by their civilian countrymen. To stroll through an élite club of mausoleal Edwardian aspect, hung with exemplary pictures of the Glorious Dead, was for them merely an everyday occurrence.

Eyeing the Bulgarian surreptitiously, he felt a perceptible wave of nonconformist, New World outrage at all jackbooted, high-marching militarists and an equal wave of pride in the different traditions of his own country and Service. But what in hell's name were they doing supporting these goose-stepping s.o.b.'s?! 'Democratic forces'? These? For Chrissake, Oblomov even smoked his untipped Turkish cigarettes like a Czarist officer, between reversed thumb and forefinger.

It was thus with some satisfaction that he heard the attractive French girls sing out:

—Your coats, Mr Shepperd, Mr Oblomov.

Mister! That was more like it, dammit! The order of the club: no ranks, no bowing and heel-clicking, just the plain title of a member and a gentleman. A gentleman is a gentleman is a gentleman. When all was said and done, Gerry Shepperd really did quite like the Brits.

—My country, said the General, stopping in the middle of being helped into his overcoat by one of the girls, – Has been invaded by every dominant culture. Greeks, Romans, Turks, Germans, Russians, all come to Bulgaria. So tell me, he laughed, batting Gerry between the shoulder-blades, – What the god-damn hell is taking you so long? Why are *we* still waiting for the cavalry, my friend? Hoh Hoh!

—Aha ha, laughed Gerry.

The two of them strode out into the night. They crossed the cobbled yard, their coats and shoes glowing blackly in the flaring light from the two great, gas-fed, art nouveau braziers that burn permanently above the gates; over their heads, a Union Jack of positively Imperial dimensions swayed heavily in the damp air.

And so they passed out into the democratic bustle of Piccadilly, by way of the gate which is marked OUT on either side, and which, together with its twin marked IN on either side, has given the Naval and Military its popular nickname.

11. A Virtual Balalaika

As Trevor and I stood, not next to each other, in the urinals at Fleet Services on the eastbound M3 (it was now 12.15 a.m. on that last Sunday) and tried to prolong our pissing, without it seeming suspicious, until the awkward old bastard washing his hands had sodded off, I was thinking how Deeny had fooled me too, for years, just like Gerry. I suppose I just wanted so much to believe his bullshit that I did. I really did. I didn't even get suspicious when he pulled that supposed coincidence in Mr Kant's house, when we got back from the restaurant.

*

When we got back from the restaurant, Mr Kant led the way into the main room of his house. It was a great hall, and at one end it had this tall, wide fireplace with a heap of blazing logs laid over firedogs. I had never seen firedogs actually being used before. They were curling, wrought iron shapes that were not really trying to look like living things at all; but in the red and orange fire, and the dark between the flames, they still looked as if they were ready to stir and move. High up, the firelight made fat shadows among the black rafters. It glowed on brass and silver. It shone waxy on the oranges of a little orange-tree that stood among deep fires in the dark polish of the grand piano. And on Mr Kant's secretary's face.

She had sat herself down at the piano, and was stroking slow, minor chords; she was looking down at her fingers not as if she needed to know they were playing right, but just because she liked to watch them move. Already, I wanted to hum along.

—Russian vodka! said Mr Kant, standing before me, proud of his drink and his English.

—Ah, *Russian* vodka, I replied quickly, and rolled my eyes suitably.

—You are learning, said Mr Kant's secretary from the piano, and looked up at me while continuing to play. It was the first thing she had said from her herself to me, and though she was ten years younger than me, I felt proud that she thought I was learning.

And why not? They say it's not the age that counts, but the mileage. Balls. It's the *kind* of mileage that counts. If you just cruise life's easy motorways, you can hit forty without a mark on your paintwork; but thirty years street-fighting your way around Amber Light City is bound to show. I mean, I have always made a big thing of having travelled rockier roads than most nice quiet Brit businessmen, but there was no doubt that Mr Kant's secretary could trump me any time. She had seen the caravans of the east, no question. She had lived more than me, I knew it without having to know it; and I deferred happily to her superior knowledge of the world, to those eyes which had seen stranger constellations than mine, in nights far from streetlights. I wanted to learn.

I was also scared. I fancied her so badly it was in danger of making me be straight with myself despite myself.

Messing about with Charmaine I could cope with. Charlie could be fitted easily enough into the well-oiled world of little maybe-lies and not-quite-truths which had somehow, sometime, become my normal way of life. If Sarah found out about Charlie (which she would not), I would be able to look her in the eye quite easily and say:

> Sarah, look Sary, it's nothing. She's nothing. It is just that I wanted, just for once I wanted to fuck someone who is not you. The only thing that made her so attractive to me is that she was *not* you. Not-you. I mean, I didn't really care if it was Charmaine or whoever, it just had to be not-you. So really, you are still the centre, you are the big story of my life, the point of orbit, even if, just for once, negatively. Do you see?

Which may or may not be bullshit. The question is not whether something is objectively bullshit. From a certain angle maybe everything is bullshit; from another angle maybe nothing is. It doesn't depend on truth, it depends on believability. I would be able to believe, so it would be real to me. And if something is real to you, you are halfway to persuading the rest of the world. Ask any priest or salesman. Whereas if Sarah had stopped the show dead that moment, right here, in Mr Kant's house, and said, openly:

—You want Mr Kant's secretary more than you want me, don't you?

I could only have said yes. Hopelessly, publicly. I could only have admitted that at that moment, she was right. I could only have been honest. Which would not be the best policy, it would be suicide. I knew I was not going to get Mr Kant's secretary, so why let anyone know how much I wanted her? We do not want to advertise our own defeats and weaknesses; the only people who react kindly to defeat and weakness are the ones who secretly like to see somebody being weaker and more defeated than themselves.

And the worst thing about this unwanted bloody honesty was the thought that Sarah could spot it anyway, without me saying anything. Maybe she could tell straight away, from my body language, that if I had the choice, if I was free to choose, if I was a free man (which is to say: if I was a man) I would not be going home with her tonight. That I would, at this point in time, have rather spent the night standing in the rain looking up at Mr Kant's secretary's window than in bed with Sarah. And when we ended up going home, which of course we would, Sarah would know I was not doing what I really wanted to do. So I would be a cowardly heap of shit, and she would be just second best. And that would make her, in her own eyes, the kind of woman who is prepared to take a man who is prepared to take her as second best.

When we got home, and looked each other in the eye, we would see only the incontrovertible proof of our own wretched compromises. The cold in my stomach was not from the chilled vodka: when you have got that far, when your lover has seen that deep into you, *sorry* is already too late (but then *sorry* always is, isn't it?). You might as well do it and see what comes out alive the other side.

Not nice. I could feel Sarah's eyes lasering into me from somewhere beyond my vision, threatening to burn through the concrete walls. I broke eye-contact with Mr Kant's secretary quickly, buried my eyes in my glass, and swamped my failing control-rods in another flood of vodka coolant.

Mr Kant watched me down it. I tried to make it last an extra second, for the simple reason that I had no idea where I was going to look when the drink was finished.

I could not look back up at Mr Kant's secretary without risking doing something crazy, like asking her to play something I could sing to, just to be near her. I could not look up at Sarah yet, because my safety-doors were not in place and she would see for sure what she might as yet only half-suspect. Experimentally, I flicked an eye past the edge of the glass to Deeny, but the slimy git was (as usual) looking at me like he knew everything I was thinking and some things I wasn't. The last drops of vodka slipped hopelessly down my throat; I closed my eyes and prepared to meet my doom.

Then Mr Kant saved me. He called to his secretary, evidently to stop playing, since she did. I almost shouted for joy as I lowered my drinking-mask and locked safely onto him with a perfectly good excuse. *OK, now we get to business*, I thought. Business. Thank Christ. Something with maths, something with facts and figures and dates, something you can get hold of and pin down and work out and punch into a PC and draw a line under. An escape from this hopeless crossfire of head-to-head feelings.

—Now Mr Kant will sing *Stenka Razin*, said Mr Kant's secretary.

And the bastard did it like he did everything else: he just opened his throat, and sang. It turned out, though, that *Stenka Razin* was actually the same tune as *Now The Carnival Is Over*, only in Russian, and very deep and sloshy. Which meant I could harmonise. So I did, lalala. I could not help it.

I let him get through the first verse alone, as one should, then I started gently putting baritone thirds above his bass melody. Like I said: a craphead I may be, but thirds I can do all night. Mr Kant looked at me, surprised, but did not falter and even nodded, so I let it grow a bit. By the end of verse three I was taking it up to almost his volume, I had the timing of the words better now, we were getting there. Verse four got suddenly soft, Mr Kant warned me with his eyes so I dropped out. Then his eyes called me in again for verse five, but I had a mad rush of blood and vodka, and decided instead to do a virtual balalaika.

The virtual balalaika is quite easy to do (assuming you have drunk three bottles of wine, a half of vodka, and are desperate to escape reality): you sing *lalala* but you click your tongue up and down very fast as you sing, while miming playing a balalaika.

Mr Kant almost stopped singing, he was so shocked. For a moment I thought he was going to shoot me on the spot for mocking his deepest national treasures or something. But instead, he cracked by the far the biggest smile of the evening. He almost laughed, and raised his tempo and volume, swinging his arms to conduct me along. I could tell by his crescendo that there could not be far to go now, we were coming to the last verse, or maybe the second last with a quiet one to come, either way it was time to go for it, so I went back to my normal lalala (or rather, this being Russian, *lyalyalya*) thirds, with the odd fifth thrown in to underline that good old coming-to-the end feeling.

We were flying, Mr Kant and I: our eye-contact was perfect, we were swinging our bodies gently together like old troupers. And then came the slow verse for Mr Kant alone, you could tell even without knowing Russian that it was the same as the first verse: everything was back where it started, the wheel had turned full circle, whatever the circle was; the old ways are the best ways and the vodka is hot in your eyes.

He milked it for all it was worth, and kept the last note right on pitch but dying away for a good ten seconds.

—Jesus lads, that was mighty stuff, shouted Deeny, strutting about and making sure everyone else was clapping too. He would have made a good bloody redcoat at Butlins, the git: – Hey, Pete, now are you *quite* sure you don't have Irish in you?

I grinned at Sarah without thinking about it, and saw that she was looking at me in a way she had not looked at me for ages: like I was an annoying but actually rather likable six-year-old. I did not dare to look for long at Mr Kant's secretary, because when I did a scan-pass on her eyes, I was almost sure I caught her looking at me in a way she could not possibly be looking at me: the way someone looks at you when you have suddenly taken them by suprise, and made them upgrade you despite themselves. I know, I know, I already said: it was impossible. Saaad, I know. But we still have dreams, even Anorak People have dreams, and where do dreams come from if they are not the wind-blown shreds of lost, possible lives?

Luckily, we then had to drink more vodka straight away. Well, if your liver is going to make it as a media-star, it might as well be black and shrivelled.

And then Mr Kant stopped grinning at me and suddenly said something to his secretary: they huddled up in front of the fire without any pretence about it at all. They murmured and rumbled and sloshed away in Russian, letting us three feel our own essential super-fluity as we tried to keep up the chat while we all knew we were actually just killing time waiting for them to finish.

Without them, we were just rather tired and (in my case) distinctly pissed people in someone else's house for no good reason. Whatever the story was, it was them running it, and we all felt like bit-part players.

Our attempts at conversation were thin and hollow against the background of their mushy, Russian mutterings: they had A Life, and we were stuck in some horrible Alan Ayckbourn script.

Have you even tried playing the Alan Ayckbourn game?

Very nasty. Also very simple. If you want to *really* screw up an evening, try it. All you do is: you are sitting with a load of friends around a dinner table and suddenly someone says *OK the next person to say anything like an Alan Ayckbourn play has to do a really horrible forfeit*. And then no-one says anything for the next ten minutes, because they know that anything they say will sound like an Alan Ayckbourn play. As soon as they think about opening their mouths they can feel Alan Ayckbourn waiting to pop out. Then they slowly realise that sitting there saying nothing is Alan Ayckbourn too, and the longer the silence goes on the more it will sound like Alan Ayckbourn when someone does eventually say something. You cannot escape Alan Ayckbourn, that is the trouble with being English.

You don't even have to know his stuff. Even if there are people around the table who have no idea what Alan Ayckbourn is like, they will still say something like Alan Ayckbourn if they say anything:
SOMEONE WHO KNOWS NO AYCKBOURN: Oh really! Why *are* we playing this silly game?
EVERYONE ELSE: (with ecstatic relief) Forfeit! Forfeit!

The bastard has got us taped. Try playing the game: as your dinner-party is slowly vivisected by self-consciousness, you will see that the only escape from Alan Ayckbourn is to stop being English.

Soon, Deeny, Sarah and I had reached the *long pause* section of the Alan Ayckbourn game, without even having meant to start it, and had given up. We were now waiting, without shame, to be saved from this situation by Mr Kant and his secretary, who were still huddled in their private Russia. At last Mr Kant's secretary coughed, and we all abandoned the fiction that we had being having this great independent chat. We looked round and waited, and she just said, without any preliminaries:

—Two million.

—? I said.

—Mr Kant will provide two million pounds to BIZVID. The money will be provided in the following form: two hundred thousand pounds immediately, the balance in three months. The terms of repayment will be: quarterly instalments of two hundred and fifty thousand pounds, the first payable six calendar months from the date of the agreement. The interest rate applicable will be the Bank of England's published base rate plus one per cent payable in advance. Further loan facilities may be made available at the same rate should the arrangement prove successful. Mr Kant may from time to time ask you to make payments for consultancy work to certain parties; these payments will be covered by separate cash payments to you. Do you agree?

—Holy fucking Mary, Mother of fucking God, gasped Deeny.

—Darling? said Sarah.

—Hmmmmmmmm, I said, for as long as I could reasonably say it, i.e. say nothing, in order to give my brain some chance to close the gap that had opened up between it and the world.

—Thresholds, darling, murmured Sarah.

—Against what collateral? I managed to say at last. – What guarantees does Mr Kant seek?

—BIZVID. If the loan is defaulted upon, Mr Kant will have the full right to BIZVID's name and goodwill.

—Ummmm, I said, – Well yes, I said, – I suppose our goodwill, and, and . . . must be worth . . .

I looked at Deeny for support, but he was still sitting there looking like he was in shock. When I caught his eye, he looked at me like I was someone he had never seen before. Mr Kant grinned and nodded, hands braced against his waist, enjoying every second. Then he spoke, long and unusually soft; she watched him and then she translated it:

—Mr Kant invests in people, said Mr Kant's secretary: – Mr Kant does not believe in material security. Mr Kant says: we have no help but ourselves. Mr Kant trusts his own judgement, not the statements of any bank or the mythical solidity of any state. States fall and banks go bust, says Mr Kant. As a small child, Mr Kant saw the invincible Panzers come, and he saw the invincible Panzers burn; he has seen the T54s crush nations and then fall, in their turn, to rust; he has watched the colourful bonds raised on a dozen forgotten states, blowing across the endless steppes. Human relationships endure, says Mr Kant.

OK, so he's a nutter, I thought.

—Two million? I asked. I managed to put the accent on the first word, not the second. In my head the central locking was flying open in all the doors I had; the new wind raced among the dusty furniture-covers I had put over my big plans. – One per cent above base?

—That is correct.

—I need to discuss this, I said. I nodded to Deeny and he stood up with me. As we walked away, I looked at him out of the corner of my eye, not daring to catch his gaze in case I giggled. I noticed that he was walking as if his limbs were powered by rather leaky hydraulic valves.

As we staggered out of the room, I was thinking: *one per cent above base! One per cent!* Christ, I could put one of his two mill away on the side and earn myself at least, *at least*, one per cent and lots of nice little points above that with zero risk. Nothing like money for nothing. And meanwhile, the main game: I could pay off the tax bastards *and* crucify those poor sods at TV CHOICE; I could blitz them with a glossy new cut-price catalogue aimed to hit the schools and colleges before the end of the school budgetary year, before the ring-fences for next year were set up. I could get a spit-new in-house editing suite to cut our costs, that would be about £140,000 . . .

In a couple of fingercounting, fingerlicking seconds, I knew that I would be able to do everything I needed to do *and* pay Mr Kant his first two instalments, no sweat. That would take us up to a year from now, and by that time, by the time instalment three was due, I would have my order-books bursting and my new equipment as collateral for a normal English bank-loan: I could easily raise the third, the fourth, maybe even the fifth repayment before I had even seen a penny from the new sales.

And shit, so what if I cocked it up?

No collateral!

So the nutter likes Drake and Hawkins and England, good for him, but say I can't cough up: bad luck to him. BIZVID he can have tomorrow.

—This is unfuckingbelievable, whispered Deeny: – The big eejit must think you're MIRAMAX or something. Fucking typical. Because you booze and sing, he loves you. Shagging Russians! Are we on the pig's back or are we on the pig's back? This is the greatest fucking deal since Adam got handed Eden.

—So do we go for it?

—Does the Pope wear robes?

—Right. OK. So how do we tie him down? He might just piss off to Russia tomorrow.

—Hey, am I your accountant or am I your accountant? What do you think I always carry about me in the old magic bag? Hold on, hold on, wait fucking for it, I jest not . . .

(he hopped across the hall, kicked his coat aside, grabbed his briefcase, knelt down on the floor, crossed himself, threw the briefcase open, stuffed a big wodge of papers into his gob, scrabbled about inside the case with his eyes flying over the docs, and at last spat out the stuff in his mouth and kissed some bits of paper)

. . . draft fucking loan agreements! Didn't my old mother always tell me that going to confession would pay off one fine day? God bless her and keep her!

I looked at the document. It was so simple even I could understand it.

—Just write in the noughts, slot in the clauses and join the fucking dots! crowed Deeny. – I jest. We have to do this kosher-like. Lawyer to check it out, write in UK jurisdiction in case of any dispute, all the proper shite. Sure we'll get Jenkins on to it now. Great excuse to get the boring little arsewipe out of his bed. Make him graft for his dough for once, eh?

And before I knew it, Deeny and Mr Kant and Mr Kant's S.S. driver were off towards the black Merc. Deeny was on his mobile, talking Jenkins, our crap lawyer, through the deal, even as they left the house. Slick as oil.

—Shit, I breathed, reaching for the vodka bottle.

—Thresholds darling, said Sarah. I looked up at her

because of something in her voice, and found that she was not annoyed. She was grinning.

—I am glad we are doing business, said Mr Kant's secretary.

—Me too, I said, and tried not to giggle.

—Tomorrow morning we will sign the papers. Your room is on the first floor, the second room on the corridor to your right.

—Are we staying? I asked, turning to Sarah as I spoke, as if it was Sarah, not Mr Kant's secretary, who had made the suggestion.

—Sounds like a good idea to me, said Sarah, to my surprise.

—Goodnight, then, said Mr Kant's secretary, and went.

We watched her go. For just an instant I got the strange feeling that a bit of me was being pulled away with her; I turned to Sarah, momentarily unsure what to say. But Sarah was already walking over to the fireplace, leading me on invisible strings by not turning round. She sat down on the big armchair, half her face was in darkness, the tall flames made the other side glow and move.

Then she threw one leg over the arm of the chair.

You know those films where they shoot a little camera down inside someone's heart? And they always put this sound effect on, that slow *BA-shOOOshhhh* noise? Well, that is what I got at the sight of Sarah's knickers between her stocking-topped thighs.

They were just her ordinary M&S white knickers, like she puts on every day, I see them every day on her as she gets up and gets dressed and stuff. I am not particularly a knicker man, let alone a white knicker man. I am not particularly an anything man, to be honest. I am (like everyone) always glad to happen upon stockings, but then I am also (like everyone except poor fixated saps) glad to happen upon jeans or leggings or long or short skirts, too. Or nothing.

But now, like I said, the mere sight of my own wife accidentally or not flashing her nicks at me between the tops of her stockings hit me like a serving-girl's ankle might have hit Mr Gladstone in 1880: scarlet and black. I could feel that old reptilian cortex wake up in the back of my forehead, I knew my pupils had got big and black, and saw hers too: her smile was slow and her lips just open. I leaned forward to kiss her. Suddenly I could feel the lost muscles in my body again, so I picked her up and crossed the room, still kissing her, and kicked the door open and took her up the stairs.

And, of course, fell over halfway up and dropped her and swore most uncool-like.

But then the great thing about marriage is you don't have to be cool. You always get a second chance, that's all the Vows actually mean: *I do solemnly swear to give muggins a second chance rather than immediately binning their toothbrush the first time they utterly fuck up.* The readiness to get hitched is just the readiness to give someone a second chance, whether from overwhelming love, growing tiredness, secret desperation, or, saving the best till last, a more developed sense of human frailty and potential.

So anyway, Sarah hauled me back up the stairs, laughing horribly, and in between her legs and up to her face. We had hardly touched lips when she put my hand on her breast and said:

—Hard.

She had her *So Do It* eyes again. So I did.

Sarah was back again: the doors of Memory Lane

whizzed well-oiledly open and three years of unlived life came charging from their besiegement as our teeth bumped, our tongues lapped and my dick uncurled at the feel of her dampening knickers.

Coo, I thought, as Sarah started to gnaw away at my dick through the denim. I thought how long it was since we had done anything like this; this was not supposed to happen any more to bald, fat bastards. I also thought that if we had been thinking sanely, we would have weighed up the possibility that attempting 69 in this position (as we now were) might result in one of us waking up with a nice friendly wheelchair salesman at the bedside. But we were not thinking. Thank Christ. How very nice not to be weighing things up for once. And not be weighed down by them.

—Halfway up the stairs is the stair where we suck, I sang, hanging weightless, upside down between her legs.

—Stop it, you're making me laugh, she said.

—OK, I said.

—This is serious, she said, and laughed.

—You're right, I said: – I'm slipping.

—Come on, she said.

So having thus established our wishes, we very soon found ourselves scrambling up the stairs and along the corridor and into the bedroom, trying to keep fondling each other as we went, as if we were both scared that this unexpected renewal of synchronised lust might evaporate before we got there.

It didn't.

It was a very very long time since we had fucked twice without me coming out of her, since just those nice little internal hugs had been able to get me stiff again. I put it down to the talking: I stayed inside her and we talked low and slow about the things we were going to do. Not *wanted* to do; were *going* to do. The world was once again a place for our wishes; we were out of the valley of the shadow of No Money.

If you ever have been in that dark and dingy place, you will understand what the break-out felt like. We had lived our lives for years as control-freaks by obligation, with the present always mortgaged in favour of some imagined future. Call us bread-heads if you want. I don't care. I don't deny it, in a way. Yes, it was to do with the money. A lot of things are.

(There was once a German who went up to a Jew and said: *Itzig, you Jews only chase money, but we Aryans chase honour and glory.* To which the Jew replied: *Hans, we all want what we haven't got.*)

I want one thing to be clear: I am not saying you *cannot* be happy with no money. Like I am not saying it is *impossible* for someone to sit for thirty days on top of a pole, chanting mantras and feeding on nothing. I am quite ready to believe it is possible. No, wrong: I am *quite sure* it is possible. All I am saying is: so try it.

We had. And now we were free. Now it was just a question of what we *wanted* to do again. And what we wanted right then was: for me to get hard again and then for us get set around so we could sit up, her around my lap, me with my pelvis shoved up and my arms holding myself high, just holding in there as she moved around, back and forward, eyes open and looking through each other's eyes at each other's dreams coming up and maybe even coming true.

After the second time, the waves of receding orgasm carried us straight out to sleep: the keys turned softly and all was well.

And if only the bathroom had been en-suite, every-thing might have stayed that way. But it wasn't, was it?

12. The End of Home

Charmaine Lee, who had naturally spent her school years suffering from the wit of teachers calling her 'charmingly' but who was known as Charlie to her pals, was not as pleased to be home as she had expected to be.

Of course, it was nice to be with the gang again, in Birmingham, out of bloody London, among friendly people and homely accents, and all that. The only thing was: it did not feel like home any more.

Yesterday, it still had. Getting off at New Street had been like coming home, she had strode to the Lion with her heart beating; she had passed Rackham's shop (all those years she had spent looking forward to her visits there!) and looked in the windows as if somehow all the things in there were quite different to any other old House of Fraser store. And she had taken her place in the pub with deep satisfaction and a kind of sigh of release:

—A decent, cheap pint at last! Bostin!

They had a great time. When she showed them the big A3 colour photocopy of her and Pete that she had made on the night of the Office Party, you should have heard them squeal!

—Slag!

—Charlie! That's *disgusting*. Give's a look again.

—It was dead funny, said Charlie, – Pete was really scared.

—Pete?

—My boss.

—This him?

—Charlie, you big tart!

—He's alright, Pete. Mad, like.

—I'm not surprised he was scared in case you flashed this round. Bloody right!

—No, he reckoned the photocopier light might be, like, bad for his sperm-count.

—His *what*?

Laugh?!

But somehow, by the end of the evening, something was missing. Maybe it was Trevor, she did miss Trev. Walking home off the bus, she realised she was actually looking forward to seeing Pete as well. But mainly, she was just kind of looking forward to being, like, around the office again. At last she admitted it: being in London again.

—Home, she said to herself, as she looked at the quiet street in the lamplit night. Memories stacked up before her with each step towards the little house and the teenage bedroom that was still called hers. Memories. She thought of Pete's password to the secret accounting-files: MEMORY* LANE. She had read it off the keyboard when he was typing it in, he was that slow, any idiot could have made it out. He was asking for it, really.

—No. 14, Memory Lane, Sparkhill, she said to herself.

I am back home, she told herself. And the day after tomorrow I will be going home again, but to London. When you go away and then come back, it turns into home, she thought. So after tomorrow, London will be home. It will be home because I have come back and made it home. You cannot have two homes. And so what will this be then?

She was crying by the time her mother opened the door.

13. Escape from Alan Ayckbourn

As I picked my moment and dashed across the M3 from the westbound side to the eastbound at Fleet Services (it was just gone midnight on Sunday now, a good time to cross a M-Way if you really have to, and I really had to; and in any case, crossing the M3 this time of night was a piece of piss compared to crossing a main road in Lada Heaven), I was trying to work out if I was trusting the right people. I mean, Gerry and Deeny had stitched me up while playing their little game, OK. But then so had Masha. She must have known I had no idea, as she waited there in the dark.

*

She must have been waiting in the dark. Unless she can see in it.

Due to the unforeseen sex with Sarah, I had forgotten to take the first precaution one has to take when bedding down for the first time in a big, old, dark house: to locate the lav for night-time use. So when I awoke, not yet hung over but busting for a piss and very unsure who I was or where I was, I had to feel my way in the solid blackness, out along to the corridor, and along it, eventually locating the door to a bog. Then, being unable to find the light-switch, I had to find the bowl with my feet, position myself carefully and then direct my piss by echo-location. Then try to get back home, with my hands vaguely stretched out in case I smashed into some painting or wall or whatever.

Which was when Mr Kant's secretary appeared, a thicker shade of black. And as if we had programmed the whole thing we just grabbed hold of each other without a word in the dark and I shoved her up against the wall.

The only way I can describe what I was thinking is: I was not thinking.

Partly, I did not dare to think, in case I woke up. This was far too good to be real, this does not happen any more: your fantasies stop coming true like this when you are about twenty-eight. From there on in it is all big dreams or little realities. I had thought.

I was not thinking any more. That was the other great thrill: the *not* thinking. We all think so much, about everything, all the time. And suddenly I was confronted, four-fifths off my head on wine and vodka, with a shadow that wanted (for clearly, she wanted) to be shoved up against a wall. So if you ask me for clarification of my actions, for some description of my state of mind, I can only say that I was out of it and thinking, if anything: what the hell.

I lifted her right leg up and she threw the left up herself, around me; I stuck my right hand under her left thigh, to get at her knickers.

Weird.

Not her knickers, me. Us. People

I mean, an hour ago or whatever, I would not have given tuppence to put my hand inside someone's knickers. I would rather have watched England batting, for Christ's sake, than bother messing around with anyone's knickers. I had been sated, done for, had enough, content: I could no longer even *imagine* what it must feel like, must *have* felt like, to have a burning erection, what *I* must have been like, *who* I must have been half an hour before.

And now I was shoving my hand up underneath Mr Kant's secretary's arse, wanting nothing in the world more than to tear off her knickers and stroke her legs open so I could feel that still-incredible-after-all-these-years smoothness all over again, or rather: not all over again, for the first time. *As if* for the first time.

How can this be?

Surely, a cunt is a cunt is a cunt and a dick a dick and so on?

Nope.

I am glad for the sake of humanity to be able to report: nopety nope.

It was not just her cunt I wanted to get into. It was her.

Sorry, but we just don't need sex that badly. We can do without it altogether if need be, or if offered powerful enough bribes (like, say, a Bishopric in the Catholic Church). Once, when I was young and single, I found myself having just got off the bed and left my girlfriend's room with the dead silence of a failed relationship worming in my ears, a goodbye that was unspokenly, yet certainly, final; and found myself wanting to wank that very night. This worried me, so I decided not to. After three months without sex or wanking – the odd wet dream was not my fault, even Bishops get them – I had completely forgotten what an orgasm was like. Until, of course, the next time I ended up kissing a girl I nearly came in my trousers at the first twang of her bra-strap.

But that is the whole point: When you fuck with someone for the first time, or the first time in ages, or having last fucked with someone else, they are not just *a piece of ass*. They are them, this person, this other person, this unknown being. In that wonderful twilight between the unknown and the half-guessed-at, they are utterly fascinating. To fuck is to know, and we are put here set up and running to get to know as many of us as possible. And the more there is to know about a person the longer we want to fuck with them, which is why everyone goes on about GSOH and unpredictability all the time. Nope, sorry Mr Biology: our wild searches for fucking are nothing to do with genes and breeding any more. We do not really need sex at all; we just have a limitless craving for each other.

Tights.

Can you believe it?

Mr Kant's secretary was wearing tights.

I was surprised. No, *suprised* is wrong. I was shocked.

—Tights, nibbled Mr Kant's secretary in my ear: – The last bastion of rationality.

She had noticed my shock, even in the dark. For a half-second, I got one of those flashes of understanding: the lights in my brain flashed on like a long crack of lightning, and I saw this person with their strong legs clung round my waist, their arms round my neck and their smooth nylon-clad arse in my grasp in the black light. I could feel what I had felt, somehow, as she translated for Mr Kant: what had first hit me about her. It was the thin-ness of her skin, the sheer emotional conductivity of her. She had nerves where other people have space about them.

Good or bad? Is it good or bad to be like that? If we do not connect with each other, we are only half-human, we are dumb less-than-animals, autistic freaks of nature. And yet: if we connect too much, what are we? What is left of ourselves, if we are prey to all the fields and forces that other people generate in us? Is it worse to be a statue incapable of stretching out, or a blowing straw not worth the clutching at? If we feel too much, we could end up blown to rags like a torn sail in a wind too strong for it; but feel too little, and we will freeze over and crack into dust. Freedom and security can both be fatal conditions.

—Rationality, huh? I growled, through the nonexistent stuff in my throat.

—One last chance to think about it, said Mr Kant's secretary.

Think about it? That was the last thing I wanted to do, I could feel my highly unexpected third erection of the night losing steam already at the mere thought of thinking about it.

—Think fast, I said, without thinking what I was saying.

—If my father saw us, he would kill you, she said.

There was a time-delay while her words shouldered their way through the booze and lust into my brain:

—Your *father*?

Her father.

At that moment, I could have entered the Nobel Prize for Speed Erection-Losing with a quiet smile of confidence. Her father. It was not the threat of him killing me that worried me, I knew that was just bullshit like it always is. But the bastard had just offered me two million quid and by fucking with his daughter I was likely to fuck the deal up too.

She slid herself down me, now unhindered by my Incredible Shrinking Dick, and lowered herself softly onto her feet. She stood in front of me again. I could see just the palest hint of her face, now my eyes were at home in darkness.

—I've got to get back to my wife, I said.

—Then I will tell my father you are a coward.

—I thought you said he'd kill me if he knew.

—He would. But he does not like cowards.

—Right.

I mean, what was I supposed to do? So I did the simplest thing, the thing that required least thought; the action that demanded the least struggle against the night and the vodka and the loony-tunes playing around us. I leaned forward very slowly and licked the tip of my tongue around the unseen outline of her lips. She took my hand.

—We only have to talk, she said.

—OK, so we talk, I said.

And she led me through the darkness into her room.

It was a big bare room with a big white bed and nothing else in it except a triple candlestick, which she lit and then lit us cigarettes off it. She sat us on the bed and she talked. She said:

—I was twelve when I lost my virginity to a fumbling sixteen-year-old. Do you think that is too young?

—Twelve? I said.

—Sixteen, she said. – He was too young. Or too old. Or I was too young for a sixteen-year-old, maybe. One of you has to know what they are doing, or else both of you should be completely innocent. I was innocent, I was still dreaming about black horses, I knew I wanted *something* to happen but I was not sure what. Mr Kant ... my father did not believe in sexual education. He does now, because I have explained this to him. This boy knew, though: he was a virgin, yet not innocent at all in theory. That is the worst combination. Practice almost always has some gleam of innocence about it, whatever it is, but all theory is unclean, don't you think?

—Sure, I said.

(OK so what was I *supposed* to say? I am English for Christ's sake.)

—I was just his first practice. That was why it was wrong: the collision between innocent desire and a conscious plan. I would rather he had been twelve like me, and we had just stumbled across sex in a game, maybe; or else I would rather he had been twenty, and had understood what it was I was waiting for, and enjoyed helping me. You have fucked with your wife tonight?

—Well, yes, actually . . .

—Good. She is very beautiful. Good because you have, and good because you did not lie. I can smell you and her on you. I will finish my story.

What had happened, had happened. We walked back along the riverbank holding hands but miles apart, and then I just let his hand go and went home. I remember there were bats in the trees, I liked bats. My mother used to go out to watch them at the bottom of the long garden. I shall always remember her like that: seeing her, as I came up the garden to stand with her in the silent evening. Her there, with her back to me, looking out at the river beyond the garden and the forest far across the river, with bats circling her head. I suppose now that the bats were after the insects that came at her; but when I was a child I thought she had called to them in a voice I could not hear.

I had a school satchel still with me, I was swinging it quietly as I went, thinking of nothing, just feeling the weight of it as it searched for the centre of the earth.

And then when I came up the path to the house, I saw that all the windows and the front door were hung with heavy black curtains, and in front of the house was a long black car. I understood: the house was in mourning for my virginity. Old men in black coats, men with hats and beards were waiting for me. My father, too. He came down towards me, crying, and I ran onto his arms and cried, Sorry sorry sorry Daddy. And he looked at me and I whispered to him about what had happened to me. For a moment I thought he would hit me, but then he looked up at the sky and nodded and then led me inside, where they had laid my mother out.

Much later, I found out he had had the boy's legs smashed for ever. I was eighteen when I heard that, and I was glad.

She looked up at me:

—Tonight you sang with my father. There is no man like my father.

And then she lay back on the bed and pulled her skirt up over her tights. As I eased them down, her eyes were looking up at the ceiling, dark with need.

I do not claim to understand her need. I do not think anyone understands anyone else. The only thing we can do is stare out from our own fogbound beach and try to hear the rhythm of their waves breaking, the beat of the muffled oars that row on the big seas inside them that we cannot know. All we can do is walk into the fog with our eyes open and our hands outstretched.

And don't, please don't say I *should have helped her get over it* or any shit like that. Get over it? She never will. We never do.

We never get over anything. That is the trouble with being alive. Once it goes down in the Big Ref's book there is no appeal. It never comes out in the wash or in anything else but our dreams. You do not get over it; all you can do is get on with it. You paper over the cracks and plaster them in and shore them up; you raise your place on top of them, with all its secret distributions of weight and cunning lines of stress, yes, and the brave flying buttresses of your daylight life. But there is always that dark little room, at the end of your longest corridor, where the mad child who never grew up howls in its chains for a freedom it can never be allowed.

Safe sex? There is no such thing. Of course it is not safe, it is to do with other people. You let someone into your jeans and who says they will not make it into your head? If *I* turns to *us* the world is kicked into a new orbit. It could be the start of a life or the night you die, the sudden discovery of impossible happiness or the dead end of hope, who knows? You may be able to take precautions contraceptively, but never psychologically. Safe it is not.

Slowly, she refocused her eyes downwards on me; downwards, because I was gently sucking her left breast while tickling the very start of her clitoris until her legs had started to shiver gently open. She smiled.

For a second I wondered if it ever really happened. Her story, I mean. Or maybe she heard it from someone, or just made it up to explain some ache in her. Whatever, it was too late now: true or not, it was real now: I felt like it had happened, and to me; not to her, to me. I looked up into her eyes and I had memories of something that had never happened to me and maybe never happened at all to anyone, pictures lit with the flat green light before a storm. Her eyes had turned into mine, we were linked by a thing without being.

And as she pulled me up and hooked one leg over my shoulder, I had the mad feeling that I half-understood whatever she was saying in Russian, not like you understand a book, but like you understand a picture; and as I kissed her, I also half-understood, with a floor-dropping certainty, that if I had still been twenty-five she would not have brought me here. For the first time in years, I was glad to be me.

163

Her tights were still hanging from her other foot.

I woke up next to Sarah with a sandblasted brain, blinking at the unknown ceiling, vaguely conscious of a great onrushing shadow filling the world in front of me. I was in a small boat about to be run down by a vast, black tanker full to the gunwales with crude Guilt and Terror.

—Hello, said Sarah.

—Hello, I said, almost grateful for the whumping hangover that now kicked in. For kick in it did, and with such force that even the looming *M.S. Nemesis* (1,000,000 tons, registered in The Realms, captain: The Big Ref) was submerged almost without trace in the pounding waves.

—Christ! I moaned, and grasped for support even though I was lying down already.

Guilt sharpens the senses and fills the world with hidden, shadowy meanings. Your mind is developing the hazy pictures of your own failure, because all guilt is about failure. Not failure like failing an exam which you pass or fail, but a continuous assessment whose verdict grows slowly and unmistakably in the mirror. My radar was tuned as sharp as razors for any sign of knowledge or intimation from Sarah.

Terror was there too. Terror of the dawning realisation that I had probably just blown the deal that was supposed to save our lives. And she had said that he would kill me if he knew. But that was just a figure of speech, I was sure. Almost.

I took grateful refuge in the hangover.

—I want to die, I gasped at Sarah.

—Not yet, she said, – Not till we've banked this. I found it on the table next to the bed this morning.

She held out a draft for a quarter of a million pounds

drawn on the *Privat und Erbgut Verwaltungsbank AG* of Liechtenstein and payable to a certain *BIZVID Business Loan Account* which I knew we did not possess.

—Bugger me, I said.

—*That* I cannot do, said Sarah, grabbing my dick.

—Come on, I said, – Three times last night and . . .

—Twice.

—Oh, yes, sure. My head . . .

Pictures of bats and funerals flicked about just behind my eyes. Turn the key softly in the oiled wards.

—Look, said Sarah, after a while, and the intonation of her voice was unmistakably a Serious Conversation intonation. I tried to clear my eyes of bats and funerals, and looked round to face her and the music.

—Yes? I said.

—Look, I know I should have talked to you first, but I didn't and I'm sorry and all that but anyway, look: I went to the BUPA clinic yesterday and had tests on my tubes and cervix and my eggs.

—Oh, I said.

An awful possibility had occurred to me: if Sarah was somehow messed-up inside, then that meant I was probably not infertile, which meant that Mr Kant's daughter might get pregnant. Suddenly, I found myself desperately hoping Sarah was OK and I was infertile. Fear had brought me to the point of view I should have reached through love. They all count, eh Ref?

—And, well, I'm all right, said Sarah.

—Yes?

—Completely. Supernormal, in fact.

—Darling, I'm so glad!

—Oh. But that means it, it's . . .

—It's *me* then, that's for sure, eh? Oh well. Infertile. Still, like you said, darling: it's better that it's me.

—Oh Peter, how brave you are. I was thinking, now we could use some of the money for IVF, what do you think? I mean ...

—Absolutely.

—I *do* love you.

As we came down the upsloping corridor, we passed an open door: I felt metal in my mouth again, because I realised it was the door to Masha's bedroom. I kept my head fixed straight, but my eyes fired helplessly left into the room as we passed, and what they saw made me close them fast: Masha and Mr Kant's driver were standing there at the foot of the bed. They were talking close-to, she had to stand almost on tip-toes to get that close to his face, she was holding onto the Sam Browne belt of his uniform to reach herself up; he was putting her hair slowly right, and frowning as she spoke. They looked round and caught my look before I could shut it off.

In different ways, their looks both scared the shit out of me. Hers, because I felt my knees going and Sarah's hand in my hand suddenly growing weightless, as if it would just drift away from her if I loosened my grip; his, because it said he knew about us and would happily tear my spine out like a sardine.

They followed us down to where Mr Kant and Deeny were waiting, in the great hall, with the agreement ready to sign. I scanned the document, trying to look like a man with a lot to lose. It was simple, just the usual crap about *hereafter called The Business* and *assures the unfettered rights to dispose of* and *in the event of the decease of one signatory*, you know, the usual stuff. But sod the small print; the small print could not hide the big pattern: it was the deal of a lifetime, the kind of deal you only have to reel in once to cover your grub-stake for the duration.

Two mill to be paid, as specified, from Liechtenstein, into this nice, new, kosher, high-street account with our usual bank. Deeny explained: we naturally had to keep these funds separate from working-capital, and with himself co-signing as independent accountant (I had to look away when he said that, to stop myself choking) everything was properly safeguarded. *And no collateral except our name and goodwill!*

I hesitated, pen above paper, for just one half-second, because I had never heard of this bank in Liechtenstein, but Deeny murmured:

—Nor me. Nor the Banker's Almanac, I should say. Jesus, that's what you have a bank in fucking Liechten-stein *for*, Pete.

And he half-nodded and half-winked and half shook his head, all at once.

I scratched my signature on the three copies as if in a dream. While I wrote, I saw Mr Kant nodding slowly to himself in the corner of my eye.

Then Mr Kant's driver took Sarah and me home; Mr Kant and Masha waved from the door of the house. As the car pulled up outside our Executive Unit, Gerry and Melissa and the kids happened to be passing. They stopped to say hi: Mr Kant's driver did not get out to open the doors for us, he just whizzed the locks open and shooshed off.

—Well, how did it go? asked Gerry.

It was good to have someone to tell, we both felt that: Sarah insisted they stayed for lunch. I think she just wanted to have them here now she was happy, since they had seen her not really happy so many times. So we sat around and I read stories to the kids as she told them all about it, and when I was asked, I nodded and smiled.

I didn't say anything about the river and the black-draped house and the bats, of course. Or about the look Mr Kant's driver had given me. Them I kept locked behind my eyes, until we were lying in bed that night, and Sarah was asleep. Then I could let them out to fill the dark above the bed.

14. Not Talking about Fucking

Gerry was ready for bed, he yawned contentedly as he checked the kids' rooms and found his brood asleep with their various soft toys cuddled up close. But Melissa wanted to talk about Sarah.

She had an idea. When she told Gerry, he looked at her in more than some astonishment:

—You didn't actually say this to her, did you?

—Of course not. Not yet.

—Shit, honey, I don't know.

—But it's just logical, Gerry. Sarah wants a baby, so why shouldn't you be the sperm-donor? I would have thought Peter would be delighted, I mean, you are his friend. Surely he would rather have his friend donate some sperms than just anybody? And you have no history of abnormality in your family.

—Phew, said Gerry: – I mean, wow, you're saying I should go and . . .

—I'm not talking about fucking, Gerry, just donating. A turkey-baster job, you know.

—Sure, sure. You are incredible.

—Just practical, darling. Are you feeling tired?

—A little.

—Oh good. I like it so much better when you're a bit tired. So much more of a challenge, don't you think?

Later, when Melissa was asleep in whatever pristine world she dreamed in, that world which Gerry could only guess at but which he was determined to defend anyhow, he went quietly downstairs, turned on his PC, and tapped in the password SURRENDER? NUTS.

Then he sat for quite a long time in the multicoloured glow from the screen, pondering the rather scanty contents of the file which he had called up by clicking with his mouse on the name SEAN DEENY.

15. Intermezzo: Mostarda Di Uva

Imagine that you are a salesperson in the Conran Shop in Kensington, you know, in that building with the twenties Michelin Man on it. This means, naturally, that if you are a man you are probably gay, or maybe you are just the kind of end-of-millennium straight man who has opted to focus his entire self-consciousness on his outward appearance, his hair, teeth, trilats and all: it is getting harder and harder to tell the difference. If you are a woman, on the other hand, it means you are probably wearing short, dyed hair (black or peroxide) with a designer-simple sleeveless minidress and heels, and your CV probably records a nice London day-school and not *quite* enough brains to get into Art History.

But who cares about all this? All this is just clues for method-actors, who are well-known to be the biggest pains in the arse there are: all you need to do is imagine *you* are there, we all see the same things, and that is all that matters now, *you* are bored (who would not be?) and *you* are staring out of the main doors absently, and what *you* see is this:

In the foyer of the building, where all those nice tile-pictures of twenties cars are, a man and his wife are eating a delicate continental breakfast at one of the small, red-check-clothed tables. At first glance they seem quite at home here, they have that authentic mortgage-free look about them: but when you look more closely, you notice that there is an edge to their pleasure, a slight tinge of self-conscious voluptuousness

171

in their butter-spreading and coffee-swigging and eye-contact, which suggests that they have not yet quite had time to get bored with this game.

Then they come in and start to browse about and yes, you were right, their voices are just that touch too loud. It is not that they are trying to impress other people. No, they are trying to impress upon *themselves* the fact that they really are here, that they really can take it home if they want it.

The woman sits on a sofa and tests its comfort with faraway eyes; the man watches her, they have no eye-contact now. Maybe it is because of this, maybe because he is the kind of man who needs to talk about his happiness to make it real to him, or maybe there is some other reason, but whatever: he raises his eyes skywards and mouths *thank you*.

They buy and buy, chatting as they go, and what they buy is this: a coffee-pot designed to look like one of those blue-and-white striped milk jugs, only with a lid for pouring, of course; some really quite cheap little Italian coffee-cups made of Pyrex and steel wire – first twelve and then another four, then only eight after all because actually they were quite boring when you thought about it; a cherry-oak dining table, distressed (as well it might be, having been battered about with oily chains in a shed in Swansea) and with kind of rusty iron band things with rivets here and there, to make it look like it was once falling to bits; a parmesan cheese grater shaped vaguely like half an avocado; a tall chrome lemon-squeezer rather like Tintin's moon-rocket, which reminded him he wanted to go to the Tintin shop afterwards to buy Tintin things.

—Who the hell for, I hate them, she says: – And we haven't got any children, remember?

—Oh, just to give out at the office party, you know,

he says, and looks at some Mostarda di Uva which, according to the pot, could *even accompany snow*, which he says sounds unlikely.

—Look, says she, – I've made an appointment to see the BUPA doctor about IVF this afternoon.

—Right.

—We agreed we would, didn't we?

—Oh yes, absolutely. In principle. I don't see how you would serve snow.

—So I thought I'd go ahead and fix it up.

—Without discussing it.

—Without wasting any more time. It's just a preliminary meeting to see what the options are. So we know.

—Oh, *we?* Am I invited?

—Thresholds, darling. Sorry. Unfair. I just … I've just had this feeling, the last couple of days, that you don't want to know. It's like, we've got this money now so you don't care any more. I bet if I'd discussed it with you you would have said we should wait a bit longer. Don't lie. Well I don't want to wait.

—Right, he says.

Then she went off to look at some furniture in peace, and he went and bought a wonderful retro-designed radio, sort of like a fifties cadillac dashboard, cream-and-chrome plastic, you know, rather offputting that you could *see* the modern speaker-things inside the grilles, but never mind, and two Citroen CV-ish toy cars marked *not toys*, made, so it seemed, by Africans out of tin cans. He almost got this strange clock that worked by projecting a beam of light onto a kite-ish assembly of white linen and sticks that you had to hang up somewhere quite a long way from it. But in the end he decided it was just too crap.

Then he looked at his watch and scanned around and

knelt down behind a bookshelf full of books to tell you how to make your house look. Holding it rather conspicuously far from his ear, he used a mobile phone to phone someone called Charlie and tell her that she would have to stall Irons and Jobson, whoever they were, because he was not ready yet, and then he said something else to her, very quietly, then put the phone back in his pocket and re-arranged his underpants surreptitiously.

If you could have looked into his head right then, you would have seen him and this Charlie a week before, hot with drink and dancing, bundling each other through the door and into the lift of an old office building in Charing Cross Road, and you would have seen her hit the button for the top floor, lean back on the wooden panelling, take him by the tie and just reel him in like he was on wheels. And if you could have looked doubly into his head, to see what he was actually thinking back then as they fucked in the lift, you would have seen a long garden far away, with a big river beyond it, and a girl turning round and looking at you from a cloud of bats.

A busy, busy mind.

All you actually saw, of course, was him hitching his dick tactfully and wiping his brow.

Then he took his big pile of purchases in their nice bags (not the table, of course, that was being delivered) and blundered over to the circular, rotating shelves of olive oil. Perhaps he did this because he was very interested in olive oil, many people *are*; or perhaps because the olive oil carousel is very centrally placed in the Conran Shop, so going there meant that he could see his wife from there and watch her, in that funny way you can watch someone you usually only see close-to; or perhaps because there is room around the olive oil to put down a big pile of bags and rest your arms. Or maybe just because he could not think what to do with himself right then and needed a quiet think while he looked at something meaningless, like the ridiculous crap they write on bottles of designer olive oil, who knows?

But anyway, he spent a long time wandering absently around the circular shelves, taking out bottles and putting them back, humming some kind of Country & Western tune to himself and occasionally mouthing words to it. Eventually, a tall gentleman, splendidly mustachioed and sporting a long leather coat, also with a substantial load of purchases in tow, came up, stood beside him, took the olive oil next to the bottle he was looking at, and smiled winningly.

Before he could re-gather his heap of things and flee, however, his wife came back. She came up in rather a marching sort of way and said it looked like there was someone to see him.

The someone concerned turned out to be a very elegantly dressed young lady of striking, distinctly foreign appearance, not strictly beautiful but quite unforgettable, who was crossing the big floor with an air that made it quite clear she was not here to shop. He staggered.

—How the hell did she know we were here? asked his wife.

—I don't bloody know. Christ, unless they're following us.

—Don't be ridiculous.

—Good morning. Mr Kant sends his regards. He trusts that BIZVID is prospering.

—Thanks to Mr Kant, it is, he replied gallantly.

—That is good. Unfortunately, Mr Kant has found it necessary to put a temporary stop on the next payment.

—What?

—Temporary. There is one small point which must first be cleared up, and for which it will be necessary for Mr Kant to meet you in person once again. Very soon.

—Great, said his wife.

—Right, um, OK, so, when?

The girl looked at her watch:

—Late today or else tomorrow.

—Right. Well . . .

—The car will arrive at mid-day, at your house.

—OK, OK, twelve tomorrow it is.

—Today. Flight BA 2880 from Gatwick to Moscow departs at 13.35. You will check in by one o'clock.

—Moscow?

—Here is your ticket.

She then produced a small, chromium-plated camera and fired off three shots with a motor-drive and flash, at his face.

—Jesus, he said, blinking.

—Mr Kant's driver will have your visa. There is an early heat-wave in Moscow, yet there are still small pieces of ice floating down the river. It is very interesting.

—I don't believe this, said his wife. For a moment it almost looked as if she was going to plant herself between them.

—It is simply business, said the girl.

—And will *you* be going to Moscow? his wife asked her.

—Oh no, she replied, – I have business on the Volga, far from Moscow.

And she left.

—Bloody wonderful, hissed his wife, and folded her

arms and bit her lip. She glared at the girl's back: –
Tweety bloody pie.

—Jesus! he shouted suddenly, so that people near
him jumped.

—Don't bloody well shout at me, she snapped.

—I'm not, I'm just ... shouting. Where are you
going? Sarah, for God's ... wait. Sarah!

—I am going bloody home. And then I am going to
the bloody BUPA clinic, all right? On my bloody own.
Oh yes, and then I am going to bin that bloody
resignation letter to school. It looks like I'd better,
doesn't it?

—All right, all right, just ... Sarah, look, give me a
hand with this, it's ...

He attempted to gather up his massed bags while
already setting off after her. He got tangled in the wire
from the retro-radio, dropped the bag with the coffee-
pot in it so it smashed, raised his fist towards the
ceiling, shouted *Jesus fucking Christ, Referee!*, looked
around at everybody, went a very bright shade of pink,
and eventually managed to stagger off after her,
unknowingly dripping Mostarda di Uva from a sagging
carrier-bag as he went.

Quite fun working in the Conran Shop, actually.

16. The Bomb Ranger

As I filled the Volvo right to the last drop at Fleet Services on the M3 westbound (it was now just coming up to midnight; as I walked up to pay, I took off my Tintin cap to wipe my brow, making quietly sure that I was doing so in full view of the surveillance cameras), I was thinking how Mr Kant and Dr Jones must have planned the final stitch-up. They had me taped from the moment I landed at Moscow Sheremetovo.

*

It was half-eight Moscow time and still warm when I arrived at Sheremetovo, having already half-surrendered to the in-flight booze. I felt sweaty and particularly fat. But not guilty.

Stupid, but not guilty: stupid, because I knew from my own sodding training-videos (*Meet to Deal!*) that many is the lad who has been bounced by freshly pressed Yanks or Japs as he staggers out blinking onto the runway, expecting only a final large one, bathtime and beddy-byes; but not guilty, because there is no shame in giving in to the miniatures when your brain is just circling like some doomed jumbo waiting for a landing-slot that is not going to come free.

For the first two hours, I had bravely resisted the cheery trolleys. I had read through the whole Agreement a dozen times, trying to work out what this *small point* was, and whether I could hold him to the contract if he wanted to change it. It was down to muggins, because I had been unable to get hold of Deeny or even Jenkins, they were both on bloody holiday, sod them. I

178

kept on saying to myself over and over again, like a mantra: *no collateral, no collateral*. I couldn't lose. Even if everything blew up now, I still had the first payment.

Trouble was, I needed the next one. One more, at least. We had our showdown meeting with the Special Compliance lads from the Enquiry Branch of the Revenue coming up, and we still did not have enough to pay them off.

I know, I know: I should never have paid off the sodding mortgage and booked that five-star hol to Bermuda. But it had just felt soooo bloody good, dishing out the dosh like that. And we were, like I said, hoping that Bermuda would fool Sarah's selfish genes into thinking I was a new man as in different man. Bollocks and bollocks and shit. And then, of course, Deeny had had to have his little, or not-so-little, whack at the dough too. Fuck.

If we had just sat sodding tight, I could damn nearly have paid the Revenue off with what Mr Kant had already given us. Then I could have just told Kant to piss off when he summoned me, and argued breach of contract if he didn't keep paying, losses as result of said breach, and all that. No UK court would have enforced repayment. Sod it sod it sod it. Thank Christ I had at least resisted trading the Volvo lease up for a Merc. Well, *resisted* is not quite the right word: Sarah had put the knackers on that one by pointing out pointedly that the Merc did not have a built-in child seat.

Sarah, that was the worst thing about it all. Her face, I mean. When I had caught up with her outside the Conran Shop, and tried to explain as I wiped the sodding mostardo di crappo off my new trousers, she had just looked at me.

You know that look. When you are trying to justify something rationally to someone, and you know you are right and all, rationally; you are doing the only sensible thing, logically; but this person just looks at you, and suddenly your voice sounds all hollow and thin and feeble. Because it suddenly comes to you that all you are really saying is: *we are not free, I am not free and with me you are not free. I am doing something I do not want to do. Someone else is calling the shots.* True but saaad.

Sarah had accepted it. It all added up, after all. I was right to go, she knew I was right and she had to accept it. But the look in her eyes as she accepted it was the look of a person taking yet another little hit of despair. No, not *despair*; nothing as grand as despair. Just tiredness. Just another petty weight on the shoulders, another weary little defeat.

But shit, I mean, OK, so I was coming when Mr Kant whistled: not very sexy, maybe. But who wouldn't? We all do things we don't want to do. And why? Because of the maths. Because we have looked at the percentages and the angles and we reckon that the maths will come out in our favour, in the end. One day all these seedy little deals will pay off, and buy our freedom. Like now, like for us: if I could just swing this next payment, that would be it. He could stop coughing up after this one, sod him: he could have BIZVID, if it came to it. Just one more payment. Just let me reel in this one, Ref.

—Just this one? Mr Thompson, asked the Tweedy Edinburgh Lady, who had appeared with her two colleagues, looking at me from the next aisle. – So you say. But perhaps one gets short-sighted with staring for years at the maths; perhaps one can no longer see the real thing when it goes riding by?

—Oh for God's sake, I moaned out loud.

—Exactly, said Sarah's look from down Memory Lane.

180

—Shrrshrshhhhh, whispered the engines of the plane, on and on.

—Tinkle-tinkle, went the drinks trolley in my ear, by and by.

Two hours I could have stood. Three, maybe. I could have made anywhere in the EC without giving in. But when I saw that two hours had gone and we *still* had nearly two to go, it was just too much.

Is there anything that feels better than giving in? As the hostess fished for the crap plastic cup, I gazed around the plane, just to remind myself that I was not exactly acting like sodding Nero or something, just having a nice little drink to relax myself, just like everyone else. No better, no worse. I poured the first wee bottle over the ice almost drop by drop, and sipped it good and long and slow. Well, it *felt* like I took much more than five minutes over it, I swear.

And so here I was now, queueing for Russian bloody immigration in an unairconditioned hell, just wanting to go and lie down somewhere and wake up on a health farm. The evening sun threw no shadows through the heavy sky and the filthy glass roof; instead, the saved-up heat of the day seemed to emanate out in a solid wave from the ground, the concrete, the people.

I mean, for Christ's sake: as a good European, I even find the arrivals building at JFK pretty horrible. If you are a lucky, whitish Old Worlder, used to sailing merrily through the nice EC CITIZENS lanes in spacious, airy places like CDG or Frankfurt, after about half an hour in the queue for immigration at JFK you start to think *Oh for God's sake, you arrogant Yank bastards, you really do think the whole world is full of people dying to get into your bloody country illegally, don't you?*

However, there is at least a certain logic to the Yanks

messing you about like this, since the correct answer is *well yes, actually, yes: we believe that because it is true.*

But Russia?

It took me three quarters of an hour to get up to the pale-faced, fish-blue-eyed bastards sitting in their cheap-rate neo-Prussian uniforms in their plexiglass cabins. Each time they got a passport, they just stared at it for a good two minutes, doing nothing at all, then stamped it. Shitheads. As I at last reached the head of my particular queue, I remembered just in time that I should get myself physically sorted (as described in that BIZVID classic *Be There for Business!*) in order to get the vital first impression right.

Skulking behind a tall German in a miraculously uncreased suit, I tucked in the shirt and belly, re-tied the tie, shiftily licked my palm to flatten down the sticking-up diehards of what used to be my hairline, and straightened my cuffs.

I was now able to throw back my head, flare my nostrils, and generally march up to the SMERSH-faced ratbag at the counter (and thus into the view of the Arrivals Hall) with the general air of man who is not here to piss about, but here to deal and sod off out (twang twang).

I maintained a steely poise despite the weight of the booze and the flight tugging down at my shoulders; I waited the regulation two minutes without once looking out at the Arrivals Hall for Mr Kant or whichever sidekick he had sent. Psychology, see: you let *them* do the looking. You have to show whoever is waiting that it is *them* waiting for *you*, not the other way around. I took the passport back with a curt nod, and swung round to strut out into the Arrivals Hall even as I pocketed the docs. Shame I missed my inside pocket and had to scrabble about to pick them up, but there you are. Ta very much, Ref. I arose, pinker and even more sweaty, and scanned the place.

It looked like the main concourse of a hideous sixties British Rail station that had been taken over by very expensive art-design teams and turned into the set for *Mad Max IV*. I mean, I knew Russia was different, but this was Moscow, for Christ's sake, the capital, the main sodding entrepot airport. And it was not first world, maybe not even second world: this was so close to the Third World you could smell it.

The first clue was the double file of shouting, grabbing taxi-drivers besieging us as we filed out. The next was the shade-toting police leaning and lounging on their blue-and-white Ladas, amidst the klaxoning hordes of other Ladas. But the big giveaway was the Army.

The Army consisted of men in various combinations of half-uniforms, many of them including blue-and-white striped T-shirts. Some wore para-like berets, some had navy-style caps with little ribbons hanging down, others sported baseball caps. They slouched about with their little moustaches and greasy hair, cradling wooden-butted kalaschnikovs. Most of them also had various large handguns stuck in the waists of their trousers, strapped to their thighs, or joggling about in loose shoulder-holsters. They were all either in the middle of a cigarette, or just lighting up, or just stubbing out. And all of them had transparent plastic ID photo-wallets slung on strings round their necks, to prove they really *were* the actual Army, just in case you were in any doubt.

Now, as a good Anglo-Saxon, I always feel that having a large and publicly displayed standing army about the place in peacetime is rather dodgy. But if there is one thing I like less than being in a country where order is obviously only maintained by a large standing army, it is being in a country where order is obviously only maintained by a large slouching army.

Especially when I have just fought a path through unwashed taxi-drivers with my dignity being sapped every foot of the way; when I have walked, masterfully at first and then gradually more and more feebly, through the Arrivals Hall, without anyone stopping me, without any nice or even any cheap and nasty sign saying MR THOMPSON BIZVID, and have, at last, ended up standing outside the door, lost, in the foul, taxi-fume-ridden air, with no-one to meet me and bugger-all idea where I am going.

I took a step outside the shade of the concrete roof, to scan for any sign of hope: now the invisible sun pressed gently down through the smoggy haze like a warm, damp towel.

—Taxi taxi sir! cried a leather-blousoned and dentally challenged thug, proudly indicating a hideously rusting brown Lada and grabbing hold of my bag. I held on to it.

—No. Um, nyet, no taxi, no!

—Yes taxi no bus no train only taxi.

—Look, just bugger off will you? I half-snapped, as rudely as is it Englishly possible to be.

—Baggeroff Viliu? the driver frowned, and his momentary puzzlement let me snatch my bag back fully. He glowered and advanced again. Two of the Slouching Army men nearby checked to see how much they had left of their fags, to decide whether it was worth stubbing them out and coming over.

So all in all, I was almost relieved when the taxi-driver fled as Mr Kant's chauffeur crash-stopped beside us, at the wheel of an especially, I mean *customisedly*, crap light-green Lada.

Almost. As glad as you can be to see someone again, when the last time you saw them you had a good idea that what they really wanted to do was peel you like a prawn, spine by spine by spine.

—About bloody time too! I said forcefully, leaning down to his window to gain the height-advantage, and trying to play it justly outraged. – You are late. Late. Where is Mr Kant? Where Mr Kant?

The bastard just kicked the door open and unfolded himself slowly out of the car, so that I finished by having to look upwards at about forty-five degrees to keep up eye-contact. He took my suitcase out of my hand like I was some bolshie teenager, flipped it into the back of the Lada, shut the back door, opened the front passenger door, and went back to the driver's seat to start her up again. When I got in, he let in the clutch before my arse touched the bouncy plastic seat. Just to check on his lack of English, I said HE IS NOT PROGRAMMED TO SMILE HE HAS A GOB LIKE A CAT'S ARSE, loud and clear. His face didn't move. As we swung round the first bend, I grabbed hurriedly for the seat belt and found nothing. The bastard smiled.

We roared at a deafening 50mph past the huge, hundred-foot tall Marlboro Cowboy painted onto the side of a crumbling tower-block. We clattered past the red steel tank-traps that mark where the Panzers got to in December 1941. We weaved along the showpiece eight-laner as if it was one big lane to be used at will, choking in our own smoke, never mind the smoke from a trillion other identical, uncatalysed Ladas. As we veered underneath the huge banner saying *Trinity Motors: Cadillac Pontiac Chevrolet*, I had already reached

185

my first conclusion about Russia. Instead of proclaiming salvation through Americana, the banner should have given more useful advice, like: *Welcome to Russia you might as well die pissed.*

Mr Kant's driver dumped me outside the Hotel Budapest and cranked straight off, leaving me to check in alone. I asked where Mr Kant was, and no-one had ever heard of him. For a moment I looked round in panic at the cloud of blue smoke that was still hanging in the fat air where Mr Nazi's Lada had been. Then I calmed myself by remembering that Masha had said *today or tomorrow.* Fine then, tomorrow it must be. Quite right. Quite sensible. Considerate, even. A nice quiet night, tomorrow we do our business, and I get out.

I had to pay for the room myself. Bastards. They just waved *Nyet* when I offered them my Visa-card; they pointed to a sign on the counter which said the room was $200 a night; I tried to pay in dollars; they told me dollars were unacceptable and illegal; they changed my dollars to roubles at 4 per cent commission and took $200 dollars' worth of roubles. It was a lot of roubles. But I did not care. At least the room had been booked; at least someone knew I was coming. I had somewhere to park my bags, scratch my arse and floss my teeth.

The Hotel Budapest was a middling attempt to imitate a western business-class hotel, though the long, high, snaking corridors still whiffed mildly of cabbage-steam, old damp and purges. At my door, I tried to tip the porter with roubles, but he looked at me like I was utterly saaad; I gave him five dollars, and he was happy.

I shut the door gratefully. I flossed my teeth, scratched my arse, peeled off my sour-smelling clothes, had a very unrelaxing fight with a dysfunctional sodding shower and then sat on the bed, doing nothing, in limbo. I walked up and down. I sat on the bed again. I lay on it. I called reception to see if anyone or anything was there for me. No-one and nothing was.

I hate rooms in business-class hotels anyway, anywhere. *Hate* is the right word. Business-class hotel rooms are where the fantasy of Executive Lifestyles crumples into the reality of industrial carpeting, portion-control menus, humming minibars and pay-as-you view porn. And the soundtrack: the roaring of emptiness, the pre-echo hiss of suspended living which all business-class hotel rooms seem to have built in to them. I had often had this feeling in pisspot hotels in England, but now I was getting the big-screen version: that old sound of nothingness was coming on in Dolby pro-logic.

I felt like I was starting very slowly to dematerialise. I could feel my willpower being sucked gradually away. I had let myself be bullied into the worst negotiating position: an away game with a nobbled ref, a hostile crowd and no interpreter.

Masha.

I called Sarah. And got the ansaphone. *Hi, this is Peter Thompson.* I had forgotten about the time-zones, of course. Sarah was zones and zones away, it must be the middle of the night there. I just said *Hi Sary, Peter, um, sorry, forgot about the time-stuff, um, everything ok here, nothing much happening yet, and no, Mr Kant's secretary is not here, ok? My phone number here is 007 yeah, really! 007 095 740 9832, Room, um, room 241, so, yeah, give us call? I'll try again tomorrow. Bye. Bye.*

Great. I put down the phone with that old feeling of having called Sarah and said nothing I wanted to say (twang twang). Then, with my hand still on the phone, I thought again. Hold on, I thought: the time-zones were not like Yankland, it was the other way round. It was only seven p.m. at home. Sarah could not be asleep. So she was out. At seven. Somewhere. With some people.

Gerry and Melissa? No, Melissa was away for a week at her parents, because Gerry was apparently working his balls off till all hours on something or other and needed a kid-free zone. Gerry alone? Would Sarah go to dinner with Gerry on her own? No. Someone else, then. Someone else.

Funny. Whenever Sarah called me at BIZVID and said she was going out for a drink with her colleagues at school, as she naturally sometimes did, I was perfectly happy. It meant I could go and get pissed straight after work, which is always the best time to get pissed.

Charlie.

For a second I had a flashback to us fucking in the lift. I smelled Charlie's sweat again. Her shoulders had smelled of warm green peppers. She had been wearing black cotton knickers with a little red flower embroidered on them on one side. Before the second time, I had let her photocopy her hand round my dick, for Christ's sake.

Lies, lies, lies.

And yet now, here, so far away, the idea that Sarah was out there somewhere, with someone else, seemed full of dark overtones. Oh, come on! Her colleagues, of course. Remember, she had been about to give the job up, and now she was thinking about keeping it on. Obvious: she would be out, talking it through with her colleagues. Her teaching colleagues. Nice safe boring teachers. So that was OK. Fine, then.

'Mr Kant's Secretary'! As if. I blushed at my lies to Sarah even as I thought of Masha. But she was not here, by whatever name.

I lay on the bed, staring at the ceiling, hearing

mosquitoes even though there were no mosquitoes. The only lights in my mental horizon were red ones, whispering sex. No, not sex: feeling. Just feeling. Whores know their business, and that is why they hang out around hotels in big cities: they know it isn't the need for sex that sends we poor travellers out into the dark alleyways. We just want to feel *something* undeniable, we hand over the hard currency just to be reminded, in the most basic, definite way, that we do actually exist after all. I am fucking therefore I must be. I am coming therefore I must be going somewhere.

I tried reception one last time. Nothing. No-one. I thought idly about having a wank. Except then I had a kind of helicopter-shot vision of the thousands of blokes, blokes of every colour and creed but all with the same suits hanging up and the same trousers in the trouser-presses beside them, who must be wanking saaadly away in business-class hotels (or rather, business-class wankeries) at any given moment of the global day. So instead of relegating myself wilfully to this lower division of humanity, I fled out into the evening air with my duty-free plastic half-bottle of alleged Famous Grouse, just to see what the other higher primates round here were up to; just to have a quiet drink away from the nonexistent mosquitoes in my head.

I was near Red Square, so I thought I should do it. I mean, Red Square is on the list. You know, The List of things in the world actually worth seeing, the things that every self-respecting human should try to see before they check out. If we do The List, then when the Big Ref blows for full time, as the roar of the crowd fades away behind us and the horizon fills with the mouth of the tunnel that leads to the dressing-rooms of eternity, we will be able to say, if nothing else: *well, at least I really did Earth when I had the chance.*

As I stared at the deep red of the floodlit Kremlin walls, and the mad sugartwist fantasy of St Basil's, with the dark, muttering Orthodox chants coming out from the little gilded chapel across the square with its cheap fairy lights saying *alpha* and *omega*, I swigged away at my plastic bottle and considered The List, in no order of importance:

Red Square.

The Great Wall of China.

Trflgr Sq.

Manhattan.

Swig, swig.

A little pub in Ireland, you amidst musicians, singing sweet black-note harmonies. Where? Christ knows. Memory Lane.

Vienna. No, scrub that. Florence for sure.

A full-moon moonlight rainbow. All the colours plus silver edging. Nice. Rare.

Red Square. Oh no, been there. Am there, in fact.

Swig-g-g-g. Oops, shagging cobble-stones.

My mother, no, not mine, someone's, a mother at the end of a long garden in the light of a summer evening, with bats.

The Piazza San Marco at 4 a.m.

Walking with pals on the Blorenge, which is a mountain in Wales and the only word in English that rhymes with orange.

Swig. Bet there's PCBs in this plastic bloody bottle. Stonehenge.

Eh? Stonehenge doesn't rhyme with orange. Well, not except in Country and Western, but then everything rhymes in Country and Western. Twang twang.

Ho Hum.

Swig swig.

What the hell do these ad-signs all say? *Cadbury's* something. K-r-a-? *Cadbury's Kranchi Nat!* Cute: sweet and cheap, a little fix of the western good time as promised by the golden arches of McD's over the way. Large or regular salvation, sir?

When I was little, you could still sit on the stones of Stonehenge. We lived near there, and I often did sit on them with my brother. Must call him soon. I scratched my name on them. If everyone sat on them and autographed them, they would fall down. In fact, if everyone just walked around them for a few more years they would fall down, just from the earth around them being packed down by all those feet. If you want it to stay there, you have to wall it off.

> (2,3 . . .)
> (Cos there) Ain't no entrance
> To Memory Lane
> (And) there ain't no children sitting
> In Stonehaynge

Diddlee dye.

Swigetty swig.

What's the time? Did I reset my watch? Why am I here? Oh fuck and crap and shit.

Elton John.

Elton John? He's not on the list. No way.

No, but he's playing.

What?

Yep, saaad but true: you come two thousand miles and they still pipe Elton John into your head. Alan Ayckbourn you might escape, Elton John will always get you.

—Do you have light sir?

Ah, so here I was (*hi Pete, this is Pete*), that explained all
the E. John naffery going on: I had somehow left Red
Square and, having evidently polished off my whisky,
was now gargling it down with beer in some flasho
little bar, with no idea how I had got here. Oiled wards,
or what? Jet-lag and cheap whisky, I put it down to.

And there was this girl asking me for a light, she had
just said *Do you have light sir?* and that was why I was
fumbling around to try to find my matches. I eventually
managed to give her a light, and she turned away with
the most surprising expression of disdain on her
chinless little, shrew-nosed, make-up caked face. OK,
Ref, so matches aren't that cool, but . . .

—Fifty dollars, said a deep, growling voice.

I repositioned myself on the stool, carefully, so as not
to turn my head too fast and lose my balance, and
looked around. It was a big, fat bloke in a purple velour
jacket and red-frilled shirt, with a lot of heavy rings and
a scar that started in the snuffling, zitty undergrowth of
his moustache, rooted up along his broken nose, and
ended with a small flourish between his yellowed eyes.
– Fifty dollars for drink with lady you talk.

Fear did the usual wonder-job of clearing the happy,
boozy mists, and I looked around again with eyes now
half-alive. I was not mad: there really *was* no sign it was
that kind of bar. Was it possible that some horrible
radar in me had detected it? I mean, I knew I had not
consciously been aiming for some place like this. But
then, doing something unconsciously is no excuse, in
fact, it's worse: you can't apologise for what you do in
your dreams or your cups. Or maybe this was just a big
rip-off. I tried to get my tongue working, despite its
unusual size.

—Look, I said, – I'm sorry, I didn't . . .

—Fifty dollars, he said, and his scar glowed red.

I turned to the barman, who had just now been the epitome of a friendly barman, no doubt due to my having left him (as I now recalled) a dollar when I bought my beer. I also remembered that he had definitely spoken English. I thanked the Big Ref that I had learned to tip unBritishly:

—Look, I said, – Sorry, but could you just explain that . . .

But my friendly barman had just suffered a hideous attack of instant deafness and blindness. I suppose a dollar isn't that much really, even in Russia. I licked my lips.

—Fifty dollars, said Mr Scar.

This constant repetition was getting on my nerves. Worse, it was pressing on my bowels: because despite the drink, I knew I had paid for the beer with a twenty, and that this twenty was all I had brought with me from the hotel, thanks to Gerry's words on muggings. Great. So now I was going to get murdered because I had not wanted to be mugged. I got a strange taste in my mouth, a taste that for some reason reminded me of an old, wet dog. Funny, because I have never knowingly eaten an old, wet dog.

—OK, OK, I said; I spread my arms and dropped my eyes in the international language of defeat. I carefully emptied my pockets, I even pulled them inside out, and held out all I had in cash, which was thirteen dollars. I opened out my jacket and patted my empty inside pockets. He hit me. Just like that.

Not hit, just bloody slapped. Bastard. Without thinking, I grabbed for his collar with my left; next thing, I was off the stool and kneeling on the floor with his arm round my neck and my mouth squashed into the stainless steel of the bar. It tasted of salt and bleach.

My ex-mate the barman was looking at me coldly as he rummaged around for something under the bar. I heard the heavy grate of a metal object on the stainless steel. I saw his arm flex as he picked something up, and then the dull metal thing was clanked down on the bar in front of my nose.

A credit-card voucher printer. Mr Scar hoisted me up by the lapels:

—You credit card. Fifty. More fifty for trouble.

And then someone touched him on the shoulder and he turned.

It was a small dark bloke with a huge moustache. His shades were lit as if from within by the red neon from the Budweiser sign over the bar and his yellow suit shone with its own, dyed-in power. All he did was reach Mr Scar a business-card.

Mr Scar took it with one hand; I sagged gently away from him, and when his other arm was fully extended, he just let go, as if he had forgotten about me. I turned through a half-circle to get the bar at my back. Mr Scar took a long time with the card, like someone who is not too hot at reading, or someone who does not want to know what he is reading.

And then he went, just like that, grabbing the girl as he went quickly to the door.

My saviour waved to the barman, who was now our best friend again, and two beers materialised. Then he spoke. In English. Not even Yank English; real proper English.

—A professional, obviously. You would have done better to find one of the many educated, attractive amateurs in Moscow: there are even more here than in

194

L.A. One could draw a most useful graph: on *this* axis, the real income differentials obtaining in a city, on *that* axis the youth and attractiveness of its prostitutes.

—I just came in for a drink. Honestly. (I smiled ingratiatingly, keen to make him like me and keep me under his mysterious protection.) —So what the hell was on that card?

—The name of Mr Kant's best-known local associate. I choked on my beer.

—Mr Kant? You know him?

—If I did not, I would merely have observed your predicament with amusement. One of the more depressing aspects of life in Moscow is watching western males indulging themselves with amateur dollar-prostitutes. It is not so much the financial availability of Russian women that attracts them, as the fact that Russian women *put up* with so much. They *expect* their men to be drunken, sadistic boors. So-called liberal journalists seem particularly happy to adapt to these conditions. Doubtless because they are not really liberals, but merely moral relativists. Scum, in short.

—Right. Um, so, you know about me?

—Clearly.

—How did you know I was here?

—You were followed. For your own protection. Mr Kant has many loyal trading partners, but he also has many competitors; and the current fashion in these parts is to take one's business rivals *out*, rather than *over*. Come. We two must be at the Kazakhstan railway station in less than three hours.

—What?

—There are no flights to Samara, owing to an unfortunate incident at Domodedovo airport. The result, no doubt, of a privatised monopoly failing to maintain its aircraft. Privatisation without genuine competition is, of course, the best formula for corruption. Fools!

His eyes blazed behind his shades, and his moustache bristled. I just goggled at him as he drained his beer, hopped from his stool and walked out. I had to follow him. Well, I could hardly stay in the bar.

Outside, he strode quickly on. I had to work to keep up:

—Just a minute, just a minute. Look, I mean, thanks and everything, but so who the hell are you?

—My name is Dr Jones. Of the London Business University. You should know me. After all, you have pirated enough of my ideas for your BIZVID productions.

I looked at him and now I knew where I had seen that mug and that yellow suit before: it was off the cover of *Man and his Markets*, a work from which I had indeed recently half-inched the odd rehashed gurubuzzword.

—Sorry about that, I said.

—There is no need. I admire your ability to distinguish between the copyright expression of an idea and its freely marketable essence.

—Oh. So look, what the hell's going on? What does Mr Kant want?

—Come along. We must gather your belongings. I believe we have some business equipment to pick up too, for Mr Kant.

—I'm not going anywhere until I know . . .

—The traffic comes from the other side here, by the way.

—Shit!

Dr Jones and I jumped to safety on the far pavement,

as six lanes of psychotic Ladas with undipped lights blared round the corner, almost on top of us. We resumed our course back to the Hotel Budapest.

—Are you Welsh or what?

—My grandfather may have been, I believe. At any rate, my grandmother gave my father the surname Jones. Not a wise move, considering the British were about to pull out of India. It made my father's life unpleasant. So much so that he elected to leave for Uganda. Which, of course, made his life ultimately even more unpleasant. And some years shorter, indeed. I was studying in London when they came for him. I returned to find our village full of bodies and teenagers with machetes. It is not pleasant, I assure you, to be chased from the ruins of your family home by excited, uneducated, rural fourteen-year-olds who know that they have the advance approval of the State for whatever they might choose to do to you with their machetes. Fortunately, I had at that time quite recently represented Kent as a schoolboy 1500m hurdler.

—Oh, I said. – So, um, look, do you happen to know, I mean, what Mr Kant's after from me?

Dr Jones did not reply.

I just took it and tagged along. Tagged is the right word. Like at school, when it meant touching someone. I was tagging along behind Dr Jones, almost without shame. Because without him, if I lost touch with him, I was on my own, half-pissed, knackered and nowhere in a giant, fucked-up, Lada-ridden building-site of a city where even a sign saying *Crunchy* sodding *Nut* had to be worked out in some alien alphabet. He was my only tie to Mr Kant, who was my only special offer out of Debtsville, the only way for Sarah and me to have a crack at living a nice normal thirtysomething life, IVF-ed if need be, instead of living in a Swedish film-script until one of us cracked. Sod pride: I just swallowed his stonewalling and kept tight to him. I tagged.

Mr Kant's business equipment (which was waiting for us in the foyer of the hotel, under the grasping eye of the in-house armed guard) consisted of a large cardboard box and three sets of evening clothes. Each set was made up of a double-breasted dinner jacket with extremely wide and sheeny lapels, silk-taped trousers and a white, starched shirt with a thick, stiff front.

The guard held the suits out to us on their hangers, with the dutiful smugness of a man who reckons he is on course for big, hard-currency drinks. Dr Jones gave him twenty dollars, which was clearly bang on the market rate: the guard neither sulked nor grovelled. We looked at the suits.

—From Mr Kant's London tailor. The outsize one is, I assume, for Mr Kant.

—Look, what the hell is this all about?

—Power, of course. This dress represents the change of the Western Male from a peacock-dressed free spirit and privateer to a disciplined functionary of State or corporation. A man in evening-dress is saying: *See how utterly I efface myself! How powerful my organisation must be, how great its punishments and rewards!* I assume Mr Kant intends us to have the same effect on his clients.

—What clients? Christ, you could bloody tell me.

—Judging by the size of the lapels, these jackets are modelled on American gangster-films. A common phenomenon. One businessman of my acquaintance enjoys regular armed escorts from the Briansk mafia in return for teaching them English from screenplays by Scorsese and De Palma one night a week. He tells me that their enthusiasm can be rather unnerving during

the shoot-outs, but that they are making quite remarkable linguistic progress.

—Jesus! Would you just listen to me? Why does Mr
Kant want to see me? What's his problem?

Dr Jones turned to the cardboard box. He opened it
up with surprising enthusiasm and strength, like a
child ripping the packaging from a long-expected
Christmas present. Inside was something that looked
like a small but powerful stage loudspeaker.

—Aha, said he.

—Aha what? I snapped, tiredly.

—The proprietorial name is, I think, the Bomb
Ranger.

—What does it do?

—Ranges for bombs. It transmits on every frequency
at once, you see. I imagine the effective radius is
approximately 1km. To jam radio-controlled devices, of
course. Such sophisticated forms of assassination are
rare in Russia as yet; there is little demand for
innovation. But Mr Kant is one step ahead, as usual.

—This is a joke, I said.

—On the contrary, Mr Kant has no doubt provided it
for our safety on the rail-journey. Most thoughtful.

—I'm not going on a train with a fucking anti-bomb
machine!

—Would you rather go on a train without one?

—This is too much. Sod this. Now you tell me what's
going on here, right now, or I'm going home; right now,
or I am *out* of here. Right! OK. So get me a cab to the
airport.

—Very well.

—You what?

—I shall get you one.

—Oh, I said. – Right then.

I did not move.

—You will, of course, receive no further funds.

—Of course, I said.

I still did not move.

I was having great difficulty moving. It was not just the growing swell of post-booze exhaustion. To move, to get out of here, was so obviously the only sane thing to do. And yet, to move from here could only mean: to go back. Back home. To reality and sanity. And bankruptcy; and sperm-counts; and taxmen. And lying to Sarah about my unfaithfulness and telling her the truth, which was that we once again (and now for good) could not afford the IVF treatment; telling her that reality and sanity meant, for us, years of poverty and no kids.

That she was better off without me. That she should leave right now and try to save something of her own life, not go down the tube with mine. It would just be the rational thing for her to do. And I saw me, waving goodbye to Sarah for ever; me, turning and going back into the house, alone with myself in Hunter's Rise, looking in the mirror: and the Interview Panel just quietly reaching me a tube of Colgate.

—Right, I said. And still did not move.

—Before you make a decision, said Dr Jones, quietly, – Let me put one point to you.

—Put away, I said, without looking round. I was feeling nothing; I was not-feeling, as if I was already dead and cold. It was like shock, but before the event. Pre-emptive shock. To go along with this was madness, but to run home was suicidal; my mind had locked solid in the face of an impossible choice. It was shutting down all my nerve-endings and closing all my airtight doors, in preparation for the inevitable melt-down to come. I heard Dr Jones as if he was a long, long way off:

—Would it affect your decision if I told you that I

represent a certain agency of the government of the United Kingdom in this matter?

—Oh, I said.

I could feel life returning. It started with the blood in my neck, for some reason. I found I could turn my head again, like a praying mantis. I did, and stared at Dr Jones.

Like I said, I would love to be different from me. I would love to be a plumber. Or a really good pub-musician, say. Someone who can turn up anywhere in the Anglo-Saxon speaking world, set up his stall, put up his little cards in shop-windows and know he has a good chance of making enough to keep body and soul together anytime, anyplace. I bet, no, *bet* is wrong; I *know* you have this fantasy, too. Except I am not like that and nor are you. I am your neighbour, you, a normal bloody person: we wash our cars and mow our lawns and dream snugly of a freedom which we actually trade in for security every time.

And Dr Jones was *with the government. The* government. *Our* government. The ones who run our lives. The ones who own the tax-inspectors and the traffic-wardens and the VATmen. And the police and the Army and the SAS and MI5 and MI6 and the slush funds and the witness protection schemes. He was with *them: they* were at my side and watching my back.

For the first time since arriving in Moscow, I felt that there actually was oxygen in the air here, after all.

—Shall we go? asked Dr Jones, with a curious smile.

17. A Short Time

It was the strangeness that she had forgotten, she decided, the sheer otherness of a man's body. You got so used to the person, your partner, to their habits and timings; you started to think of them as just part of the world: something just as natural (and just as pointless to investigate) as trees or tarmac. They were what they were, and you were with them and that was that. It was not that you felt any identifiable oppression from this sameness: you just forgot, really, just forgot it had ever been any different.

The Greeks thought the river of death made you forget.

Suddenly, she wanted to cry out at the waste of all those years. Not the way she had been feeling bad or anything, just the way she had not *been feeling* for so long; the way she had been insanely acting to all intents and purposes as if she had secretly been guaranteed another shot at living when this one was done with.

In her rage at her own frightening capacity for not living, she bit hard into his shoulder (by now she was half climbing on him and half staying up that high by chimneying between his body and the rough brick wall behind her) and grabbed with her nails, deep into where she expected his love-handles to be. But she had forgotten who she was, and that he had none. She noted his lack of love-handles with some curiously far-off part of her brain, without especial pleasure or satisfaction, simply establishing a fact: this is what this man is like. Different.

It was absurd: she had stuck with her husband through the bad times and now that things were getting better, she was cheating on him. Ridiculous. But then, perhaps it was only the never-quite-absent misery of the last years that had kept her from desperation? Perhaps having to worry about the little problems stops you noticing the big miseries?

Or perhaps it was just the sheer weightless delight of fucking with someone who had obviously never thought of kids. She almost giggled: the idiot thought she was doing without a condom because she was so desperate for his dick. To stop herself laughing, she bit harder and made a little crying noise in her throat.

He understandably took this as a sign of impending orgasm. She went along with that, for she knew that he was waiting for her; not out of consideration, not even out of a feeling of duty, but out of pure, self-regarding stud-pride. She knew that he had taken her grab and bite as a welcome signal that now he could really start to bang away for his own pleasure, so he did. Nice enough, but not good enough: she calculated that he would come a few moments too soon as this rate. She could feel his knees starting to twitch. His feet were shuffling like some Lipizzaner in the ring now. So she took hold of his ears and forced him to open his eyes, and made herself talk slower and lower than she felt like:

—Aren't you going to turn me round then?

Of course, it was a dangerous offer, she thought, the idiot might think she meant she wanted anal, which of course she did not. Though maybe (she thought, as she slid him out and cutely spun around to press her left ear into the brick) the nearness of something one did not want lent a spice of choice to the thing one did want? Or was it the reliance on the other person's good sense and radar, the risk to the whole event, that made her do it? Or the impersonality? After all, it was not his personality she wanted. Or maybe just the feeling of the cold brick wall on her hot cheek, the paradoxical sense of being purely, objectively enjoyed by someone whom she had set up herself for that very purpose? Or just the extra depth and comfort and not having to worry about him sliding out, and that strange feeling of being held up on tiptoes, as if she were wearing invisible heels, not trainers?

He was good, no doubt. Not only had he gone straight back in, with no hint at all of wanting her arse, he had actually reached around too and was stroking her clitoris with almost just the right degree of simulated roughness. She altered the lie of his fingers just a touch, and pressed them a little flatter, he obeyed quickly and correctly. He was good. She congratulated herself: she had been right. He was the kind of man who liked being good. She had done the right thing when she had taken her courage in her mouth and come down here at the end of school, to the swimming pool. She had known for a long time he fancied her, and she liked the look of his bum in his shorts; he was really quite a boy.

And it was the memory, now, of the moment their senses locked on as she came up to him in the quiet changing room, of the first daring touch that could not be disguised as an accident, of the mutual recognition of intent and desire, his surprise and his delight – both so very flattering to her – and the quick yet unpanicked decision she had seen come up into his eyes, the decision to go with this, to just go with her without thought or planning of his own . . . It was that memory that fired up the fact of them actually doing this thing, of her incredulity and pride that she had finally done it, at how easy it had been, easy and good, too; that memory made her delight in his strength, and in her own being shoved about like a rag doll now, he liked what he was getting and he was just what she wanted, this was just what she wanted, right here with her mouth now tasting brick-dust:

—There, there! she shouted into the wall. For a long, swooping moment she was pure honesty, that really was all she wanted, right there. And he kept right there too, kept doing just what he was doing, and she reached back as she came and grabbed the sides of his buttocks with her hands and clawed deep; and he came too, right with her.

She leaned back against the wall, wiping the taste of the brick from her mouth. She could feel his sperm running down the inside of her left leg. Why the left, she thought, absently? Which side does madam fuck on? She laughed and put her head back and breathed deep.

—Christ, Sarah, said a voice in her ear from some faraway planet. Him. She looked up, he was watching her with an attempt to be content in his own satisfaction, or in his having pleased her. But she could see there was just that little light of unease in his gaze that men still get when they know they have, in the end, been dancing to a girl's tune.

—That's me, she said.

Later, she sat at home in Hunter's Rise (ugh!) and tried watching telly. The first thing that came on was one of those horrible, lying ads for pet-food which are actually aimed at desperate spinsters and widows – but which show beautiful (though sensibly dressed) late-twenties working women, indulging their cats and small dogs in return for what the ads call love. They are clearly doing it out of choice; clearly because they are happy in their bright flats; clearly not because if they did not have these small, imprisoned animals then they would go mad with loneliness.

Hell has easy-to-clean surfaces.

She turned the telly off. She sat and thought with hatred of the wasted months, never mind years, and of the eggs; the lifelong, lifetime, life-old supply of children that were slowly degrading in her body, waiting vainly for their sperm, for any old sperm for God's sake, to come along. She hummed to herself:

—Some day my sperm will come. And then she put her hand inside her jeans and felt the dry spunk sticking tight, like an overdue face-pack, on her inside leg, and thought: Ho ho, and tasted brick again where there was no brick.

To her surprise, she was filled with a vast desire for Peter. Not just for anyone, for him particularly, for the little uniquenesses of his face and body and the special sounds only he made when they made love.

So then she turned off the ansaphone (the metal, Pacific Rim voice said THE UNIT IS OFF) as if she could somehow make someone call her by doing so, by sympathetic magic or sheer need. No-one did. She felt herself freezing into immobility as she sat on the sofa, as if the entire weight of all this brick and mortar about her, their house, was somehow concentrating itself in the room, compressing the air, making motion impossible. She remembered something Peter had said in one of his rants, something about it being time to have an accident while shaving.

—What, while shaving my legs? she said out loud, and then laughed out loud. The laugh broke the spell; she got up, fixed a stiff vodka, and settled herself down to read *Emma*.

Then Gerry called round to make sure she was OK while Pete was off in Russia. She was glad to see him, so she took another large one herself when she got Gerry his, and they talked for a long time.

Except naturally, she did not talk to Gerry about the one thing she really wanted to talk about right then. She was not bored, though: because she could not deny that it gave her a strange kick to be talking to Gerry when she had just cheated on Peter. Her secret made her feel big and strong and relaxed. She just kept nodding.

But then she began to wonder if her own secret had somehow sharpened up her senses, for it soon occurred to her – the certainty of her insight almost made her blink – that Gerry was not being straight either. It felt like a curtain was being drawn back; she realised that for a long time she had wondered if Gerry was not too good to be true. Too good to conceivably fancy, for example. And now she knew for certain: as he talked to her about Peter and Russia, there was a thick filter in between his words and his mind.

The air in the room began to crackle with lies.

They had another drink. Gerry lit up one of Peter's cigarettes from a pack that was lying about; Sarah had never seen him smoke a cigarette before. It was an admission of unbalance, an admission that she knew was meant to be noticed. So she took one as well: as she did so, she felt him watching her, and she knew that he had never seen her smoke either; he watched her, and she knew that he saw she was returning his confession.

Lies and truth mixed and tingled: when Gerry struck the match, it seemed to flare too brightly and too strongly, as if the room was full of cool, sweet oxygen. When Sarah looked at his hand as he lit hers, she already guessed what she was going to do. She did not know if it was because she wanted him, or because she knew he wanted her. The world was just suddenly full of pure want, not want for anything, just want want want.

A little later, as she closed her eyes and started to suck his cock – it was quite different from the gym-teacher's cock – she could hear him repeating her name like it was the key to some enormous mystery, and all she was thinking was that time suddenly seemed very short today, somehow.

18. Life is Butter

As I drove down the empty M3 westbound at 11.30 p.m. on that last Saturday, I was thinking:

> *No Memory Lane factory this morning, twang twang*
> *(cos there) Ain't no Entrance (twang)*
> *To Memory Lane (twang twang twang twang-ang-ang)*
> *(but) I don't care, cos I'm in*
> *The outside lane (twang twang twang)*

and also shaking my head with wonder at the thought that, when I filled her at Fleet, one little tank of petrol and seven hours in the Volvo would take me (well, take Trevor) almost to the other end of our country and back again. Ridiculous. In that other country, or that other world, rather, I had boarded the train with Dr Jones for an eighteen-hour ride to the next big place down the line.

*

At the pre-revolutionary, iron-and-marble Kazakhstan Station in Moscow, nearing midnight, the slouching army was at the doors to check we really did have tickets before they let us into the arclit concourse. Now, the thought that I was halfway to being some kind of bloody spy made the AK47s and other assorted hardware even more worrying. I kept even tighter to Dr Jones as we shoved our way through the criss-crossing waves of people.

The men and boys were monochrome in cheap, dark suits and pale shirts; in the hard, white light, the bright scarves and central Asian robes of the women stood out like hand-tinted parts of an old photograph. They sat about in sub-tribal groups, surrounded by bulging plastic sacks; they milled in crowds around the dozens of little kiosks selling fags and poisonous-looking sweet drinks in plastic bottles; the men stood in little huddles, smoking and muttering; small children sat beside their mothers with otherwordly patience, their big eyes simply watching. An old woman was standing alone, dressed in a scarf and cheap apron, holding up one loaf of bread and one packet of milk, which was all she had to offer, chanting incessantly to the passers-by. I supposed she was chanting *bread and milk*. Or maybe she was chanting *milk and bread and you're better off dead* (*twang twang twang-ang*), who knows? Well, the Russians knew, I suppose, but they all ignored her too, whether she was offering bread and milk or Russian C&W despair. There was a man sitting cross-legged on the platform with four kippers in front of him, placed in that ancient way that says For Sale in any language. The kippers were lying directly on the diesel-blotched, greasy concrete.

At last, we found our carriage, handed over our tickets to the pretty, half-uniformed train-hostesses at the door to our carriage, and piled into our first-class sleeper.

—East German, said Dr Jones, patting the wood of the compartment, – Everything that works in Russia is German. The army was imported from Prussia, hence the goose-stepping, and the secret police from Austria: *those* always worked. I suppose we ought to start the Bomb Ranger immediately.

—Why is the army everywhere?

—Do not worry, it is nothing to do with us. The Chechens, presumably.

—We're going to Chechnya? Christ!

—No, only three-quarters of the way. Now, if I cover it with a coat, so ... The army is at the station because control of the transport infrastructure is, of course, one of the minimum claims a State must make if it is to be regarded as a State at all. Furthermore, within the station concourse it is the State that claims the taxes from the little stallholders. Outside, it is the State *and* the mafia that demand a percentage, and usually only the mafia that gets paid. Personally, I would prefer to pay the mafia, although their grasp of economics is lamentably ...

—You what?

—Of course. It may seem dreadful to be obliged to pay a percentage to armed men, on pain of retribution. But why? Protection money is all taxation *ever was*. The vast majority of mankind lives under States which are simply the biggest and strongest of the protection rackets. If you doubt me, try *not* paying even the British State its percentage, its tax and VAT, and see what happens to you. But then, of course, you *have* tried that, have you not? So you already know.

At that moment, the train jerked to a start; but it was not the jerk that made me feel I was losing my balance.

—How the hell do you know about that?

—Why, your accountant told me, naturally.

—Deeny?

—I assume you have only one accountant.

—But he's not supposed to bloody talk to every ...

—He is not *supposed* to cheat the taxman.

—Shit! Who are you working for? I mean, which *bit* of the Government?

—Here in Russia, the issue is at least refreshingly clear: the State is merely a group of largely unreformed

Communist Party apparatchiks who control large numbers of armed men. The mafia too has armed men. But at least it pretends to be nothing except what it is: a business. Whereas the State pretends to be God. All States do.

—Excuse me, you just said everything that works here is German. The Germans have a state. And the Japanese. And Koreans and Singaporeans. They have states that intervene in your precious bloody markets. And pardon me for thinking they don't do badly on it.

—Oh, the idea of a benevolent corporate State has always been a highly tempting model for those who would evade the fundamental issues. Fashionably advanced Englishmen have been entranced by this notion since Bismarck's day. But one must look at the broad historical canvas, and in that light the Anglo-Saxon model has one decided advantage.

—Such as what? Such as short-termism? Such as speculators? Such as asset-stripping and leveraged buyouts? Such as bonuses for laying people off?

—Such as not producing murderous dictatorships.

—Look: are you MI5, or what?

Dr Jones put on his shades and turned to the window.

As we rolled past the endless rust-belt-and-highrise outskirts of Moscow, I was reeling backwards and forwards through everything that had happened in the last few weeks, trying to work out what the hell the Government could want from me. I tried to relax. I tried to tell myself: look, it's out of your hands; if you have no power you have no responsibility, you can't even fuck up now. It's all down to *them*, now.

But it wasn't working. The truth was I was stuck here utterly helpless, with a ticket I had not bought to somewhere I had never been and never wanted to go, with a man who would not tell me how he knew all about my life. And a bloody Bomb Ranger. And all I could do was wait until the future came up to join us in that unknown place up the line where the rails met and vanished.

I stared out of the window and the hours rattled by, endlessly and yet timelessly. Somewhere in the night, hopelessly awake, I saw mile upon mile of huge, identical, black, mothballed steam locomotives. You could see the shape of the hammer-and-sickle cast on their anthracite snouts. I watched them pass by and pass by impossibly, until it became so like a dream I had fallen asleep at the window; then it was dawn and we were still trundling on. I felt like a child recovering in a hospital bed, drifting without will or desire through changeless days.

Maybe I missed the good stuff while I was half-asleep now and then over the next twelve hours, but I don't think so. I think I got what there was to get, which was: ten miles of birch forest, then a horrible, scratty village with people wandering about with long hoes, or idly prodding cattle along tracks. Then another ten miles of birch forest. Hour after hour. In the occasional gaps in the birch forest along the railway, you could see for ever, and for ever consisted of: birch forest with occasional plumes of wood-smoke about ten miles apart. For the first time in my life, I realised how very kind the Big Ref has been to not let us see too far. Here, whenever the forest closed around us again, it was a mercy.

—Christ, I said, at some time or other, looking out at the sheer, endless size of the place.

—Indeed, said Dr Jones, removing his shades, – Imagine a country four times the size of Europe, run entirely by a White Trash Vengeance Militia, convinced that they are being cheated of their place in the sun by a vast and probably Jewish-led conspiracy of foreigners. And armed with eight thousand-odd nuclear bombs and an enormous number of perfectly adequate tanks. It is by no means an impossible nightmare. Little wonder the remaining Jews are so keen to emigrate; little wonder the Poles and Czechs are so *very* keen to join NATO.

I tried to catch him off-guard:

—Do you work for NATO?

—Such impatience.

—We should have supported bloody Gorbachev better, then.

—And exactly how many thousand billions do you think we should have thrown at him? No, no. All we can do to help Russia is: keep our guard up, our tariff barriers down and our aid firmly linked to political liberties.

—You think doing nothing is going to save this? This is the end of the bloody world.

—On the contrary. This is the Russian equivalent of the M4 corridor or the American Eastern Seaboard. These lucky villagers know it. See how those pretty girls bathing in the river are waving to us, let us wave back! The express-trains rattle by as constant reminder of their good fortune in living here. Oh no, I assure you: the end of the world is two thousand miles *that* way. But size is not an issue. The problem with Russia is that there has scarcely ever been a time when Russians could sensibly expect to make, and then *keep*, a reasonable return on their investments. The result you see before you.

After a long pause, a Russian-style long pause, in fact (we were getting used to the scale of things, his pause and my boredly expectant silence took in maybe another dozen miles of forest), I asked, yet again:

—Look, I mean, shit, shouldn't you be, I don't know, *briefing me* or something?

And Dr Jones replied, staring out:

—Car-park Earth has many spaces left, does it not?

I looked at the forest and thought about the girls waving. They had been just near enough to make out their smiles. I thought of Sarah, and what she might be doing, what time it might be there. I felt that sudden vertigo that comes when you have a vision of the sheer size of the human world. These girls, waving from a river somewhere in the middle of nowhere in Russia, were ordinary girls with ordinary dreams. If you met one of them in a bar in Berlin, say, who knows, maybe you would fall madly in love: we are all only people, and there are really not many variations on the theme. And yet these same girls waving the mainline train away would probably never even read about it in the papers if your house and your family and friends and everything you know were to be simply wiped out in some natural catastrophe or industrial disaster. And you will never know the slightest thing of what is going to happen to these three girls who are waving you goodbye as they wave hello. You do not even know what your own wife is doing three thousand miles away, you cannot even get your head around what time it is for her, over there, back home.

It is a mercy when the forest closes around you.

But at last, the forest opened on something which looked like ten Liverpools rolled into one, you know: it had that indefinable look about it that says nothing has really been done here since about nineteen sixty-six, that next-to-the-scrapyard feeling that makes you doubt that anything anyone really *wants* could possibly come out of here. The Lada complex, Samara, the Detroit of Russia. We were there.

Dr Jones was fast asleep, lying on his back with his hands folded across his chest and his shades on his belly. I scuttled up the corridor to shave, rinse my armpits, and change into a clean shirt. My body-clock was shot to pieces by now (it was getting on for seven in the evening), and I was running on will-power overdrive. Right. The bastards might have forced me to spend a day and a half on a train, but I would show them what the West was made of (twang twang).

As I shaved (careful, careful) the Interview Panel assembled behind me, crowding into the train lavatory with some distaste. The Tweedy Edinburgh Lady looked at me quizzically:

—But surely, Mr Thompson, you must have *known* this deal was too good to be true. Did you *really* believe that you had discovered the source of the legendary free lunch?

—Fuck! I yelled, having inevitably cut my chin.

As I finished brushing my teeth in non-Colgate, we were already slowing down, so I was just in time. I carefully plucked the piece of crap Russian bog-paper from my shaving-cut, and was relieved to find the blood had staunched. I tucked in my nice clean shirt and returned to the compartment, where I found Dr Jones inexplicably perfect in his yellow suit and ready with his luggage, but glaring out of the window at the passing factories with an expression bordering on fury.

—I don't suppose that now we're here there's any chance you'll tell me . . .

—*Negative added value!* cried Dr Jones, in tones of moral outrage, his nose pressed against the window. –

The steel and rubber and oil that goes in here is worth real money, hard currency; the Ladas that come out are practically worthless on the world market. The more this place works, the less value exists. So much for the labour theory of value and the State-planned economy!

He turned off the Bomb Ranger with a sniff, and gathered it up in his arms. His miffedness made me feel irrationally good. Sod him. I laughed, grabbed my case, and strode to the window. I stuck my head out, pulled in my tummy, raised my nose into the air, breathed deeply, two three four, gagged on a sudden cloud of diesel, recovered, centred myself again, and prepared to knock them all dead and get back to Sarah a.s.a. bloody p.

The first person I saw was Masha.

She was standing with her arms folded, wearing a simple little polka-dot dress and flat shoes, and talking to a large, very fat man with a moustache and a tiny man with a club-foot, while Mr Nazi watched over them, figuratively and literally. All the men were wearing highly coloured western tracksuits with big logos. As we rolled up towards them, they were talking in that Russian way that seems to consist of pure eye-contact. Like Belfast people, you know.

Masha turned, and her eyes hit straight between mine. My first instinct, I only just resisted it, was to pull my head back in and hide.

It was not her that scared me; it was letting her see how much I was glad to see her. You know all that crap about hearts leaping and stuff? Well, it is. Crap. My heart did not leap. It just got suddenly small and hard, like someone had dropped it into a bucket of iced vodka. My mouth tasted like it was full of leaching dental amalgam. I could feel the skin around my eyes drying up in the heat of her gaze.

I had been living without thinking overmuch of her for weeks. Not overmuch. You know, nothing unbearable, just the occasional silent 3a.m. howl when I awoke to find I was me here and now, not me how I should be. But nothing I could not cope with, because we all have to cope with those moments anyhow. They come with our oxygen, we just have to bear them. If you pluck the Big Ref by the sleeve and ask how much more extra time he plans to add to this thankless slogging-match, he will look at his watch and say *Why, just as much as you can stand*. The only consolation is that you can always take yourself off if it gets unbearable. Any time you want, you can swing the wheel, cross the central reservation, put your foot down up to John O'Groats, and then, when the land ends, just put your foot down some more. And if you choose instead to sit in your traffic-jam and bear it, then it cannot be unbearable, can it?

Fair enough, really. Well, as fair as it gets.

Sarah and I had been having a good time, the best for years, and I had really and truly believed that Masha was receding steadily away down Memory Lane: soon she would be safely gone. And now, she was here and now. She was filling my eyes as we slowly drew up to her, level with her, past her. Now, the possibility of her being in the same place as me but not *being with me* made my solar plexus implode. I could feel myself crumbling spine by spine, I could not unlock from her unreadable gaze; it was only pride that kept my life-support systems ticking over as we trundled and jolted to a slow, squealing stop.

—Welcome to Samara, said Masha, and we shook

hands very formally. I was blipping gigabytes of feeling at her, but nothing was coming back; my questions just ricocheted off the hard surfaces of her eyes. There was a distinct warning in her first two words:

—Mr Kant will meet us later. This is Alexander Zhakin, Vice-President of the Regional Government (Mr Clubfoot). This is Andrei Zenkhin, Minister for Sport (Mr Fat). You already know the Kick-Boxing Champion of the Volga Region Interior Ministry Police.

—I thought he was Mr Kant's driver, I said, in order to let her know that I had got the message that he was *Mr Kant* for today, not *My Father*. To reinforce the idea of a conspiracy between us, I shook Mr Nazi's big hand with what I hoped was a cunning mixture of manly comradeship and cheery condescension.

—Driving is his hobby, she said, and turned away.

Dr Jones presented the Bomb Ranger ceremoniously to the Regional Vice-President, who accepted it with enormous formality, and we all got into two big white super-Ladas called Volgas. The Vice-President and Dr Jones got in Mr Nazi's one, while the Minister for Sport showed Masha and me to his own car and rat-faced driver, as if he were inviting us into his house. For a moment I thought that Masha and I were going to end up in the back seat together; for a second that was as high as the Grand Canyon, I heard the bats flying and saw the house by the river with the long garden; every inch of my skin prepared to be close to her again. But then she sent me into the front passenger seat with a nod of her head, and the vision died.

I sat and stared ahead, twang twang.

Instinctively, I reached for the seat-belt. Almost before I did so, I remembered that no car in Moscow had one. Then, to my surprise, I found that this car did.

That little touch of normality came as an absurd relief: people who had seat-belts were people you could deal with.

As I went to fasten it, the Minister for Sport tapped me on the shoulder and shook his head strongly. I turned and shook my head back, questioningly, the clip poised above the anchor. He was waving a finger at me in an avuncular but Stalin-ish manner. He spoke briefly in Russian. Masha translated, her eyes meeting mine head on but giving no hope or quarter, just translating someone else's useless words:

—The Minister for Sport says his car is a very good car.

—Oh, I see, um, right. Please tell the, er, Minister for Sport that I meant no comment on his car. It is a very good car indeed. It was just that I am used to English laws, and in England, it is the law to wear seat-belts.

—The Minister for Sport says it is also the law in Russia. But not when you are with the Minister for Sport.

—Right, I said, and let go the belt. As the reel snaked away through my hands and over my chest, it felt like the last dregs of sanity had just drained away. I looked at Masha, and pleaded openly:

—What is going on?

But she simply broke contact and looked away. I looked at her mouth:

(Cos there) Ain't no entrance (twang)

to Memory Lane

and then I was about to say to myself:

(And) You're never going to kiss

Those lips again.

Except I only got halfway to thinking that, and then those stupid, crappily simple words scorched through the concrete walls and burnt my throat. They turned into a wail that I had to fight down. The thought that I would never kiss her again was truly beyond bearing. It made me want to howl out loud and bite my fist. I tried one last time with her:

—Look, you have called me here and . . .
But the Minister for Sport cut me off with a barrage of Russian, and Masha looked away at him. Then she translated, and as she did so, she looked at me as if daring me to talk again.

—The Minister for Sport owns several of these yellow steel kiosks you may see in the street, said Masha. – He owns them in partnership with Mr Kant. He says they are very good kiosks for businesses. They are proof against small-calibre weapons and standard-issue ex-army grenades.

—Really? I said, without turning round. I was actually thinking whether I should just grab the wheel, stop the car and get out right now.

—Really. I myself will tell you what they sell: drink, cigarettes, lottery tickets, porn. The usual short-cuts to heaven for a people in despair.

Her voice made me look round at her, but she was not looking at me, she was watching the market go by.

Then the Minister for Sport started talking again, and she re-entered Earth's atmosphere to translate:

—And now the Minister for Sport says we must make a trip in a small yacht to see the panorama of the city and the Zhiguli Gates on the Volga. The Zhiguli Gates are very famous, and you will like the Volga, says the Minister for Sport: it is very wide.

At last, Mr Kant was there.
We bumped down an evil little muddy track, followed by the other official car, and parked on the bank of a slow-moving river. It was not even twice the size of

the Thames at Waterloo. However, along the banks were the weirdest structures I have ever seen: they were great floating buildings on pontoons, like Tara out of *Gone with the Wind*, neo-classical wooden things four or five storeys high and eighty or a hundred feet long, half a dozen of them swaying gently up and down just off the bank of the river.

From one of them Mr Kant emerged, dressed in a very colourful shell-suit and carrying a large aluminium pot shaped like half a milk-churn. He called merrily to us and pointed to a little green metal boat that was lying just in the water, pumping out diesel smoke. In it sat two fat women, not old but nevertheless evidently many years past worrying about their looks; they were slicing great, greasy chops of cold pork and ham, and adding to a vast pile of sliced cucumbers and tomatoes.

The Minister for Sport engaged Mr Kant in a long conversation across the ten feet of water, the subject of which was clearly the contents of the aluminium pot.

—Mr Kant says this is a very famous soup, said Masha: —It is made of pikes' heads and onions.

—Really? I glared at her. – Please ask Mr Kant what details of our business he wishes to discuss.

As she spoke to her father, I looked steadily at him. He looked from her to me, glowered, but then cheered up again and spoke briefly.

—Well? I asked her.

—Mr Kant says he understands your concern. Pikes heads and onions *do* sound quite boring. But it also has vodka in it.

—Christ, I never . . .

But she had turned away and engaged the Vice-President in some other discussion. Mr Nazi grinned at

222

me. Dr Jones emerged from behind some bushes, having evidently just had a piss.

—OK, now look . . ., I started.

—Play up, play up and play the game, murmured Dr Jones, and passed right by me, heading to examine the soup.

I looked at Masha. *Mr Kant*, she had said; Mr Kant. Last time she had called him My Father. But then last time, we had been in bed. And now I was relegated to just another guest. It felt like exile. Now my heart had changed again: it was big and hot, it filled my chest.

Then everybody was boarding the boat. If I had had anywhere else to go, I would have stayed. Mr Nazi helped her on. He held her hand like he had held it a thousand times before. He suddenly looked round and caught my gaze before I could drop my eyes: I was still firing pure hatred at him. He just grinned again, and my impotent fury rebounded; it came back, turned inward and brewed a bitter, unswallowable poison in my throat.

We sat moored for some minutes: me in a cloud of despair and all of us in a cloud of mosquitoes that only dispersed when the wind blew the diesel fumes back onto us. The smoke was a relief if you timed your breath-holding right, otherwise it was marginally worse than inhaling mosquitoes. Dr Jones asked various questions of the Vice-President, which Masha translated dutifully. I tried to chip in, and she simply ignored me. My new shirt was starting to feel tight round the armpits already. In my suit, I felt like a prize twat. I had been bounced. The bastards were playing me like a trout.

At last we set off. After some minutes, the river began to grow wider and wider. We chugged past large, and then larger, and then full-sized, sheer, terrifyingly looming oil-tankers swaying at anchor or rusting hugely away at unsafe-looking angles in the mud. The towering hulks and the knowledge of what depth of water must lie beneath us began to make me shiver. Then we rounded a bend and were suddenly out in a very, very large lake: that, or we were heading out to sea.

—This is now the Volga. The Vice-President asks you if the Volga is wider than your Thames, said Mr Kant's daughter.

I nodded, dumbstruck. They all laughed.

I suppose that to Gerry, say, there might be nothing that mad about sailing across a river that has huge oil-tankers bearing down on you and takes half an hour to cross and is still just a river. I think they have those in Yankland too. But I am just a Brit, and I was gobsmacked to the power x. This was evidently the correct and anticipated reaction, since it clearly made the day of the assembled Russians.

—The Vice-President says that he hates the dams upstream. In his youth this was a real river. One day he will restore the Volga; when the Volga Region is fully privatised from Moscow's control, he will blow up the dams and the river will be free again, and full of large fishes, and great again.

—But I thought the economy of Samara depended entirely on the hydro-electric power from the dams? asked Dr Jones. Masha translated. The Vice-President nodded, as if to a simple and obvious statement of fact. – Ah, said Dr Jones.

We anchored the boat on a little island with a beach, and ate pike's-head soup and drank vodka. The eyes in the pikes' heads looked like halves of tiny boiled eggs; the soup tasted of water, onions and vodka. The fat wives continued to heap up gherkins and tomatoes while the men got down to serious drinking. Masha sat and watched the river; Mr Kant's driver watched Masha.

My head was on fire with vodka and uncertainty. It was time to sort bastardface Jones out. So after a while, I downed the latest vodka and jumped up:

—And now (I had got into the formal Russian mode):
– And now we as Englishmen must swim in the wide Volga.

—The Minister for Sport says it is only ten degrees, said Masha.

—Tell the Minister for Sport that Englishmen do not mind. The nation of Nelson and, um, and Richard Branson adores cold water. What could be more refreshing?

I strode to the boat and grabbed our bags from the deck. Dr Jones eyeballed me. He asked, via Masha, if swimming in the Volga would make one fall sick. But he was too late: the Russians had no intention of missing their Mad Englishmen now. Mr Kant and the clubfooted Vice-President called out mockingly across the tomatoes and gherkins to Dr Jones. Masha almost grinned as she translated:

—The Vice-President says that this is the problem with the English. The English are sick. The Germans are not sick, says the Minister for Sport: dangerous, but not sick. Mr Kant says . . .

—Yes, said Dr Jones, – I heard. I presume Mr Kant says that Drake and Hawkins would naturally have swum naked in the Volga as a gesture of good-will to their business partners?

—Why, Dr Jones, your Russian is improving.

—This is ridiculous, said Dr Jones, as we spluttered

away in the Volga between our little island and another one, barely resisting a powerful current.

—Good for the sperm-count, I called out.

—Pardon? he gasped.

—Nothing, I said, and concentrated on not drowning for a few strokes. It was slightly worrying to think we might both get dragged away out here and if the real world, I mean, *Home*, ever heard about it all they would hear would be *love rat businessman drowns in naked romp with freemarket loony*. None the less, I managed to wave merrily at the Russians on the beach, to make sure that Dr Jones and I were out of even lip-reading range.

I trod water:

—OK, this is far enough, Jonesy. Either you tell me what the hell is going on here, now, or I ask them straight out and I don't sodding stop till I get told.

—The vodka appears to have improved your morale.

—That's what it's for, Jonesy. So: what's this got to do with the government? How do you want me to play it?

—I want you to do business. What the British State may want you to do, I have no idea whatever.

—You what?

—I do not represent the British State in any way.

—You said you did!

—No, I asked *what if I said* I did. But I do not.

And he struck out for the bank.

I trod nothingness.

Gasping and spitting, I followed Dr Jones back onto the shore, to the little patch of sand, shielded by bushes, where we had left our towels and clothes. My knees were wobbling, and it was not just the cold or the exercise that was wobbling them.

—You bastard!

Dr Jones began to dry his head and armpits.

—You imagine the State to be a creature composed of linen, country-houses and benevolent National Plans. What utter nonsense!

—What the fuck is going on!?

—Consider. (Dr Jones dried his back with brisk double-handed motion.) What end does a corporation serve? That of its shareholders, of course. (Dr Jones struggled into his shirt; his wet arms made it hard.) The State is merely the biggest of the Big Corporations. Except that we, the shareholders, have forgotten this. We have yielded all shareholder power to our own management! How ludicrous!

—Shit! Shit shit shit!

I couldn't think of anything else to say. Or think. The only possible thing to do was to smash Dr Jones in the gob. I could see in his eyes that he knew what I was thinking, and was totally unworried by it. For a moment, sheer, outraged pride made me want to prove him wrong about that one, just for the sake of it. But then I remembered that this man had been chased through the jungle by murderous fourteen-year-olds with machetes: even if I beat him, what did he care? What did it change?

So I just sagged and watched him, helpless, as he sat down to dry his feet. He worked the towel carefully between each toe.

—Extraordinary. You would feel more comfortable with the thought that I work for MI5, who topple elected governments and arrange assassinations, than with the thought that I am a free agent associating with another free agent, Mr Kant?

—The kind of free sodding agent who carries anti-bomb machines about? I hissed.

—Well, why should the current State Management

have a monopoly on bomb rangers? Or bombs, for that matter?

—Are you trying to start a civil war or something? Dr Jones began to dry his balls and dick with care.

—I do not desire one, but it is very probable.

—You are evil.

—No, I am an unsentimental liberal. England had a civil war, after all. And America. Kings were killed and pitched battles fought before liberalism triumphed, you know.

—And what if it doesn't? What if the baddies are just harder and madder than you?

—Well (Dr Jones had stood again: now he began to dry his thighs and arse), – if you assume there are more baddies than goodies in the world, or that the baddies are cleverer and harder than the goodies, then why pretend to be a liberal at all? Why not confess that you are a conservative: that is, one who believes that the vast majority of people are incapable of self-government?

—This is ravings. The vast majority of people just get shoved about by Exxon and General Motors.

—If one quarter of potential car-buyers signed a pledge that the next new car they bought would be one that ran on liquid hydrogen, what would happen? (Dr Jones bent to dry his lower legs) Why, General Motors and Exxon would race Ford and Texaco to get hydrogen-powered cars onto the road, of course. The technical problems are small; all we need is the triumph of informed demand.

Dr Jones gestured theatrically with his sodden towel, his balls swinging along with his arm-movement, and I followed his accusing finger.

—Who, pray, built that crepuscular nuclear power-station we see so alarmingly close on the horizon?

228

—Not Westinghouse?

—I give you another graph: the more dominant the Big State in any given country, the more nuclear power-stations that country will have in it. There is no *demand* for nuclear power, except of course from the Big States. And why? Because Big States desire a centrally-controlled power-supply and plutonium for bombs. Who declares wars and whips up ethnic cleansing? Business-men or State-ists? Did classical economics build Auschwitz? What, indeed, were both Nazism and Stalinism, economically speaking, but vast attempts to buck the liberal market?

Dr Jones's waving arms unbalanced him as he tried to stand on one leg to get his trousers back on. He fell, sat down hard on his backside, and glared at me:

—Can it really be that in this day and age an educated, intelligent person can believe that the Big States are likely vehicles for the advance of humanity? I suggest you dry more carefully between your toes; one of the few pieces of maternal advice I have never felt the need to repudiate.

Dr Jones stood up again, this time successfully re-trousering himself. I grabbed my jeans from my bag. Bugger the suit, I would play them at their own game.

—So just what the hell are you? Right-wing or what?

—Right? Left? Who is on the extreme right today? The gentlemen with the tanks outside Moscow and the large, braided shoulderboards? The ones with such alarming tendencies to talk about the *sacred genetic stock of Russia*? But they *call* themselves Communists. And if they are lying, if *they* are actually the *right*, then who are the *left*? The international businessmen they hate so much? No, no, no: the terms *right* and *left* meant nothing in 1788 and will soon mean nothing once again. The only battle is the only real battle there has ever been: between those who believe in the slow, hard-fought advance of mankind towards economic and psychological autonomy, and those who do not. Lest you continue to misunderstand me, let me say that Trades Unions are very frequently to be found on the former side. I suggest you decide where you stand. I also suggest that you dress more quickly, because malaria is not entirely unknown hereabouts, and these large mosquitoes are particularly voracious so early in the season: blood is in short supply and high demand.

—Wait, I said, – Just a minute.

Dr Jones turned back and looked at me. His visionary gaze had gone now; he put back his shades. – If you don't work for the government, how the hell come Deeny has been telling you about my taxes?

—Mr Deeny will do almost anything for money. As you of all people should know.

I could feel the sand running slowly between my toes. The vodka suddenly seemed much stronger, and the Volga even wider. I felt like our island itself was about to break loose and start floating crazily down the river, towards the sea. Dr Jones was already going, I had to half-call to him now:

—What does Mr Kant do?

—Mr Kant trades in the informal business sector. His interests I know to include Ladas and caviar. As to what else he trades, I suspect the answer is: anything at all. I did once ask. I still remember his daughter's answer. She said: *those who should know, know.*

—You know she's his daughter? Who else knows?

—Those who should, presumably.

I watched him go back.

I looked through the bushes at Mr Kant's picnic-party on the beach by the Volga; at himself and the Vice-

President and the Minister for Sport drinking and talking; at the big wives cutting gherkins; and at Mr Kant's driver smoking lazily by the bow of the beached little green metal launch as he watched Masha looking out across the evening.

I was miles away, I could feel them receding in backwards telephoto. I looked out over the wide river, and felt this terrifying wave of loneliness, the kind of feeling of complete and utter loss that you only get when waking up after crashing out from a lunchtime drinking session: you open your eyes and have no idea what day, time, or place this is, or who you are. For a terrifying few seconds you are in free-fall.

Sarah.

I put my hands up to my head and inside my skull I saw a garden with bats, and no mother, and a child looking at a house in mourning.

I was free, and lost.

I was also freezing.

I was freezing and being eaten alive by mosquitoes. I was half-pissed on vodka and belchingly stuffed with tomatoes and bloody gherkins. I had been stitched up by everybody from the start, I had just been shat on from the ozone layer by a free-market nutter and I was stuck in the middle of nowhere, in the hands of a bunch of Russian loonies who did their Christmas shopping at the Executive Terrorist Gift-Shop of Mayfair and even had my accountant in their pockets.

—Sod this, Ref, I thought, – I'm off.

And then I thought about Sarah, and the overdraft, and the sperm-tests, and all the horror and expectancy and mindcrunching emotional drain of the IVF-ing to come (if we could afford it, for Christ's sake) and how if it did not work we would grow old, grow poor and grow cancerous together from our unspeakable, unthinkable resentments. Or else break up. Sarah would leave me because she needed to find better sperm. Or one of us would fall madly in love and lust with someone just because with them we did not have the weight of failure hanging on the edge of every word we spoke, overloading our caresses.

I had nowhere to go. I had only got into this because everything was falling apart. I looked at the picnicking party, and heard their voices easily again, they were so near. I imagined them getting on the little green boat and leaving me. I felt panic rising at the thought of my own helplessness.

Then Masha looked around, and it was me she was looking for. She waved privately to me as she ate a piece of tomato, a little wave of her fingers, like she was playing an invisible flute. Then she looked away again. I looked quickly to see if Mr Nazi had seen this, but he was still smoking on, and showed no sign of having done so. I looked at Masha.

She was staring out at the river. There was something in her eyes, something you rarely see in anyone's eyes anywhere, let alone in the sodding home counties. It was like she was looking down from a mountain onto a vast, wide plain: she really was not thinking about herself, there was some bigger story going on in her head. It made her look sad and serious and even more beautiful. I felt my forehead grow cool. I knew right then that I was not going to do anything that voluntarily took me away from her. I was in this to the end, one way or another.

So I looked up at the big sky through the clouds of mozzies and took a deep breath, two, three, four and said to myself, quietly:

—Fair enough, Ref: no more psychology.

And instead of thinking, I walked. And as I took that

first step, I felt like I had not felt since years ago in Spain, waiting to face Death by Cow.

I say *cow*. Somehow I had ended up as the sole gringo in this bloody great bullring packed with trumpet bands and cheering folk, standing in a circle with twenty-odd Spanish laddos who were, I could not help noticing, all damn nearly as edgy as I was. Edgy, because in the middle of us was this long, tall thing with big curling horns, looking to see who was going to move first. Its eyes said Death.

I still have no idea why it was me. Pure adrenalin, maybe. Or the sun coming up already hot over the stands, or the trumpets playing their high-noon, death-wish Paso Doble. I have even less idea why it thundered just past me and under my leather jacket. The whole stadium shouted *olé!*, and for three seconds, I was happier than I had ever been. I stood there and spread my arms. The crowd laughed and cheered. Then they laughed and cheered even more, because the cow came blasting up behind me and its big head hit me square up the arse. I could hear the trumpets and the cheers *oooooOOOLEE* as I did double-axels in the air. The world went slow-motion, and then I was on the ground trying to remember how to breathe, with this big head butting at me and hooves crunching the sand by my head. At which point the laddos decided they had better save this craparse Brit from actually dying, and made it chase them instead.

I suppose if I been a foot shorter, like most of the Spaniards, that charge would have mashed my lower spine, but there you are: the difference between two weeks having to shit standing up and a lifetime in a wheelchair, between farce and despair, is only as big as the way things work out.

But that was the feeling: the knowledge that you are

233

going to do something mad, for the sole reason that if you do not do it, you will never stop wishing you had. It scares the shit out of you, but something is telling you that this fear is Nature's Way, maybe the only way Nature has, of letting you know what you are meant to do next.

And in any case what else *could* I do?

So now, on this sand-bank in the Volga, I brushed the mosquitoes away, buttoned my jeans and tightened my stomach and raised my neck spine by spine by spine and pushed boldly through the bushes, back towards the picnic, aware of nothing but the speed of my approach and the fact that I had omitted to dry my arse properly.

I sat down dynamically (squelch) in the middle of the Russians and drained the large glass of vodka that (of course) was immediately presented to me. I held out my glass boldly for a refill and said to Masha, with flashing eyes:

—Tell Mr Kant I am now refreshed by the waters of the Volga and ready to plan our business.

At the word *business,* all the Russians quickly raised their glasses and repeated it: *beeiznis, beeiznis, beeiznis.*

—Mr Kant says you are almost right. But we do not plan. Communists plan. Mr Kant has schedules.

—Then let us schedule our schedule.

—Mr Kant says that first we must eat small crabs and have saunas at the Minister for Sport's dacha. Also, we must first see the Zhiguli Gates, which are famous.

I did not blink; I did not let this be seen as a defeat. Was I the co-auteur of the classic crap training-video *Deal to Close!* or what? I nodded wisely to Mr Kant and her in turn:

—Crabs and saunas are very good to prepare for

business. And I long to see these famous Gates of yours. I presume that they are very wide?

—No, they are a small island in the river.

—Ah. But the river is wide?

—Exceedingly.

—I toast the wide Volga.

—The Minister for Sport asks if you truly have no Russian blood.

—You should hire yourself out to visiting business-men, said Dr Jones quietly, – I will be your agent.

I passed him an uncut cucumber, which he took with some surprise.

—Sit on this, arsehead, I said.

Then we were sailing up the river again.

This time the wind was directly astern, and so the diesel from the exhaust was travelling at about the same speed as us; it clung to us as we floated, our own little dedicated cloud of toxic gases. But I was so pissed by now that I did not care. I stood at the prow of the boat, with my feet stoutly apart, hoping the breeze would dry between my legs, adjusted my balls privily and surveyed the small clump of trees on a sandbank which (I had been told about twenty times) was actually somewhere on The List: the allegedly world-class Zhiguli Gates, home of the allegedly world-famous pirate Stenka Razin, whose viking-style boat can be seen to this day on the crap Lada Samara logo.

When they said that for the twentieth time, I remembered that *Stenka Razin* was the name of the song Mr Kant and me had sung back in England, that lost world. Ridiculously, the name of a medieval Russian pirate made me long for Surrey. So now, up on the prow of the boat, I started doing the virtual balalaika again. I was not sure if I was doing it for me or for them; but in a few seconds all the Russians joined in behind me.

At the end of the song I turned and found myself looking into Masha's eyes with an unlustful smile, to my own surprise, and I saw some new thought in hers too. I was just regaining hope, when the Russians murmured at Masha and she asked, loud in the post-song silence, the question that every Englishman with a taste for singing most dreads:

—Now you must sing us an *English* folk-song.

In desperation, I called for another drink. While we were getting them poured, I scanned boozily around in my virtual hard-disk to think of anything except bloody Greensleeves that I could sing. Nothing. I will not sing Greensleeves. I refuse to learn Irish songs (though I will harmonise with them, naturally) because that is what saaad German hippies do. And I would rather be shot in the mouth than let some crap, defeatist, sentimental, sixties protest-ballad pass my lips.

Then I got it. I looked at Masha very seriously and asked her to translate the meaning of a very old song. She nodded attentively. I explained that this song was sung to the tune of Frère Jacques. They all knew it, thank God. So then we first practised the round-singing without the music. That got us well warmed up. I called for another drink and they all sat and watched, beaming with drink and expectancy, as I searched the horizon for the right words.

The swallows over the river had now turned into bats. The stillness was coming out from the wooded banks, hand-in-hand with the evening mist. We had turned the key (softly) and cut the engine: our fumes now blew slowly away from us. We were floating in the middle of the fat, slow river, like some silent pilgrim-ship on Memory Lane itself.

I was nothing; I was purest vodka; I was made of glass. And suddenly, it was one of those holy moments, you know, those moments when, for once, that gap between the way you live and the way you ought to live slides softly shut, and you are doing just what you are thinking. The river *was* wide and the sky, now turning dark purple, really *was* incomprehensibly vast. And, as I stared into Masha's eyes, I really would have done anything she asked. Anything at all. I would have chiseled off a finger, *kthunghk!*, like that, just to kiss her once:

—This song we will sing is an old, simple song, but it tells us a great truth. The music brings us together, friends on a wide river singing to a pretty tune we all knew as innocent children, and yet the words tell us that underneath: *life is merely a bloom of sadness.*

They ate it up. They sighed with pleasure. They murmured various things Russianly to each other. Dr Jones raised an eyebrow at me, but I just nodded at him, slow and serious, so he shut up. One of the ageless wives silently passed me a piece of cucumber, which I accepted with a solemn nod. Masha leaned sideways towards me to translate quietly, but remained facing towards the men. In the setting sun, I could see that she had tiny, downy hairs on the edge of her ear. I wanted to kiss her ear. And I knew she knew, and was not playing games.

You know, one of those moments when you catch yourself looking at someone's ear, or the veins in their hand, or the colour at the tips of their eyelashes or whatever, and they are suddenly lit up with their own reality. For an instant, this other person, their whole life, is truly as real to you as you are; and your brain floods with longing. No games.

—The Vice-President says that your song sounds like a line of Chekhov. You know Chekhov?

—Your Alan Ayckbourn, I believe.

—The Minister for Sport says he is now quite certain you have Russian blood.

—Tell the Minister for Sport I wish it were true.

Masha looked up sharply. The Minister for Sport raised his glass. Mr Kant looked at me carefully and said something that made Mr Nazi smile to himself:

—Mr Kant says perhaps your children will have Russian blood, if God desires it.

I swallowed, and tried to concentrate on the song. I climbed onto the highest part of the boat.

—This had better be good, murmured Dr Jones, as I clambered past him.

—Now we must sing the song, I said, – You must copy my words, the words do not matter, words are merely sounds, the feeling matters, this feeling that life is merely a bloom of sadness, set to a sweet tune.

Fuck, half of me was thinking, as Masha translated. *Does he know?* half of me wondered. *Has she told him?* half of me trembled. *Is this a marriage arrangement or something?* half of me stammered. *This bloke keeps a Bomb Ranger in his boot,* half of me warned. His *driver could snap me in two like a gherkin,* half of me gulped. *Just who the sodding hell is running my life?* half of me screamed.

But the other half of me was not me; not any me I recognised, anyway, or at least not any me I had come across for many years now. It was me mixed in softly with the evening and the vodka and the river and the thousands of miles from home, and now the sudden, flashlit certainty that it was not all said and done between Masha and me. And stronger than everything:

238

the strange, half-fearful delight in feeling, for the first time in my life, truly, truly lost. Yesterday was packed away in some far-off time-zone and tomorrow was still unknowable light-years away: I was adrift in currents without charts, with nowhere to go but here and now, and nothing to be but me.

And singing, as the night fell, floating back through the Zhiguli Gates on this vast river, singing rounds in a small, green boat, to the tune of Frère Jacques:

> Life is butter
> Life is butter
> Melancholy flower
> Melancholy flower
> Life is but a melon
> Life is but a melon
> Cauliflower
> Cauliflower.

19. A Film of Milk

Brian Irons came into the little kitchen off the main landing at BIZVID and closed the door behind him, pulling hard on the handle to make sure it had caught. He looked at Toby Jobson. Jobson was observing the mug of coffee in his hand as if it were a natural phenomenon of some interest:

—Coffee? said Jobson, without looking up.

—Eh? Yes, yes, OK, said Irons. Jobson shoved a ready-made mug over to Irons, and raised his own mug (it said Filmies Never Die They Just Get Edited Out; Charmaine had brought it in one day) towards his mouth and blew over it, long and slow. Jobson watched Irons through the steam that rose off the coffee:

—Good day?

—Sorry? Well, you know, not too bad ...

—Memorable?

—What do you mean, memorable?

—Oh, you know, any people falling past your window? Any little green men popping out of bins?

—Toby, are you all right?

Jobson continued blowing, Irons could see a film of milk starting to form on the coffee.

—Toby?

—No, and neither are you. Had a call from the accountant.

—Deeny? What's he after now?

—He says we're bankrupt. There's a towel over there.

—This is a joke. Do you think it'll stain my jumper?

240

—Yes, and no it isn't. It seems that dear old Pete's been cooking the books for years, and now the taxman is onto us.

—The bastard! Quick, let's get into his hard disk and find out what the fuck he's doing.

—Tried that. Charmaine says she doesn't know the password.

—She must do.

—She says not.

—He's shagging the bitch!

—Possibly.

—Right, she's out.

—I think you'll find our ex-friend Peter has got the small print on the hiring and firing sewn up, Brian.

—The bastard!

—Deeny wants to meet us.

—But he must have been in on it, Pete can't have cooked the books on his own, can he?

—We've got to find out, and Deeny seems to know.

—We should call the police.

—Deeny says not.

—Of course he does! He's in on it, I told you!

—No, he says for our own good. It seems Peter has arranged some kind of finance, and we could keep going if we play it right. Also, he says, for our own safety.

—You what? He's threatening us?

—He claims that dear Peter has got us involved with some very heavy people. Money-launderers. With guns.

—*Money launderers?*

—With guns. You know, bang bang. Are you going to drink that coffee, Brian, or just pour it round the room?

20. La Penultima

As I drove quietly out of our drive at 11 o'clock Saturday night (as the song goes), and swung round, leaving Hunter's Rise for what, logically, would probably be the last time, I was thinking that, even if I woke up tomorrow, I would still have to tell Sarah about Masha. I knew I could not tell her; but I knew I would have to. I had known since the night in Samara.

*

I woke up in the house in Samara, next to Masha, already half-consciously trying to work out what had dragged me from my vodka-heated sleep. It was rain, pattering on the roof just above our ceiling.

Rain, and something else, something lurking in my mind like mist caught between trees on a mountain: something I had not done before going to sleep. Floss my teeth, maybe? No problem, all that vodka would have disinfected anything. Have a chat with the Interview Panel? Sod them. Then I remembered: I had promised Sarah to take 1000mg of VitC+Zinc every night if I went drinking, just to keep the sperm-count in with half a chance.

I got up silently, without disturbing Masha, and opened the curtains, so that the moonlight would come in and I could root about in slow-motion in my luggage to find the tablets. As I grew fully conscious with the effort to keep quiet, I began to realise what crap this was: as if somehow, by taking such ridiculous trouble

242

to keep this stupid little promise to Sarah, I could make up for the big one I had just broken.

The moon was half-full; it hung bright above the dark forests across on the other bank of the Volga. I had never seen the moon over an endless, flat forest, let alone hanging at that strange angle. A southern moon, the kind that shines on Holiday Romances. It was like even the moon was saying: see, you are right, this *is* all a dream. Only I did not know if that feeling was quietly reassuring or unbearably sad.

As I was swallowing the long tablet, I thought *hold on, hold on: how the hell can the rain be pattering on the ceiling?* There were three floors above this one.

I looked up and in the moonlight from the window I could see that the noise on the ceiling was not rain pattering, it was the sound of thousands of midges and mosquitoes tickling away at the sagging, heavy-embossed ceiling-paper high above.

And now, as I lay in the dark again, next to Masha again, attempting to bring the slow convoy called sleep home for the night, trying to turn the key slowly, twang twang twang, the midges flew top-cover while the guilt dived ground-attacks in my head.

No, not *guilt*: certainty. The certainty that this was too big to hide, that what was happening to me was too much for my life to hold, it was going to split me apart. Charlie had been OK, Charlie and me I could keep hidden easily away. But not Masha. She was too strong for my locks. I tried to picture myself *not* telling Sarah about it as soon as I got back: but all I could imagine was me standing in front of her, trying to lie, and the skin on my face just tearing open like it had been softly slit with a cut-throat razor.

I would have to tell her. The thought of it scared me

like the thought of dying; it set the blood banging in my neck.

Then Masha turned over and lay on my arm. For just one second, the only thought I had was to adjust my arm without waking her up. And that tiny window broke the encircling horrors, it punched a hole in my own hopeless siege of myself: for just a second there was someone, something real out there, warm and beside me, my only thought was to keep her asleep, to keep her here. That half-second of freedom from the cog-wheels was enough for the massed vodka to rush through and wipe me out. The last thing I saw was an eyelash on her cheek, and the last thing I heard was thunder, somewhere across the Volga . . .

Have you ever fired a heavy handgun in a confined space, without ear-defenders, while mortally hung over despite 1000mg of VitC+Zinc?

Free advice: Don't.

I have never been one to say Never Again after boozing, partly because there is enough bullshit about anyway without us wilfully ignoring the Design Tolerances of the human soul and partly because I think the Spanish are very sensible to refuse ever to say La Ultima when they are drinking: they always say *OK lads lets have La Penultima*, in case it really did turn out to be the ultimate drink; I mean, the last one ever.

You have to watch it, because who knows, maybe the Big Ref, or the Big Matador, or whoever, is taking notes:

YOU (clutching head and reeling): Never again, never again!

THE BIG REF (looking at his watch): Is the correct answer.

Nevertheless, I was tempted to say it the morning

after our cruise down the wide river Vodka and the sauna and the small crabs. I was learning the first thing you have to learn about Russia, which is: *no Westerner can drink with Russians and live.*

I was turfed out by Mr Kant's bodyguard. Masha was gone from the bed long ago, the sheets her side were cold. The only proof that she had ever been there was the fact that I was covered in some kind of body-oil, and I knew that I had never yet covered myself in body-oil however pissed I had been. The scent of it on my fingers brought flashbacks of ear-lobes and dark hair, like something that happened to some dead king a thousand years ago. I closed my eyes with the pain of the hangover and the sweetness of the memories. My eyelids rubbed my eyes like cement blocks.

I staggered half-dressed from the room and was ushered out of the house and into the dull heat again, then decanted into a pale-grey Lada; I lay unstuffed on the springless back seat and felt each lurch in the road bring my guts closer to my throat.

We drove to somewhere outside the centre of town. Samara turned from an old city into what it really is now: endless miles of tower-blocks, even viler than Birmingham, with old women sitting and children playing in between. All of them waved little birch-branches, to ward off the mosquitoes, as they talked or ran.

I was still not properly awake when I found myself hauled out of the Lada, taken down some stairs at the foot of one of the blocks, and surrounded by Mr Kant, Masha, Mr Bodyguard and the Mayor of Samara, learning what a big handgun sounds like when fired with a hangover and without ear-defenders in a concrete bunker.

What it sounds like is: a lot sharper and higher than you could ever expect. Nothing like the boom of guns on a film. It sounds like a twenty-pound lump-hammer hitting a full-swing glancing blow off a stainless steel anvil right next to your ear. You have this thing that feels a lot heavier than you thought, like a big German electric drill held out straight in front of you; you pull the trigger and you are blinded by the noise, you can feel the hairs inside your ear singe and sing.

The next thing that happens, if you have an X-cert hangover is: your muscles melt, you drop the gun, your knees start to go and you feel yourself about to throw small crabs up all over the concrete floor.

I hate throwing up. Thirty-five years old and still doesn't know how much drink he can take: a wasted life. I blame it on my Northern European genes. We are all arsetight control-freaks, we Northern Europeans. I suppose we *had* to be control-freaks in the horrible old days just to get through the winter; anyone north of the olive-oil-growing line had to spend 95 per cent of the time worrying about what was going to be left to eat come March. I mean, the idea that tall blond people are racially superior is not only unpleasant, it is obviously plain bloody crackers: if we are so great, how come we ended up with the coldest, wettest and generally least sexy bits of Condominium Earth? The cool, dark-haired, stylish people were obviously harder or cleverer than the blond, pink, fleshy ones. As a result, we poor clodhoppers have been so bred to control-freakery and the occasional break-out that we have lost the secret of life, which is well known to Latin folks: be slightly drunk every day and never get utterly twisted.

You know the way everyone says the real secret of happiness is just to *be*? Well, if I had been happy just to *be, be myself* and all that crap, I would have thrown up right then and lain there groaning like a big sack of shit, which was my objective medical condition. Except I had my pride: because Masha was watching me and we were not yet even on blackhead-squeezing terms. I could still not believe that this amazing woman could actually like me; and I did not think that heaving small crabs up over her elegant shoes would help to persuade her against all rationality that she was glad she had spent the night with me.

OK, so she had not actually been there when I awoke, so that was one step we had not taken, but we had gone to sleep holding on to each other. We had spent the night together. Spent, like money: used, used up. Instead of saving up the night for Sarah, I had spent it with Masha.

I would love to be able to save up my nights. I would like to pile them up and build them into a high tower with deep foundations. I would like to be so strong that I could lie awake in any pisspot motorbreak motel, happy in the half-dark and the full knowledge that I was saving another night, adding to the vast reserves of nights behind me, nights conquered and saved. But who does that any more? Who has the big stories? Priests chase little boys and we commercial wanderers of the west throw off the bed-clothes, slink to the minibars and check out the cheap satellite thrills. What is the point of saving up your nights if you do not know what you are saving for? So we spend, spend, spend.

But maybe nights are *there* to be spent freely, maybe time is the one thing you can spend without earning it. You cannot earn more time, time is like Sarah's eggs: you get your ration free, and that's it, the Big Ref starts his watch and there is nothing added on to make up for what you waste.

So was Masha my escape-route from the real world, or my door to it? Was this just the desperate consumer-kick of a sad, lost, old tosser who has saved his nights up too long and now blows them on the first thing that comes to mind, because he has gone mad with oversaving? Or was it a man saying: at last, at last, *this* is what I have been saving my nights for, this is it and I am not going to miss it out of any tightarsed fear of spending my life, it is mine to spend and here it is?

When you lay yourself totally open, are you a lost windsock crying *Help, I have no life, give me some of your big life, take me where the real people and the real feelings are! Take me with you, please, take me any way you want but take me*, or is it maybe possible that when you stand there with your eyes and arms spread wide you are saying *Look, I have so much life! I can wreck it if I want, and throw it away, because it is all mine and I have paid the full market price for it and I am free: look, here, I spread my life before you, for you. Enjoy.*

Hard to know.

Hard to think straight this hungover.

Hard to keep down the small crabs.

But a little pride goes a long way.

I looked at Masha and made myself swallow. The challenge in her eyes gave me strength: I straightened myself up, spine by spine, and shook out my shoulders, and sniffed. I looked round, took the ear-defenders the Mayor now offered (he having had his little Russian joke), picked up the gun and set myself side on to the target again. I pulled the oiled hammer back softly (clunk) with my left thumb, lined up and down on the target with a slow arm, and blasted off the other five rounds.

I now discovered the great secret about shooting handguns (secret at least to a nice ordinary Brit who has never done it before because Brits don't): it is very, very easy. No bloody wonder any sane government is keen to keep the streets gun-free. I mean, at fifty feet it is almost impossible to *miss* a non-moving, man-sized, man-shaped target.

—Dreck and Gherkins! said Mr Kant, and clapped me on the back so hard it nearly undid the pride-cure for a nasty moment. Then he took the gun from me and made sure it was empty, the shells clattered on the floor around my feet.

And then he looked me straight in the eye through the barrel, and then lowered the gun and kept on looking at me, and said a few sentences. Masha translated, her eyes taking over from her father's gun-barrel:

—My father says that he loves me more than his own heart. He says that he always has difficulty in deciding whether he should treat men who make love to me, or to whom I make love, as his sons-in-law, whom he should love and respect, or as black beetles. At present, he does not think you are a black beetle. But some black beetles are well-disguised, says my father. And now the Mayor of Samara wishes us to see his Musical Academy. The Kick-Boxing Champion will escort you to your hotel first, to dress suitably.

And Mr Nazi hustled me out. As I slumped back into my personal Lada, all I could think was: Sarah, Sarah, Sarah!

But Sarah was a long way away, she was at the end of a long tunnel, she was almost part of Memory Lane, I could see her outlined against the light at the end of the tunnel, but I could not even tell if she was facing towards me or walking away.

Back in the hotel room, Mr Nazi pointed to that ridiculous bloody dinner-jacket gear that was ready laid out on the bed. I thought of objecting, but there was clearly no point. I struggled into it, sweating under his critical gaze, half-wondering if he was just waiting for me to get my arms stuck in the sleeves, say, and would then smash me in the face. But then I realised that he had no need to wait for that, the bastard could have torn my liver out with one hand tied behind his back. I was stumped by the bow-tie; it was a kosher, knot-it-yourself number, and I had never really got round that one. As I tried and tried in the mirror, Mr Nazi appeared behind me. For a moment I thought this was it; then he spun me round by my shoulders and flicked the bow shipshape in ten seconds flat.

Before I had time to wonder whether I should thank him, or even dare catch his eye, Dr Jones walked in. He too was dressed in evening clothes, and thus looked even madder than usual. He went over to the long mirror on the door of my fifties Formica dresser, and looked at himself with puritanical disapproval; I joined him and gazed at myself in shame and horror.

I just cannot get used to this fat, balding person being me. I suppose I am not *that* fat or *that* bald. Just a lot fatter and balder than *me*. Fatter and balder and older and less fertile.

—Well, said Dr Jones, – As I said, we must just assume this charade is for business purposes. The market justifies all.

—Great, I'm fat and bald but it's only for business purposes. Now I feel much better. I don't suppose you're going to tell me what this is all about?

—No.

—I thought not.

—I am so glad you have learnt to accept the situation.

—I just happen to be totally wrecked. Christ, how much bloody starch did they put in this shirt?

—Enough to show, presumably.

Then we got back into our Ladas and drove two blocks to the Music Academy. Before I realised it, I found myself left all alone in my bloody DJ in the middle of the middle row of seats in the big hall, having massed balalaikas played at me by thirty ten-year-olds. I never knew there were that many different sizes of balalaika.

At the end, they waited for me to clap. So I had to. I thought sod it, and clapped with my hands out in front of me, like Khrushchev, and nodded and smiled, and they clapped back. It went on for a very long time, and I found myself sweating and feeling sick again.

Then a bunch of twelve-year-old girls did a terrible sixties rumba-dancing routine with umbrellas and mad smiles fixed on me like I was some adult they had to please for some unknown reason. And then a load of fifteen-year-old girls did a very long ballet to Chopin, with radiant smiles fixed on me like I was a party boss they had to please for reasons they now half-guessed. I could feel the B-movie Hangover Hormone tears coming into my eyes at the same time as I was growing desperate to scratch my arse and itch my armpits. The mutual clapping seemed to go on for ever this time.

I was about to suffer a simultaneous collapse of all bodily functions, right in full view of everyone, when Mr Nazi reappeared and escorted me over to the Mayor's office in a large fifties building on the square. There was a statue of Lenin in the foyer, a scratty little market on the first few floors and the Mayor's Interior Ministry paramilitary police everywhere. Masha and Mr Kant and Dr Jones and the Mayor welcomed me into the Mayor's suite in a way that made it quite clear they had been talking about me. In the silence, I saw

251

brand-new German office furniture, little Volga Region flags in little flag-holders everywhere, and wine-glasses full of vodka. I looked at Masha:

—Please thank the Mayor for the wonderful performance. And please, please, Masha, tell me what is going on.

She spoke to the Mayor, and he replied. She turned back to me:

—The Mayor is glad you enjoyed his school. It is a very good school. Especially for balalaikas.

So what the hell: vodka it was.

After that dose of vodka, I was cured, in the way that you can be cured by drawing on your slush-fund reserves of health and life: you are keeping going at the cost of making your body a vitamin-free zone. But getting through is the main thing, and now you are able to survive what follows, and what follows is:

You get taken for another hour's suicidal drive in another horrible Lada, flying and bounding past mad gypsy palaces, brick-built fortresses with crystal minarets on the roadside. When you ask if Mr Kant's Nazi Chauffeur would open the window, he takes his right hand off the wheel and fishes about for a screwdriver to lever it down, and you wish you hadn't asked, because the road is a laneless job used mainly by giant oil-tankers whose priority is clearly not avoiding squashing Ladas. In desperation, you reach for the non-existent seatbelt and (to your astonishment) find one and then find there is no anchor point anyway (sucker!) and the bastard grins, so you sit back and think *Oh Well, better than dying of senile decay to Queen, and anyway, Masha does not seem to care, maybe it is true that the people who really live do not care about dying; maybe fear of dying is what you get when deep down you know you never really lived (twang twang twang).*

And so you arrive at last, impossible as it seems, at a linoleum factory somewhere beyond nowhere, in a landscape of oil-sodden fields, ancient donkey-pumps, clouds of black, heavy smoke and bright, billowing petroleum flares. You wonder how anyone has *any* sperm-count at all here; how the hell come *they* have all these nice balalaika-playing kids, Ref?

As you park, you see, about fifty feet away, these two blokes polishing up a funny kind of car, a sort of black Lada estate, but longer than they usually are, and much blacker, and with extra chrome. As you get out of the car you catch a glimpse of the inside through the open tailgate, and see: dark Formica and brass floor-rails.

But now you are being led, feeling not yet human but maybe almost neanderthal, through the factory. There are big green machines, very new, made in Hamburg, twenty feet tall and a hundred long, roaring and humming; light is breaking in shafts from the high roof. In each shaft of light, you can see the thick, godonly-knows how poisonous dust rising and falling, and you try to breathe through your nose. But that cannot stop the sweet, chemical fumes biting into your throat as you go on through, watched by the big glass eyes of pig-faced gas-masked workers tending their nameless, terrifyingly unguarded rollers and belts. You are staggering and swooning with the vodka and the heat and the cancerous air by the time you push gratefully through a wall of heavy, scratched, plastic hanging-strips, into the fat, dull sun again, and step out into a large dusty courtyard.

Then you step back in an attack of horizontal vertigo, because what you see is:

about fifty western businessmen in over-nighted, jet-lagged suits, looking like death, looking much like you, looking at you with weary, condemned interest. You suddenly realise that they are all horrendously hung over and would happily file out to the Square of Executions if they were told to. And in their midst stands one of those large, crap, portable exhibition-stands you see everywhere: it reads *Free Your Intangibles*, and in front of it, on a makeshift podium, stands Dr Jones in his dinner-suit, beaming at you like a mad preacher greeting the converts.

—Welcome, said Dr Jones through a radio-mike system of some kind; his voice came from all around. It made everyone jump; it made him seem omnipresent. – You are all here because you have entered arrangements with my client, Mr Kant, for the take-up of loans on notably generous terms. The terms are indeed so unusually generous that this may not escape the attention of the various Inspectorates of Taxes of the States in which you reside. Vicious minds may even consider that the terms are so generous as to suggest impropriety. It may be opined by these State authorities that you do not have sufficient collateral to justify these loans on a legitimate business basis. They may, indeed, suggest that you are involved in money-laundering (Dr Jones smiled his smile again). – What nonsense! Your collateral is, of course, your intangible assets, your names, your goodwill. Who is to say how much these are worth? The name Dr Jones's Market Tools may be worth nothing to a producer of toiletries, and a substantial amount to, say, Mr Thompson of BIZVID Educational Productions (he looked right at me, some

254

of the people near me turned to see). – Or to Mr Kant. Who is to say, what Inspector of Taxes could ever *prove*, that Mr Kant does not heartily desire the Western brand-names that you represent? Perhaps Mr Kant hopes that you *will* default, thus giving him control over your names. Perhaps he wishes to abuse those good names in the new markets of the East, among unsophisticated consumers. Who is to say? Value is what someone is prepared to pay. You are not your brothers' valuers.

My point is simple: rest assured, no investigation can ever *prove* that your loans, and your repayments, are not strictly legal transactions based on the collateral value of your intangible assets. Remember this, and keep your courage if your national authorities attempt to impose upon you.

And remember one other thing: it may have occurred to some of you, yourselves, that your intangible assets are not in fact as valuable as Mr Kant appears to imagine. It may have struck you that my client is far away and that in many countries, the UK notably, it is extremely easy to fold one business and commence trading under another name. You may suspect that my client is unlikely to be able to invoke State authorities to recoup his money, should you act in this way. What, you may have asked yourselves, is to prevent you merely defaulting on your loans, having transferred my client's funds offshore, for example?

Let me suggest an old and admirably simple answer to this question.

Dr Jones paused. I yawned and stretched and scratched my balls. Except then I stopped mid-yawn, mid-stretch, mid-scratch, because I realised he was looking straight at me again, and had already been doing so for so long that slowly, all the hundred lost, knackered eyes in the courtyard were turning themselves on me.

All of a sudden I could hear the poisonous machinery clattering inside the factory. I tried to make eye-contact with Dr Jones to ask him what the hell he was on about, but all I got was the sheen of his specs. I tried to shrug a joke to the other businessmen about me.

Which was when I noticed they were not looking at me any more, but at something behind me; looking, and shuffling quietly away, as if scared that whatever was behind me would see them moving and lock onto them instead. I felt a little breeze on my neck as the hairs shifted. I looked around.

Masha was slotting bullets into the magazine of a small chrome automatic. Mr Kant was watching me. Mr Kant's driver had drifted up close; now he grabbed me, spun me off my feet and slammed me one-handed, flat-back, into the wall of the courtyard, just by the plastic-strip door where we had come out of the factory. It did not even occur to me to fight him.

—What is this? I asked. To my surprise, the words came out quite normal. Mr Kant smiled and said something. Masha said, cold and loud and without looking up from springing the shells carefully into the clip:

—Mr Kant asks you what Drake or Hawkins did to men who betrayed them?

—Betrayed them? I asked.

Just sounds, the words did not mean anything. I looked past them and saw Dr Jones smiling, and saw that I was alone now in a big semicircular clearing, with the wall at my back and everyone watching me, fascinated. From somewhere down Memory Lane, the trumpets began to sound the slow Paso Doble, the music of death. I focused back to Mr Kant: – This is ridiculous, I said.

Then Masha clunked the magazine softly into the gun and pointed it at my face.

—Masha! I said. I thought how it was the first time I had said her name out loud, out of bed. And then I thought *no*, maybe I had said it at other times: maybe I had shouted it in my dreams, or cooed myself to sleep with it. And then she fired.

Amid the steel bang and the singing ears and the heat, I heard the bullet whirring away. It had hit the bricks about a yard from my head. All I could think was *right, so you really do hear bouncing bullets making that noise, kind of like a pheasant taking off, but much higher and faster, that's interesting*. Then I looked beside me where the bullet had hit the wall and thought *yeah, got it, so that's why those walls in Berlin look like that*. And then I realised that I was only thinking like this because I was too scared to think about what was actually happening to me. So I swallowed and looked back at Masha.

She was still looking at me over the barrel, but suddenly I knew she would not shoot me. And it was true; she shook her head and sobbed and turned away, into Mr Kant's, her father's, comforting arms.

And she passed the gun to Mr Nazi bloody Body-guard.

A hard lump of sour, metallic ice rose from my chest, up my throat, and into my mouth as he juggled the little gun round in his big paw like some shagging cowboy, grinning at me. He came trotting up happily and just kind of lined me up against the wall like a guy lining up a block of wood he is about to split with an axe.

So I loafed him.

Well, I tried.

He was so much taller than me I did not have to squat, I actually had to jump a little to aim for his nose, which is about ideal for loafing, but all I hit was thin air because he was much too quick as well as big. I loafed nothing, and he just kind of shoved me on my way, with my own momentum; he took my legs out with one foot as I staggered past him, and in a second I was eating the lino-dust off the concrete. Almost certainly carcinogenic.

—Fuck you, you Nazi bastard! I screamed, and I broke for the door, sure that any second I was going to learn first-hand what a bullet in the back feels like. As I half-scrabbled, half-ran, I saw all the other businessmen twitch back a step further away, faces rigid, feet dancing with the desire to leg it, as if they were scared that I might tag them and infect them, too, with imminent death.

I breast-stroked through the heavy plastic strips, back into the factory; the chemical-soaked air bit into my lungs; up loomed half-a-dozen of the pig-faced gas-mask men, and, since I could do nothing else, I went straight at them. I felt almost joy in the impact as I took two of them out and down. I thought I heard a crowd shouting *oooOOOLEEE!* But as I tried to get up and run on, the others grabbed me. Their clothes smelt of creosote and acetone.

Then Mr Nazi had me again, by the collar, like a kid. I was swung off my feet, back out head-first through the plastic strips. The dull sun hammered on my head as I landed on the concrete again. I stayed there.

—Mr Kant says you may die on your feet, said Masha.

—Masha! I said again, but she looked away. Mr Kant was watching me. So was everyone else.

258

OK, so this is what it's like, then. Not exactly what I had expected, Referee, but then again maybe it is better unexpected. Certainly better quick. So I miss out on the old people's home after all. I mean, sod it, so what, every little bank-clerk has to get this, one way or another.

So I got up, my knees were actually working quite normally, I thanked Christ for the vodka-dulled hangover, it made everything completely unreal. I even wanted to laugh, I was thinking how I could now at last have told the world something truly profound and useful for everyone: *vodka helps you die*. I was also thinking how glad I was I never gave up booze or fags. Mr Nazi seemed to be waiting for something, so I stuck with tradition and took a fag out and lit it. It didn't taste right. After the first drag I shouted up at the big square of grey sky:

—WHAT DID I DO, REF?, and then I stopped laughing. I wanted to scream or something, but I just looked at Masha and Mr Kant. She was in his arms, I could clock them with one glare: – You bastards, this is so fucking un*fair*!

And then Mr Nazi raised the gun and fired pointblank. This time the big steel hammer came with hot flames and hit me high in the chest. I felt no pain, just the deafening blow: I was knocked off balance, the fag shot out of my mouth, I took a step back and my knees went as I realised that I was dead.

I sprawled on my back. The pig-faces gathered round above me, fists and spanners raised and ready. I gasped for air and then doubled up as the pain hit me; I grabbed for my chest, now I started to chuck up half-digested small crabs at last, and I hardly cared any more as I felt, rather than saw, Mr Nazi stroll up, stamp out my fag-end, stand over me, and aim the gun at my face. I could see the black barrel out of the corner of my right eye as I coughed and vomited and squirmed on the floor.

He squeezed slowly and easily; I saw one of my own arms flapping pathetically at him, like a baby trying to ward off pain; I winced away and closed my eyes; I saw bats, and a woman at the end of a long garden in evening light, holding a child by the hand; only this time, beyond the long garden was Stonehenge, and the woman was Sarah, and as she turned to look at me, so did the child, and it was me.

And then the shining hammer smashed into the anvil.

21. Need-to-Know Stuff

—I tell you straight, lads, Pete is in it up to here. Seriously in it. I mean dead serious, and when I say dead I mean dead as in dead dead. I jest not.

—Christ, said Brian Irons. Toby Jobson looked out of the window.

—Can't we help him? asked Charmaine.

—No offence now, but would you mind toddling along, Charmaine? This is need-to-know stuff, know what I mean. Thanks for the coffees.

—OK, sure, said Charmaine, and went.

—Nice tits. Like I said, Pete has been a silly boy lads, he has gone and got himself in with some mightily dodgy people. Like, it's easy enough to play the hardball business-head over here, but these guys play for keepsies. I am talking oil-tankers of caviar, I am talking container-loads of gold, I am talking bucks to kill for.

—So what do we bloody do?! shouted Irons, suddenly.

—Nothing. Not yet.

Toby Jobson looked round from his window and said quietly:

—You're not just an accountant, are you, Deeny?

—I work with the security forces, let's just put it that way.

—Christ, said Irons.

—Was our saviour, and I may be yours. We can protect you, whatever happens to Pete.

—Why would you do that? asked Jobson.

—If Pete does end up getting bin-bagged, I'm not saying he will, but if, then Sarah inherits his share of the partnership. But the partnership is only debts anyway, you know the lie of the land now. So now: H.M.G. will take Sarah's debts off her hands, and a certain tax-inspector will find a nifty little note from on high telling him to lay the fuck off this one. BIZVID stays BIZVID except instead of Pete you get me. Lucky lads. Instead of not asking Pete any questions about the books, you don't ask me questions. You keep on filming your corporate bods and drawing your pay and my friends square it with Pete's new business pals. Hey, lads, you might even get to make that movie one day!

—This is if Pete doesn't come back?

—Iffityiffityiff, lads. But think about it. And keep listening to the news. Hold on now . . .

Deeny yanked the kitchen door open.

The landing was deserted, the roof of the lift-car was just disappearing downwards, the black, oil-shiny cables clunked and whirred. Deeny looked for a moment as if he was going to dive after it, but he stopped, turned and smiled.

—Did he ever fuck her?

—I think so, said Jobson.

—Definitely, said Irons.

—Hmm, said Deeny. – Oh well, fair play to him so. Nice girl. Lovely tits. Be seeing yous, lads.

22. Dark Matter

As I sat in my Volvo after Gerry had left (the clock on the dash read 10.33 p.m.) trying desperately to think of some irresistibly erotic scene, I kept spoiling it by thinking: I had fallen for it all hook line and sinker, and that was why they had chosen me. Just the right kind of sucker.

*

Not starch. Kevlar.

Eighteen layers of Kevlar: 8 in the hard-fronted shirt, 10 in the fat, stiff, silky lapels of the double-breasted DJ. Enough (I gather) to stop a .45 firing a 230-gramme FMJ; enough (I bear witness) to stop whatever that small chrome thing had been.

Not a big target, just the area where the lapels and the shirt doubled up. But then Mr Kant's driver had been very close, and he was supposedly very good, and everyone told me that he made sure he aimed to his right and too high, if anything, rather than to his left and too low, if anything: so that if he had missed the sweet-spot he would only have blown away my left shoulder, not my heart, if anything.

Nice bloke, Mr Kant's driver.

Some sort of poor-relation cousin, apparently, a butcher's son they had brought to Samara from the arse-end of nowhere, and who was now twenty-one and married with four kids. Not the world's speediest intellect, perhaps, but a whizz at kick-boxing and totally devoted to Mr Kant and Masha. And handy with a gun.

The first shot had been fired by Masha to miss, of course, and the third, the head-shot, the alleged coup de grâce, had been a blank, of course. Hence the careful loading she had done. Of course. Now they tell me.

Or rather, Dr Jones told me.

Dr Jones explained it all as Mr Kant's driver took us from the lino factory to Samara airport, in a black stretch Lada hearse allegedly containing my dead body, for the internal flight to Moscow Domodedovo. I slithered about on the shiny formica as we bounced along, and learnt what the hell had been going on in my life.

It had all been a show, just a piece of theatre to encourage Mr Kant's other western debtors. The last words Mr Kant had hissed at me, with a big grin, as the pig-face gas-mask men dragged me out of sight, had been:

—Dreck and Gherkins! PR!

So now all the other nice western clients went away scared shitless, quickly dropping any plans they might have had to elope with their secretaries and Mr Kant's dough. Now they knew what the Free Market was *really* about; now they had seen the black stretch Lada carrying me off; now, when they got back to Surrey and Sussex and Kent, they would look out of the UPVC windows of their Executive Housing Units and know that the petrochemical flares are never far away. Now they knew Mr Kant.

—That is why you could not be told, of course, said Dr Jones, as we sat on the hot vinyl seats in the tiny little early-sixties lounge at Samara airport, – You had to believe it yourself. Or rather, you had to *not* believe it, to be totally unprepared; Mr Kant's other clients had to see the unbelievable truth of immediate mortality dawn on you. It was somewhat risky, true: but then, the statistical likelihood of Mr Kant's driver killing you accidentally was almost certainly lower than the statistical likelihood of our dying in the Aeroflot Tupolev we are about to fly.

—Great.

—For myself, I fly on them without a second thought. Not that I claim to be courageous, merely rational: I have five healthy children and a quite bewildering array of insurance policies, so what should I fear?

Our flight was called, and we went out into the yellow, late-afternoon sunlight. The beauty of the plan, Dr Jones explained, was this: if anyone squealed, so what? If some brave but stupid type decided to tell Interpol that I had been killed, Interpol would find me alive. Not, Dr Jones stressed, that Mr Kant shied away from decisive action to protect his interests: it was just that at present, actually having to go and bump off recalcitrant British businessmen who had done bunks with his loans would have been a little awkward. Potentially. Awkward for MI5.

—MI5? I shouted, and stopped dead on the runway at Samara.

—I suggest we continue, cried Dr Jones, over the whistling of the engines, – The attitude of Russian pilots to passengers on runways is rather similar to the attitude of Russian drivers to pedestrians on roads.

We dodged the taxiing Tupolevs and crossed the runways. Our plane was battered and bulged, the ladder creaked as we filed aboard. In front of us was a lone American businessman, bald, fat, bearded, sweating and joyously happy. He could not resist turning round to talk to us, so happy was he:

—And to think I always promised my momma I

would never fly a Tupolev. But hey, shit: I'm getting out of here! I'm going home! Due West! You guys know what my report is going to say? I'll tell you. It is going to say that only a certifiable maniac would *ever* consider investing *shit* here.

—Allow me to give you lunch in London tomorrow, said Dr Jones, handing over his card.

Inside, the seats were bare metal and frayed orange fabric; the two in front of us sagged forward, broken-backed. As the engines squealed up to speed, steam rose into the passenger compartment and condensed on the patched ceiling. The Russians began to swig vodka from bottles in brown paper bags; the make-up-caked air-hostesses gripped their seats and stared grimly ahead. I would have been shitting myself, except that I had not yet recovered from being dead anyway.

Below us now, the forests dropped away and spread out for ever, until our height swallowed them mercifully.

Mr Kant, it seemed, was seen as a regional bastion of pro-western forces. So MI5 were into helping him and his pals buy high-tech weapons, mainly the latest Marconi hand-held antitank stuff, in case the Communist Fascists tried to make a come-back. Russia is full of tanks, and one tank can hold down a hell of a lot of people with rifles; but if they also have modern hand-held antitank weapons, Dr Jones explained, a Communist-Fascist tank quickly becomes a big sardine-tin full of not very determined men with a very short life-expectancy. MI5's problem was that after all this stuff about the anti-crime war and Matrix Churchill and ORTECH and so on, it could not risk being *seen* to be helping Mr Kant, and certainly could not risk being associated with someone who stiffed UK businessmen in lino-factories. Also, Mr Kant and his pals did not want any sign of any Foreign Government help, because that kind of thing is as unhelpful to the cause in Russia as anywhere else. He just had to have legitimate money, clean money, money that real British companies like BIZVID had deposited properly in real British banks, which would then go to a collecting-point in Liechtenstein, then be used to buy Eurodollar Bearer-Bonds which would be put through various meaningless transactions via holding companies and end up in Chase Manhattan or suchlike. And thence to Marconi or whoever.

—Jesus, so we're laundering money? Christ!

—Think of it as a blow against State Currency Control.

—But you just said Mr Kant is working for them.

—Oh no, said Dr Jones, with a frown of surprise. – Though MI5 would like to think he is. The Volga Region is vital for oil-pipelines from the Caspian Sea. Whoever controls the places the pipelines meet, is guaranteed enormous royalties: enough to finance a large army, which means a substantial State-in-embryo, out of one single, raw resource. So much easier to control than a market. MI5 wants the pipelines to meet in a friendly Volga Region. You should not underestimate the British State. Underneath the viyella and the red setters, Britain is by far the most efficiently centralized and militarized State in Europe. After France, of course. But so much better than France at pretending *not* to be. And so very much more concerned with the international oil trade. And so very, *very* much more friendly with the Americans, which is all that really matters.

—But Mr Kant isn't going to play ball?

—MI5 is blinded by the eurocentric ideas of its

imperialist forebears. It assumes that because Mr Kant is European, Mr Kant and his associates look to Europe. On the contrary. Mr Kant has no ties or prejudices of place or culture. Wherever there is a market, and there is always a market, there were even markets in Auschwitz, Mr Kant will be at home. He intends to re-route the pipelines eastwards. To China. That is where the future markets lie. But MI5 naturally does not know this.

—I don't get this. Are you in MI5 or not?

—Both.

—Of course. Ah, Cardinal, allow me to present Zorro, Master of Ambiguity.

—Quite. I work for them occasionally on a consulta-tive basis, as I would for any commercial organisation. In this case, MI5 comes to me and asks me to comment on the suitability of a company which they have located. I comment.

—You commented on me?

—Of course. BIZVID is too small, really, but then a company involved in legitimate filming and recording has, naturally, other potential usefulness for MI5.

—But how did they hear about me?

—Come come.

—Deeny?!

—Of course. He works for the British intelligence services.

—But he's Catholic Irish.

—So is half the SAS and the Foreign Office. Deeny is one of those alarming people who actually *desire* to be unfree, to be told what to do, to take orders and so on. To belong, in short. A horrid word that scarcely hides its own secret: Deeny desires to belong *to* something, in the sense in which a slave belongs to his master. Deeny is a natural soldier, in other words. He is a Territorial

Major in the Intelligence Corps, where Territorials are of considerably higher status than in most units.

—That bastard! He shopped me to the taxman?

—Exactly.

—And he was planning to shop me for months?

—Years, I should imagine. That, after all, is his job: to spot firms in trouble. To encourage them to get into trouble, indeed. And, of course, to find the right sort of people.

—And what sort would that be?

—Unscrupulous but ultimately conformist.

—Thanks.

—My pleasure.

—I've been stitched up.

—You have hardly done badly out of it.

—Badly! I'm stuck with a gang of money-launderers and you think I haven't done badly?

—Yet the State peddles alcohol and arms, and you think that perfectly normal. I think you may be a lost cause. Well, remember: all you have to do is repay Mr Kant, and you may go free.

—Great, and go bankrupt.

—You can hardly blame me for that.

—Well who the hell should I blame? The State?

—I should have thought it was obvious whom you should blame.

—Why did they choose *me* for Christ's sake?!

—Oh, in principle, our little charade could have been acted out on anyone. It appears that Mr Kant *likes* you. I should not seem so surprised. That is the basis on which business is conducted the world over, and always has been. The notion of a meritocracy is a very recent, and very limited fantasy, designed merely to keep the C1's hard at it on their career-ladders by day

and on their stair-climbing machines in their supposedly free time. There is, of course, the question why Mr
Kant should like *you* of all people, and there I am afraid
I must confess myself as ignorant as you. Would you
like a lift into town?

We were at Gatwick by now, and Dr Jones indicated
the large, dark-green car that had evidently just arrived
from the chauffeured-parking lot. But I wanted to be on
my own; I was totally off balance by now, I needed to
get my bearings back.

—Very well, said Dr Jones. Then he paused before
getting into the car: – I would be surprised if Mr Kant
were not to make you some kind of new offer in the
near future. I should consider carefully before accepting. Mr Kant may like you, and his daughter too. But do
not forget that they are business people.

—What do you mean? You mean they might be
lying?

—I mean that as a modern Westerner, you are
accustomed to a mode of life which involves neither
material peril nor intellectual rectitude. Mr Kant's
business methods are rather less safe; they are very
much less sentimental.

And off he drove.

Or maybe I was *on* balance for the first time in my life?
Maybe I needed to get my bearings newly calibrated,
not back? I mean, I did not know if it was jet-lag, or
vodka-lag, or being-shot-lag, or just the curtains of
reality being drawn back: but as the Gatwick Express
trundled through England it all looked like some
incredibly rich man's playland fantasy.

Here we are again, all the twee little houses and tidy
little fields and smooth little hedges and new little

roads and neat little Hunter's Rise-style estates every-where. You could imagine some huge hand coming down from the sky, like in the lottery advert, and dusting off a county or two in passing.

So was this reality? Or the Volga and the petrochemi-cal flares?

Opposite me was a small man in a dull-grey nylon car-coat and cheap shoes. He had a tatty plastic briefcase balanced across his thin knees and was avidly reading a copy of *Astronomy Today*. The headline on the cover read:

DARK MATTER SPREADS TO
SMALLER GALAXIES

but it might as well have said ATTERTHORPE YOUTH XIII IN CUP TRIUMPH or something: the too-big things and the too-small things meet at the point called meaninglessness in the heads of the terminally saaad.

Dark Matter be buggered: if there is one thing for sure about the future, it is that all that crap about wormholes and timestrings and whatever will one day seem as real as St Thomas arguing about angels on heads of pins. At the edge of what we can know and say, we make images: faced with infinity, our fact-fetishist lists dissolve, whether we want them to or not, into visions. I coughed, and my chest jumped in agony.

I had a bruise the size of a dinner-plate on my chest, a great splash of black and purple and yellow. Like when you were a kid at school and they got you to drop ink onto a piece of wet tissue-paper, remember? The shirt had come from the same Mayfair shop that supplied the Bomb Ranger. I thought maybe I should offer myself to them as an advert: *Kevlar saved my left tit, says grateful Brit businessman.*

At Victoria, I called Sarah. She was out. My own voice on the ansaphone told me to leave a message for me: *Hi Pete, Pete's not here.* I knew it was five in the afternoon, my watch told me it was, although my body was unconvinced; but I had no idea what day it was. *Saturday*, said the papers. So that was the strange feeling in the air: Saturday night starting to yawn and stir. Alone on a Saturday night. Great. And with lovely Sunday to look forward to. Fab. Suddenly the thought of going home did not feel like going home at all, I pictured myself alone at home and it was a picture by Hieronymus Bosch with a sound-track of scratchy nothingness and very loud clocks. Un-nice. So I went to BIZVID instead.

At BIZVID I could at least be in town. I could at least look out at Charing Cross Road and wish I was young again, or gay for once, or Harrison Ford, or whatever the hell it is you have to be to just wander into some pub early on Saturday night in the West End and have a quiet drink and maybe a quiet chat with whoever happens to be around, without everyone thinking what a saaaad bastard you are.

And at BIZVID I would at least find my own crap office and my own crap chair and my own crap desk with its pile of crap memos and messages for me, and that would at least confirm that someone, somewhere in the wide world, needed this bloke called Peter Thompson, who was allegedly me.

So half an hour later I was revolving in my gas-suspended chair, sitting in the dark with the lights and noise and longings of Saturday night firing up from Charing Cross Road all around me and into the office windows. I listened to the parade of life going on below and past me, and stared at the reflected neon, and wanted to howl. I called Sarah again but she was out again, or out still, probably. Somewhere with someone. I saw the bats again, and Sarah again at the end of the garden.

Then I heard the lift jerk into motion outside. Eight o'clock on Saturday night, and someone was coming up.

I leaned over and could just see through the mesh window of the office door. The cables shone with dull oil, it looked as if they were turning slowly around and around, not moving vertically. I knew, I just knew that the lift was coming to this floor. It did. It stopped outside with a soft clunk.

Silence. The cage-doors did not open, the car just stayed there. I watched and listened, frozen. I could hear myself swallowing. I thought it must be so loud that whoever was in the cage could hear it too. I waited for the doors to open. I expected them to move very quietly: – quietly, in that noisily quiet way that things open when someone is trying very hard to open them quietly. I looked around the room, my instincts were screaming *hide hide hide*, but I could not move.

Then someone burst through the door of the office, holding a large spanner in one hand and a pair of black stilettos in the other.

—Pete! cried Charlie.

Charlie. She was dressed in the shortest possible skirt and the littlest possible top and a kind of PVC mac thing and heels. Her hair was up in some kind of mad pineapple affair, and her make-up was taking no prisoners. She shouted with relief, dropped the shoes and spanner, and ran to me so fast that the chair spun round and landed us both on the floor. I could smell the plastic off her mac and see the tiny grains in her lipstick.

—Charlie, what the fuck are you doing here?

—Oh Christ, thank God it's you. I was going past, like, I'm just off to meet Trev and the gang, you know, going to the pictures, and then I saw this light on up here, and I thought, well, I'd better come and have a look, like.

—Bloody hell, that's very brave of you.

—Well, I thought it would only be them.

—Them?

—Brian and Toby and Sean. Sean, mainly. They've been trying to get into your hard disk, but I told them I didn't know the password.

—*You told* them you don't? Do you?

—Course.

—Oh.

—So they hired some whizz kid to get in.

—Fuck!

—Oh, he didn't get nothing. Soon as they first asked me, I nipped back at lunchtime and took everything off onto disks. Then I re-formatted the c-drive and put back everything except your *Memorylane* stuff, like. Me thick or what?

—Charlie, you're a genius! So you know? I mean, about us being bankrupt?

—Course. I knew yonks ago, Pete.

—You did?

—Course.

—Oh.

—But Sean said you might be, like, in serious trouble. Physical like. Is this about your secret account with Sean?

—Look at this, Charlie, I said, and showed her my bruise.

—Buggering hell, who did that?

And the next thing I knew, Charlie had brought coffee in and we were sitting down, chatting and smoking fags. And I was telling her everything. Me and Charlie, like old mates, amazing!

We soon sussed it out. It was obvious: Deeny was definitely trying to take BIZVID over. He was going to scare Irons and Jobson with stories of debt and Russians, then put the knackers on me with his MI5 boys, to make me sign over Mr Kant's money to his sole control. So I asked Charlie straight if she was with me or not, and she frowned her nice frown, slightly offended, and said *course*. We arranged that on Monday we would confront Irons and Jobson: I would offer them a take-it-or-leave-it deal to get out; Charlie would become Production Manager and full partner. I knew Irons and Jobson. They would not have the madness in them. They were just craphead Brits who wanted a quiet life and a guaranteed pension. But I had seen the Volga and Charlie was a tough young Brummie with nothing to lose: we would call Deeny's bluff.

Then Charlie had to go to meet Trevor, who was now (it turned out) engaged to her, and her mates. She invited me, and she meant it, and part of me was raring to go, but part of me said it would be a disaster. I was so wound up I could not slow down: I would act like a loony in the pub, and start singing balalaikas; or else the drink would turn the key softly and knock me straight out.

—Thanks, Charlie, really. But I've got to get home.

She looked at me carefully:

—If you're sure, Pete. But look, if you need a hand with anything, just ring, right? Anytime. Trev's always got his mobile, like, and you got the number.

—OK Charlie.

—Night night then.

It only occurred to me then, watching her go, that I had never even thought of anything happening between us except what had happened. A week ago you could not have left us alone in the office at night for five minutes without us tearing each other's clothes off; a week ago I would have chewed through plasterboard to get at Charlie. And now we were the safest non-couple on earth, old friends and future business partners. Thanks for making the rules sooo easy to understand, Ref.

When I got home, I stood for a while outside the house, in the street. Hunter's Rise was catatonic and the house was empty. I felt like some ghost, come back to haunt the places he lived because he never really had a life there. Then a sound, familiar yet unusual, chipped its way through the invisible screens and into my brain: it was my mobile, ringing away inside the garage. I dived for my case to get out my keys and ran, like this phone-call was some kind of hotline to the world; I was scrabbling in my pocket for the remote as I ran up the drive; as I heaved open the up-and-over door, I was already blipping the locks open. I was hoping, no, *hoping* is wrong: I was madly *assuming* that it was Sarah, and that I would hear her voice any second now, and that this would somehow make everything OK again.

I threw the door open so hard I whacked it on the side of the garage; I dived in and jammed the phone to my ear (I was so keen to hear Sarah's voice that I even forgot about the microwaves). The ringing stopped just as I got there. I dialled 1471, but it was only bloody Deeny who had called. Not being Sarah seemed like another offence to add to the growing list of Deeny's crimes. Sod him, the bastard, let him sweat; I had him taped now, I would see to him on Monday.

I sat for another while in the car, thinking about nothing. I got out, mechanically checked the bang I had given the door, cursed the price of Volvo repairs, kicked it shut for good measure, blipped the doors shut (clunk) and swung the garage door closed. I had never realised my garage-door squeaked so much: the noise seemed over-amplified, like when you are a kid and you flush the lav and suddenly you think that maybe the bogeyman will jump up on you when you can't hear because of the noise. I padded up the drive to my own dark house and went in my own front door with a strange beating in my heart and a strange taste in my mouth, like I was walking into a chamber of horrors. I wondered if it would have been different if I had ever really liked the place anyway.

In the dark of the lvng rm, I saw three flashes on the ansaphone. Two were from me, I knew. *Hi again Pete.* So first I listened to myself telling me I was at Victoria.

—You lie, schweinhund Pete, you are here!, I shouted out loud, and laughed like a loony, and decided I had better have a drink, so I fixed one while I listened to myself telling me that I was at BIZVID now.

—Ah, so now you change your story!

And then it was Deeny's voice:

—Hoi, Pete, my man, where the fuck are you? Call me back anytime. But *call* me.

So I thought about it and decided I might as well call the arsehole back to see what bullshit he would shoot me. I was on to him anyway, thanks to Charlie:

—Hi, Sean.

—Pete, thank fuck! Can you talk?

—Sure, no-one here.

277

—Pete, we *have* to meet soonest. Tomorrow, I jest not, Sunday or no Sunday, really, this is so serious. Be at your office at 7a.m. tomorrow, or we are just *blown* out of the water. Please. And for Jesus sake don't tell Brian and Toby, those boys have to be kept *right* out for now. Nor Sarah, neither. Not yet. Be there, Pete.

—Sean, what the hell's going on?

—Can't talk on the ould dog and bone, Pete. But *no way* can this wait till Monday. And don't tell *anyone*. I jest not, Pete: you have got us into some hot shit, there is a possibility of danger, and I mean *danger* danger, to us both. And anyone else who's in on it.

So I calmed him down and promised to be there tomorrow and promised to tell no-one, and put down the phone.

—Sure, let's Berni tomorrow, Deeny, I said to myself.

As I walked about the room, bumping into the furniture that someone had scattered about in it for some reason, I was trying to remember what Charlie had said Deeny had said to Irons and Jobson, and trying to work out if that matched with what Deeny had just said to me. I thought maybe I should phone Charlie on Trevor's mobile.

It was no bloody good, I couldn't think straight. I was knackered but twitchy, my thoughts just went in circles, getting nowhere, rattling around inside my head like a mouse on a plastic wheel, until I felt sick.

I thought maybe a nice quiet shave would cool me off, shaving is often good for morale. Except when I got to the bathroom and took the razor in my hand, I suddenly felt that for some reason it might not be a good idea to shave right now. Even with a safe little Gillette. I looked at myself and tried to work out how it had all gone so wrong; how I had become me.

But then the front door opened downstairs and I heard Sarah laughing and a man's voice, Gerry, and my first, mad thought was: *saved!*

And then my second and even madder thought was: oh well, it's only *Gerry* she's been fucking with while I was away, that's OK then. But there then came another voice, which was Melissa, so that was OK anyway. I shouted:

—Hi, it's me! Don't shoot, Gerry!

Then I ran out of the door and bounded to the stairs, grinning like some abandoned labrador at the prospect of my life starting up again. Sarah was waiting alone at the bottom of the stairs, looking up at me.

—Sarah, I said.

She held out her hand.

—Come on, she said mysteriously.

So I went. Downstairs, they were sitting, waiting for me in silence, and on the coffee-table was a bottle of champagne with a glass beside it. Gerry and Melissa already had their glasses ready, and raised them as I entered.

I was about to talk, about to ask what the hell was going on, but Sarah put her finger over her lips, so I shut up and watched. She walked over to the ansaphone and pressed the switch. Every movement she made was exaggerated, like she was playing charades; she kept up 100 per cent eye-contact to make sure I was concentrating. As the tape clunked into gear, she sat down again and looked at me with a brand-new kind of smile on her face. She patted her stomach and the metal voice said THE UNIT IS ON.

—You're kidding! I yelped.

—As in goats, she said.

So then Sarah and I hugged and kissed and then

Melissa and I hugged and kissed and then Gerry kind of half-punched me in the ribs and I kind of half-thumped him on the arm, and he said:

—Is this WASP crap or is this WASP crap?

—It is, I said. So then we bear-hugged, and then we all kind of huddled, and suddenly we were like a tribe, which is the nicest thing to be like, and next thing I knew we had already scoffed the bubbly and we were drinking some crap white wine from the fridge (except Sarah, of course) and I was thinking about this great idea I had suddenly had:

When I met Deeny tomorrow I would offer to sell out to him, which was obviously what he was after. I reckoned I would sell him my partnership and my debts for £250,000 dead, and sign over sole access to Mr Kant's money to him, with no questions asked. I would leave Irons and Jobson to his tender mercies, and leave him and Mr Kant to their war-games. I would negotiate something for Charlie. I felt a bit guilty at letting her down. But I had to look after number one. And now numbers two and three as well.

Naturally, I didn't tell Sarah and Gerry and Melissa about this, not exactly. But I did say that I thought I had a buyer. I said it might mean we could start all over again. Clean slate time.

—Your organic restaurant! said Melissa. – Let's go for it. We keep to a strictly limited menu and everything, *everything* is organic. Even the drinks. The menu has photos of the little smallholders we buy from, and we put in exact descriptions of everything. The more people pay, the better they feel about it. In a year we are franchising.

—America would love it, nodded Gerry.

—Organic Shack, said Melissa.

—Wow, said Sarah, and she patted her tummy: –

Hear that? Lucky baby!, and then she looked at nothing and said: – Thank Christ.

And then I drank a very large glass down in one and found myself listening to her tummy and singing, to the tune of *Bobby's Girl*:

You're going to be (clap clap) Middle Class
You're going to be (clap clap) Fi-rst World
White and WASPy, lucky as can be-ee

And then we all stayed laughing and talking for a while, until Sarah suddenly decided to tell the tale of how we actually fell for each other properly in the first place, which I had never heard her tell anyone before:

Thing was, I had at that time just had my foreskin half ripped off of me by this nutty French girl, in a vain attempt to get me hard after a dozen pints. So, soon after this, it came to the first real get-together between Sarah and me (we having known each other for some years through friends). Now, this foreskin thing turned out to be the luckiest break (ha ha) I ever had, because it went again, even worse, during our third or fourth bout: I didn't even notice in the general enthusiasm (well, you don't), but just as we were recovering and I was watching Sarah's face with the unexpected but certain pre-echo of unknown feelings to come, I saw her begin to frown. Then she moved her hand round the sheets, frowned more, opened her eyes, sat up, pulled back the sheets, saw this blood everywhere and bounced out of bed screaming:

—I had my period last week! Jesus Christ what have you fucking done to me?!

(I think it was the big laugh afterwards that sealed our fates. Sarah said she had never heard anything so funny as me screaming in the shower as the shampoo hit my torn membrane.)

She did the scream right then and there in Hunter's Rise, and laughed out loud, with her head thrown back and her mouth wide open and her tongue on the top of her bottom lip. We all laughed too, but as I laughed, I was watching her laugh, in amazement, and watching Gerry and Melissa laughing with her: it was like I was seeing her for the first time, or the first time in years. Then she suddenly had tears in her eyes, and before I could move, Melissa jumped over to be at her side. Sarah shook her head and said it was nothing, it was just because she was happy, but she did not look at anyone as she said it, and I thought maybe she was crying because all at once all the bad times we had had just seemed so bloody *unnecessary*, you know, it would have been so bloody easy to have avoided them: we could have laughed like this so much more in the last three years. We had let it run so long, and so close to the edge, that our last-gasp happiness had almost become a might-have-been even as it was happening.

When Sarah turned to get her drink, I caught her eye at last, and she seemed to guess what I was thinking. She touched my hand very briefly but very deliberately. Then she said she was going to bed to *gloat and gestate*; Melissa said she would come upstairs to tuck her in. I lit up a cigarette, but Melissa threw me out:

—Outside from now on. Think of placental growth, Peter!

I was happy to be ordered out. I needed to think.

Well, not *think*: just sort of contemplate. I smoked my fag and looked up at the sky. The evening was warm, one of the first warm evenings of the year. All around me, in the suburban quiet, I could hear the tiny patterings and rustlings of the world that goes on without noticing Homo sapiens. A bat flickered for a half-second in the corner of my eye. I looked around. More than that, I *felt* around with all my invisible feelers; long tides of oneness with nature flooded through me. I was part of the Big Story too now. All the fluttering insects and scurrying little furry things; the buds on the rose-bushes; the daffs looking ghostly in the sodium light; the night sky as vast and deep now as when the first super-chimp looked up and saw gods in the stars. And down here me, little me with my DNA duty done at last.

I looked up at the sky:

—Now I see, Ref, all that was just the warm-up. Shit, and I thought it was my life. So the real game starts here? You could have told me. But here I am: OK, you want to check my studs? Ready when you are, Ref. No more messing about. Just do my bit, nothing flash, no sliding tackles or hassling the keeper. I will stay clean, start over and just have a nice quiet game. A life like anyone else's. Nothing fancy. Nice and quiet. No need to tell Sarah about Masha and all that crap, eh? And sod the organic restaurant too; much too much like hard work. Now we are part of the Big Game, what should we want except to see it through in peace and quiet? Three or four kids, maybe. Why not, now we know we can do it? And Sarah and me will get old and the kids will grow up and we will become Mum and Dad and I shall drink halves of mild and have a shed. And if I ever look up at the sky and think about how it all happened, I shall just shake my head with gentle resignation and think: que sebleedingra, funny old world, innit?

—Really, Mr Thompson? asked the Interview Panel, which had appeared in the rose-bushes. The Tweedy Edinburgh Lady removed a twig from her hairdo.

—Yes, I said.

—Nice and quiet, Mr Thompson, nice and quiet? *Can* life be quiet, do you think? Can it *be* life if it is quiet? It might be argued, Mr Thompson, that we were not born for peace and quiet: we are, after all, alive and kicking long before we taste air. What will happen when you have put your children to bed, Mr Thompson? Will you sit happily with your slippers and your pipe? Will you really never hear the faraway music? Will you not always be half-looking out of the window, half-listening for the knock on the door? Will you not stand in this little garden, as the evening falls, and look at the toytown houses and the little rooms full of people boggling at the television, and think of the wide, dark river halfway across the big world, and want to cry for nothing you can name?

—For Christ's sake! I said aloud.

—Sorry? said Gerry behind me.

—Oh, hi Gerry, it's nothing, I was just, you know, thinking.

—You have plenty to think about, take it from me.

—Yeah. Accounts at Mothercare, sleepless nights. Tell me about that later. For now, let's just have a drink and celebrate. Here's to built-in car-seats. Nazdrovye!

—Look, Pete . . .

—Yes?

—Before you celebrate.

—What?

—Look, I have something to tell you that will make you think I have not been a good friend to you. It may make you hate me. But I want to promise you I *am* your friend. Or I would not be telling you now.

—Telling me what?

He came up, looked around back at the house, and

284

led me up the garden by my arm. He bit his lip and spoke softly.

—Sean Deeny is planning to kill you tomorrow.

—What?!

—As you know, Deeny is a kind of freelance MI5 operative.

—Just a minute, how the hell do *you* know I know?

—He wants to kill you in order to have sole access to your new account and thus to Mr Kant's money. I guess you didn't look at the small print on the loan account agreement? If you die, he gets sole control.

—Gerry, what . . .

But I stopped dead, because I got a photographic flash-back to the agreement I had signed that night at Mr Kant's, and I knew Gerry was right.

—He will probably get a frontman to buy Irons and Jobson out very cheaply from the legitimate side of BIZVID, Sarah too, as your heir, of course. He will show them openly that BIZVID is bankrupt. They will be very frightened, because he has already told them that he thinks you are in danger of your life, and they will see that he was right, because you will be dead. If you do not go to meet him tomorrow he will very probably kill you anyway, at the next opportunity. You may be able to convince him that he has no need to, but I would not bet on it. He has already set the story up: your death will be blamed on Russian gangsters.

I could think of nothing to say. It all fitted. What Gerry was telling me was insane and impossible, but it worked. Like one of those nature programmes on telly where it just *cannot* be possible that ants and bees and orchids or whatever work together like they do, but they do. All I could do was gape, and wonder, and ask:

—What the sodding hell *are* you, Gerry?

—N5 reporting to sink US Navy Forces Europe.

—To sink US Navy Forces?

—CinC, said Gerry. – Navy Department 5, Plans and Policy Branch, reporting to CINCUSNAVEUR, Naples. Do you have *any* idea how much law-school costs stateside, Pete?

—Naples? What has Naples got to do with anything?

—Well, we define the Mediterranean retroactively. The Sixth Fleet is the Mediterranean fleet; therefore wherever the Sixth Fleet goes, is the Mediterranean.

—Nice.

—The Black Sea Republics think so. The ex-Soviet Black Sea Fleet is something of a loose cannon. Rusty, too. Which is, of course, where Mr Kant comes in.

—You know about him too? Christ allbloodymighty.

—It's my job, Pete. Deeny lines you up for MI5 and Mr Kant, I shadow you, and thus him. Look, it's time to show; I engineered our first meeting. In the supermarket car-park, remember? My broken-down car?

—You set that up?

—Of course. There was nothing wrong with my car. It's a Volvo, Pete: they don't *go* wrong.

—They bloody do. Mine does.

—It does?

—Yeah, twice.

—You never said.

—Of course I bloody didn't. Jesus, I've got *some* pride. Christ, Ref, he even gets a better Volvo than me.

—Well, shit, I guess you just got one of the bad ones, Pete.

—Make that my epitaph, Gerry.

Gerry too. Even Gerry. I felt like all my strings had just been cut. I was a puppet hanging on nothing, or a parachutist drifting towards the sea. I snarled feebly at the sky, and kicked an innocent bush:

—Referee, what did I do? What is so fucking special about me?

—Nothing. There are dozens like you.

—Thanks.

—We're all small fish, Pete. Except that I happen to like you. Really. I wasn't lying about that, not after a while. Shit, Pete, we both had to take sperm-tests! You are my friend. And I really don't like men like Deeny who seek personal enrichment under the pretext of serving freedom.

—Great! You fucking spy on me and pretend to be my friend and persuade me to buy a heap of Swedish crap and know when I change my sodding underpants for years, and now I am supposed to believe you did it all out of friendship and morality. Very useful people, moral friends.

—Don't do this to me Pete.

—'*Don't do this to me Pete.*' Sod you, Gerry, you lying Yank shit.

—Fuck *you*, Pete, you whingeing Brit. Let me tell you something. I am supposed to do *nothing* here. My orders are to let Deeny just blow you away, you understand? I am going counter-procedure bigtime just by fucking *talking* to you. Get it? What do you want? You want me to send in the marines? We do *not* off MI5 operatives. Not in England, anyway. Well, not without five-star justification.

—And I don't rate that?

—You don't rate one star, Pete. Sorry, but there it is.

—Great. Right. So I'll just go along and let myself get topped. Well, thanks, Gerry, you are *such* a good friend. Yes, thanks to you I have just about got time to take out another insurance policy with some all-night phone-bank. Gerry Shepperd: my unborn child will bless you. Jesus fucking Christ. OK, OK, so I start packing right now. I'm out of here.

—Deeny can't kill you if you kill him first.

—Why, thank you, Mr Wittgenstein. Sure, Gerry, I just go and strangle him with my underpants while he's trying to stick me with a poison umbrella or whatever, and then MI5 just let me walk away. Hey! Tell you what, why don't *you* just do it now? Come on, just put me away right here and collect the sodding brownie points. Come on, come on, I'll make it look like self-defence for you, if you want, I'll hit you first, if you want, you . . .

—Pete, this isn't fair.

Unwillingly, I looked into his eyes and saw that it wasn't. I had actually been about to hit him, and he was right: I was not being fair.

—Shit. Oh shit shit shit. I'm sorry. Gerry. Oh God. Look, I mean, can't I just . . . hand myself over to the ordinary police for Christ's sake?

—They might protect you. You'd get several years for tax-fraud and money-laundering even if they did. But I wouldn't rate your chances of getting out of prison alive. It is very easy to arrange an accident in prison, Pete.

—Is that the voice of experience?

—Not *personal* experience.

—Right. Shit. Whooof. OK, OK, so, so, so . . . So I go to the press. I tell them everything, I go public. It's good story, they'll run it for sure.

—That might be better. Yes, the publicity might make it tough for MI5 to take you out. Though you would still get the prison sentence and the bankruptcy and all.

—But I'd be alive, Gerry.

288

—Until Mr Kant gets you.

I lit up another cigarette, numbly. I was not even surprised when Gerry took one too. For all I knew, the bastard smoked forty a day in reality, just never in front of me. He inhaled, and coughed like someone who certainly does not smoke forty a day. But when he recovered, his voice was much more nervy.

—Listen to me, Pete: MI5 is not in love with Deeny. I know this. All they want is to secure the conduit for Mr Kant. Deeny isn't really one of them, he's only halfway in, he's not much more than a hired gun. If you could kill him, they wouldn't care. They'd help to hush it up, if anything. I guarantee it.

—So let's kill him. We could go and . . .

—I said *you*. You on your own.

—Gerry!

—Pete! Will you listen! I cannot help you. My superiors cannot ever know that I even *talked* with you tonight. Understand? I have to be watertight on this one, or else all that happens is we *both* get thrown to the lions. OK? Now: *you* get him, you on your own, and all you have to worry about is the ordinary police angle. All you need is a watertight alibi.

—OK, so I'll say I was with you.

—No, no, chrissake, I just said: I *have* to be clean.

—So I was with Sarah.

—Well, yes, in theory a spouse is the ideal witness, since she is competent to testify for the defence but cannot be compelled to testify for the prosecution.

—Right then.

—In theory.

—In theory?

—In practice a loving spouse's unsupported alibi is weak. No way are they going to believe her. The cops really are *not* slow when it comes to spotting guilt and innocence, that's what they do for a living. This will be a bigtime murder rap with you the number one suspect: if you depend on her, they will hammer at her to break her. They may succeed. And if they do, she could be in big trouble: perjury, accessory to murder. Even if they don't, they'll give her a real bad time. It would be one hell of a lot better (he said, looking at me carefully) if you had the guts not to involve her.

—Can't you try putting it more bluntly, Gerry?

—I'm putting it how is is, Pete. You just have to think of something else. You just have to find some way to prove, beyond any doubt, that you were somewhere else when you were actually killing Deeny.

—Oh for Christ's sake, Gerry, this is all bullshit. How the hell can I do that? And even if I could, which I can't, how can I kill the bastard? I mean, he's going to be tooled up for Christ's sake.

—Ah well, there I *can* help. I have given you the best thing of all, which is surprise and prior knowledge. And you already have the next best thing, which is a kevlar tux. And I may be able to give you the third best thing, because when I met Mr Kant today ...

—Today? You met him today? But he's in Russia.

—Ever hear of private jets, Pete? He's in Exeter. He has business down that way, apparently. And it seems he always wanted to see Exeter and drink in the pub where Sir Francis Drake used to go.

—Says who?

I knew, of course, before he even told me. She was here, in England. The orange Greater London sky seemed to flicker for a moment when he said that: like it was not the light from a million crap little sodium lamps, but a vast petrochemical flare somewhere beyond the horizon. The thought that Masha was here, walking on England, made the ground shake beneath my feet. I swallowed hard as it hit me again, that strange cocktail of fear and longing that says: *Hi, this is your fate calling.*

—I must say Pete, it looks like you wowed them out there.

—What? Drink, sing, and get shot? Great.

—It seems to have worked. Mr Kant said if you were not married you'd have made a good husband.

—She translated that?

—Of course.

—What did she look like, I mean, did she . . .

—She laughed, she just . . . Pete, are you saying . . . ?

—No, Christ. Hey: in my dreams, Gerry.

—Well, you never know, Pete: she sent you a present.

I waved him to keep his voice down, because Sarah and Melissa might hear us through the window:

—What present?

—This is as far as I can go, Pete. From here in it's up to you. Like I said, if I try to go any further, I just ensure that we both go down. Hey: welcome to the free market, Pete. When this is over, do you fancy that hill-walking weekend? We could talk the whole thing through. All of it. We could do the Islay distilleries.

And he fished in his jacket and pulled out a small parcel. Small, but heavy.

—Christ, what is it? A gold bar?

But Gerry just slipped a small tube of cream into my pocket.

—To clean your hands with afterwards.

Then he held up his hands, shrugged, and turned, hands still high, to go back into the house. I know he had *said* he had to get out of this, but hearing him say it and seeing him do it were very different. I suppose we are just too used to saying one thing and doing another, I realised that I had half-consciously thought he was half-kidding: in my heart of hearts I had been thinking that when push came to shove, good old Gerry would never *actually* leave me alone in this shit.

And now he had.

As I looked at the door he had shut behind him, I pulled absently at one of the strings. The parcel came open far more easily than I had thought it would: the wrapping unrolled under the weight of whatever was inside, and the heavy something fell out and landed with a big, soft clunk on the dark grass at my feet. A large sheet of paper fluttered palely earthwards. I caught it as it fell and held it up to the light from the kitchen window.

It was hand-written, with two of the words in big Russian capitals. I do not read Russian, but I could read this: and as soon as I read it, I knew damn well what had made that soft, heavy clunk on the grass, because what it said was:

ДРЕК and ГЕРКИНС!

23. The Rooshians Go By

The queue of dubious-looking Russians at the German chip shop Fish'n'Fritz, which stands just off the seafront at Weymouth, was backed up out into the street, as it had been most evenings for the past month.

British holidaymakers, used to every sort of swift pap on demand, often grow restive at the time it takes Fish'n'Fritz to cook each bratwurst to order (a process which the owner defends publicly as guaranteeing freshness and privately as eliminating all wastage); but the sailors from the laid-up factory-ships out in the bay appeared not to mind. Maybe queueing for sausage reminded them of home.

Or maybe they had nothing better to do at night. A bratwurst and chips was as far as they pushed the boat out; whatever drinking they did, they did on board their ships, courtesy of the local Asda off-licence. They had no money to waste on pointless luxuries; their hard eyes did not need the little hits of spending without which most westerners start to doubt their own existence. Over the winter, unable to continue their summer trade of scraping the North Atlantic clean of all living organisms, they had stripped Dorset of Ladas and spares. They intended to steam off with this seasonal booty in a week or so, to their hard, grey countries, before returning to the now unfrozen north.

It was actually surprising just how much hard currency they had, when you thought about it. And if you thought about it any more, you certainly might wonder exactly what the fishing-boats down from

Fraserburgh were bringing out and taking back on their nightly visits out to the big, grey, rusting ships. There was no point asking the Scotsmen, because they would not say anything; and even if they did, their accents were so thick that they might just as well have been Russians.

But then Weymouth folk are of seafaring blood themselves, with an inborn tendency not to worry themselves unduly about night-tide comings and goings. One of the town's many pub-musicians had lately been going great shakes with an updated folk-song, the chorus of which went *'Watch the wall my darling, while the Rooshians go by'*. Some of the more enterprising hardware and electrical goods traders had gone so as far as to put up signs in remarkably accurate (though old-fashioned) Russian; welcome extra pocket money for Mrs Janet Fry, retired schoolteacher of the parish.

It had to be said, though, that things had been getting a bit beyond a joke recently; the knifed body of the Scottish bosun under the clock-tower on the Esplanade was not going to help fill the vacancies in the massed B&Bs this Easter. The local Police Superintendent had expressed the concerns of many when he stated on SouthWest FM that this sort of thing was bad for business and had to be stopped.

Perhaps it was just a coincidence that tonight, the very night after his speech, as the Russian sailors stood in their usual queue inside and outside Fish'n'Fritz, they suddenly nudged each other and fell silent as the long, black Mercedes rolled slowly past them.

The front window was down, and the tall, blond driver was scanning the straggling line with his pig-killing eyes: those who were fairly sure he was not looking out for them whistled silently with relief; those who suspected he might be, found their bratwursts suddenly no longer quite so tasty.

And none of them were really surprised when, shortly after midnight, the *Kalinin* first went up like a magnesium flare and then went down with all hands.

The sound of the explosion took a full two seconds to reach the underage drinkers who, at that time of night, maintained sole possession of the rainswept promenade.

24. As If

So now it was 5 a.m. on Sunday, the deadest time of the week, and I sat hunched behind my filing cabinet, wearing Mr Kant's kevlar shirt and DJ over Trevor's leather trousers and with Mr Kant's un-numbered, silenced .32 revolver on the window-ledge by my head, flossing my teeth and humming the C&W tune (twang twang) as I waited for Deeny to come up the stairs so I could send him for an early and everlasting bath.

And as I huddled and flossed (the flossing was hard with gloves on), I was thinking about what I had thought about in the garage: Sarah and Masha. Both of them.

*

I wondered if maybe it really was possible. Sarah once said *Fatal Attraction*, you know, that crap movie, was really all about how men were cowards. If Michael Douglas had only had the guts to introduce the two women and smile and say: *Hi, I think we need to sort this one out*, she reckoned they would have done so, one way or another. But the feeble tosser wanted to have his cake and eat it.

—Yeah, I had said at the time, it was so obvious.

I supposed now that the Big Ref had been listening in and writing it down so he could remind me of this at some future date and see what I said then. Or rather, now.

—As if, I said to myself now, and checked the gun was still in the right place for a half-second reach-and-shoot.

Gerry had told me where to sit. He reckoned that two thicknesses of filing-cabinet metal with a foot of documents in between would take a lot of the power out of a handgun bullet, maybe even stop it. It was all to do with layers, he said: combined with my kevlar shirt and DJ, it would certainly cope with anything Deeny was likely to be carrying, especially since his piece, too, would surely be silenced.

—What if he hits me in the face? I asked.

—Well, that's the trouble with a kevlar tux, Pete: you land yourself someplace you need a kevlar tux, you probably need more than a kevlar tux.

—Right.

So naturally I was keeping the door well in sight while I flossed, and listening with all my ears in case bogfeatures had got hold of a key to the street-door; in case he could just turn the key softly and sneak up the stairs. Every now and then I reached over my shoulder and picked up the gun and aimed at the door quickly, so that I would get its position kind of radar-locked into my head. But actually I was wondering, as I looked at the stuff clinging to the floss, if it would not be easier to just let him get me instead.

I mean, shit, so what? My genes now had at least a provisional booking for a walk-on part in the next episode of Life on Earth. I had already been shot dead once, so I knew what it felt like, except for the actual dying, and I found (to my surprise) that I was not scared: I had been through all that before. And thanks to the miracle of life-insurance, I was quite literally better off dead, so Sarah and the kid would be OK. What better excuse to die?

And anyway: just how the *hell* was I going to tell Sarah about Masha?

There was no way out now. My alibi made it inevitable that Sarah would know.

Because at this very moment it was (I hoped and prayed) happening. Right now, while Trevor was already cruising back up the M3 in my Volvo; while Gerry was preparing to cover his back by digging in to ye olde kippers and toast in the In-and-Out club not half a mile away, surrounded by Admirals of the Fleet and Air Vice-Marshals; and while Sarah was sleeping and dreaming of whatever nice things I hoped she was dreaming of, Masha would just about be putting the final touch to my alibi.

I had told Gerry when the idea came to me. He said it might work; he gave me Mr Kant's scrambled mobile number, and I called from my car in my drive, to explain the plan. It was Masha, naturally, to whom I had actually talked:

—Right, so in about an hour I'll get to Fleet westbound, fill the car, let the cameras see me at the pumps, pay with my Visa-card, then cross the motorway to meet Trevor at the eastbound lavs. We swap some clothes, he crosses over. He takes the Volvo and comes down nice and slow and legal while I take his bike to London. He should be with you at about 4 a.m.

—Can you trust this Trevor?

—If we get away with this, his fiancée becomes my Production Manager, and he becomes our permanent motorbike messenger on a ridiculously generous salary. If we don't, they become unemployed.

—This is good positive motivation. Also, he will have great respect for you because he will know you are able to kill to preserve your livelihood.

—If you say so.

—I do. This is good business, Peter.

298

—Thank you. Trev will leave you by 4.30 a.m., by 8.00 he'll easily be back at Fleet eastbound in my car. Charlie will tip the police off from a box in Finsbury Park at 8.15. By that time, I should be at Sunbury or thereabouts. The police will go to BIZVID and break in; they will find Deeny still warm. They will find out about BIZVID and naturally call me at home. They will find me not there and Sarah will be authentically gobsmacked. So they will immediately suspect me, and call me on my mobile. But by that time, I shall be in the caff on the eastbound M3, in my normal clothes, swilling coffee, with my Volvo parked outside. And the Visa stuff and my empty tank and every police camera from here to Exeter will prove that I have been there and back, tonight, to see you. Which you will confirm.

—My father says it sounds like a very good plan, Masha said, after some Russian conferring had taken place. – When the police log your mobile calls, this will be the call that you made to arrange our lovers' meeting, will it not?

—Exactly, I said.

—Very well. You have called this Charmaine?

—Of course.

—That call will also have been logged.

—So I talked to my secretary about work out of hours. I often call her out of hours.

—About work?

—Look, I have often called her recently, OK?

Now Masha was making me feel guilty about cheating on Sarah with Charmaine. Busy, busy life.

—Very well, Peter. The difficult thing will be to make them believe us. After all, it will obviously have been *possible* for you to have been there to kill Mr Deeny and then get to the M3. They will check out our story very carefully. There is . . .

—I hope they do check. I hope they check very carefully. I'm counting on it. I hope they check your house. I hope they check your sheets. I hope they check you.

—Peter?

So then I took a deep breath and told her what Trevor would be bringing to Exeter, in my Volvo, in a bubble-wrapped, insulated package.

—Yes, she said, – Your sperms will be a very good alibi for you. No-one will doubt the story because when they tell your wife Sarah where your sperms have been discovered, she will be truly shocked, horrified and enraged, and they will see this.

—Yes, I said, – She will.

—I hope she will understand.

—Me too.

As if.

—I hope *very* much she will understand. Because you see, Peter, there is another very good reason that everyone will believe you were with me tonight.

—What's that?

—I am pregnant and it is yours.

—Well, I said, – I don't think that just *douching* with a sperm-sample would ... You're what?

—I am pregnant, and it is yours.

—Oh.

—You are not happy?

—Well ... Yes. Yes. Yes.

—I am happy too.

—Does Mr ... um, your father know?

—My father is very happy.

—He is?

Now there was another lengthy bout of dark, sla-vonic muttering:

—My father longs for grandchildren. He says that the identity of the father is not of great importance. Provided the father is not a black beetle, of course. It is his daughter's child, whoever's child it is, therefore it is his grandchild. That is the advantage of daughters, says my father: you know who your grandchildren are.

—Well, yes, I suppose so.

—My father says that this is one of the many ways in which the Old Testament is a very fine guide to life, although he considers the New Testament a book to be opened only with gloves on. My father despises all metaphysics. He considers all prophets of short-cuts to heaven to be dangerous men who prey on the tired. Heaven may be a long way off, says my father; but if it is anywhere, it is here on earth. The meek do not inherit the earth, says my father: the rich inherit the hard currency and the meek get the roubles. So let us make everyone rich through increased trade, and then worry about heaven. My father wishes you a straight aim, and suggests that as Mr Deeny enters your sights, you model your behaviour on . . .

—Yes, yes, I can guess. Look, I don't suppose your father's driver could just kill Deeny instead? I imagine he's a lot better at killing people than me.

—Undoubtedly. However, Mr Deeny is our partner at present, and has not failed us. My father does not consider Mr Deeny's plan to take over your company as a breach of *our* trust.

—Yes, but shit, Masha, you're pregnant now, we . . .

—If a man cannot defend his own businesses, what use is he as a partner? Or a father?

—OK, OK, OK. But you'll provide the alibi?

—That is quite legitimate. And of course, I personally would like to help you all I can, within the bounds of business.

—Thanks a bunch.

—We must be enlightened, Peter.

—Was that enlightenment when you told me about your house with the black curtains? Was that just business?

—I am glad you remember the story. Tell it to me now.

So I did.

I sat in my Volvo in my dark little garage in my little plot of little England, and told her her own story, which was now mine too: about the girl and the black-draped house by the wide river. When I ended, I could see a woman at the end of a long garden, with bats flying round her head, and a baby on her hip.

—That is good, said Masha. – Yes, that night I wanted you to die with me. Naturally, we all long to die in love sometimes. But that is merely romantic foolishness. Better to long for life, which is by no means assured us. Very well, Peter, I will do as you ask with your sperms, and tonight I shall think of you so hard that when I lie to the police, I shall be telling them a kind of truth. I think it likely we shall meet again, do you?

—Well, yes, I mean, surely we must, the child ...

—We *must* do nothing, Peter. Our child will not lack the love of a family or access to hard currency, whatever happens. If you wish us to meet again, and if I wish it at the same time as you wish it, then we shall meet. We are free.

—Sarah is pregnant too.

—That is very good. I congratulate you both. Of

302

course, you will now have to tell her about us, even if the police do not. That is good and enlightened, though it may be hard for you, briefly. You must tell Sarah I am glad: our children can perhaps help each other in their businesses. We shall await Trevor and your sperms.

And she hung up.

It was all true, you see. My alibi, I mean.

I was lying so that tomorrow, everyone would believe I had been with her tonight. Which was the truth in a different way, because part of me *would* be with her tonight, and every night. For weeks, I had been lying through my teeth to cover up cheating on Sarah, and now I had to lie through my teeth so that the world would think I had been cheating on Sarah when I had not. But still was, in a different way. And always would be, until I told her.

Maybe when this was over there would be no more lies.

Twang twang.

Then I just sat there in the Volvo and listened to the old music awhile on the CD until Gerry came to see if I was OK.

—Memory Lane, I said.

—Sure, he nodded: – Reagan's inaugural speech. That's what it does for me, anyway. Well?

—They're on.

—OK.

—Jesus, Gerry, I can't get my head round this. All this and now Sarah being pregnant . . .

—Yeah, said Gerry, – Yeah.

—Hey, Gerry?

—Yeah?

—Do you mind?

—Sorry? Oh. You want me to go? Yeah, sure, I guess

you need to think, I guess it's all a little too much right now.

—No, I need to give a sperm-sample, Gerry, remember? Not my idea of a spectator-sport.

—Oh, oh sure, right . . . Shall I shut the door?

—Please. Better go and cover your ass. Sorry.

—Yeah. Good luck. You OK with the gun now?

—Thanks Gerry.

—See you soon. Islay?

—Yeah.

In the dark, in the closed garage, I turned the car on and flicked the headlamp stalk, so as to get the light that bounced back off the wall in front of me. I looked at the keys dangling by the wheel and thought how very easy it would be to just turn them softly another quarter of an inch, and ease my eyes shut. I put out my hand and held the key and shut my eyes.

I saw the black stretch Lada coming up a long, flat road, under a cold blue sky filled with vapour-trails.

Then I let go the keys suddenly, as if they were red hot. My heart was banging in my neck. I blipped back my sunroof and looked at the garage ceiling:

ME: Referee, I need your help. Sorry, but I can't bloody wank. So much for practice. I need inspiration. And I need you tomorrow. Look, how's this for a deal: just let me wank now, and let me live tomorrow, and this will be the last time I ever wank. The ultimate.

THE BIG REF: Let's get this clear. You promise to quit all forms of wanking, physical or mental, and start living?

ME: If I get safely to bed tomorrow, every day will be physical/mental shag-or-die day.

THE BIG REF: And you realise that the term *wanking*,

304

for the purposes of this agreement, includes all and any forms of lying, dishonesty, time-wasting and general saaadness?

ME: Check.

THE BIG REF: I'll hold you to this, boy.

ME: Strict but fair, Ref, strict but fair.

Then, having at last successfully wanked, I went in and crept upstairs like a burglar in my own house, to check that Sarah was asleep. She was: I stood and looked at her and thought how I was looking at two people now, and how I would have done anything to not be doing what I was going to do. Except, of course, not do it. Twang twang.

At Fleet Services, I filled the car as blatantly as possible and then parked her in the darkest part of the car park. I nipped into the trees, took off my Tintin cap, put on the old parka I had brought, and zipped across the silent M-Way with Mr Kant's kevlar togs under my arm.

I clocked Trevor having a coffee in the eastbound caff. He had chosen a good Sheriff's Table, you know, one where you can see the whole room. Nice one Trev: I didn't even have to slow down and let anyone get a good look at me.

We mimed pissing, three urinals apart, and when the coast was clear we both just about managed to squeeze into one cubicle, with me standing on top of the closed bog to make more room and keep an eye out in case the door opened.

—Here our boss, these jeans am a real squeeze, like!

—Yeah? I said, delighted; maybe I wasn't *that* fat.

Five minutes later, we opened the lav door quietly

and made sure no-one was about. I was in Trevor's smelly old leathers, with Mr Kant's bullet-proofs in Trevor's rucksack, on my back; Trevor stood resplendent in my hideous old parka, under which he had my normal clothes on. He tried the Tintin cap for size.

—No! Trev! Not yet. Just keep the bloody hood up for now, understand? The cap only goes on after you get into the bushes the other side and lose the parka.

—Sorry, our boss.

—Right, Trev: keys to the Volvo. Don't go getting bloody squashed crossing the motorway. She's full up; just cruise her in fifth at sixty-five and she'll make it there and back. Don't stop *anywhere*, Trev. If you have to piss, don't. And for Christ's sake put your hair up in the cap before you come out of the bushes and into the light. And keep the peak down. And keep the gloves on all the time, I only want *my* prints on the car. And for fuck's sake *please* don't get stopped for speeding or prang her, or we are all totally and utterly buggered in more ways than the Kama bloody Sutra. Understand, Trev?

—No sweat, our boss, he said. (Actually, he said *now swit*.)

—You OK with this, Trev?

—No prob, our boss. Always wanted to do something like this, like. You alright on the Kwacker, our boss?

—I'll take it easy.

—She's bit sticky-like from 2nd to 3rd, but you'll soon get the hang. I put some horrible gunk on the plates, like, so you can't hardly read them. Best be off then. What's in the parcel?

—You don't want to know, Trev.

—You're the boss, our boss.

—You go first; walk straight out the door and get in

306

the shadow as quick as you can. Just walk nice and easy into the trees, like you're going to take a leak.

—Right you are, our boss. See you at eight.

And off he scuttled. I counted twenty, put the helmet on, took a deep breath and clumped out of the lav, past the shops and into the night. I just saw Trevor slipping through the line of pine-trees, towards the dark, dead motorway, with the parcel in my Tesco bag.

I took it very easy on his Kawasaki 500 all the way into town and through to one of the little back-alleys behind Neal's Yard where no-one is going to notice anything at 3 a.m. on a Sunday. That black cab gave me a nasty moment, though I was reasonably sure he hadn't clocked me properly. I was hours early for Deeny, but then that was the point: Deeny might be aiming to get here early himself, maybe he had got hold of a key and would be lying in wait. But not *this* early.

Even so, I commandoed up the stairs like Gerry told me to: I pressed the old-fashioned lift-button, and watched the tendrils of steel cable and piping coil and wind until the lift-car came into view. I covered it as I opened it with my left hand. Then I pressed the button for BIZVID, jumped out, slid the doors shut and followed the cage up the open lift-shaft, aiming ahead and up the whole time. SAS-style. Except I suppose the SAS have slightly more style: I imagine they don't sweat that much, or hear their hearts so loud.

There was no-one there.

Three hours ago. More.

And so now, at last, was now.

As I sat now in BIZVID, I was thinking about what I had thought about then in the dark garage, eventually, in order to have my unwanted wank. The fantasy was:

307

a very, very slightly pregnant woman, strobing between Masha and Sarah, Sasha or Maria, leaning on a green Mini in front of a house decked in black, beside a river in England bigger than any river that ever ran through England, hitching herself up against the side of the car and pulling up her long skirts.

A cocktail of light and shade, of memory and premonition.

I woke up again and realised that for some reason I had got up from behind the filing-cabinet and I was sitting in my swivelling, gas-suspended chair, with an incipient erection. I revolved gently round; there was some wire or other caught up around the base of the chair, I counted how many turns it took to wind it right round tight around the black plastic stem. I realised that something was wrong, and sniffed my fingers. The smell reminded me that I had slung the used floss in the bin. Evidence. Bad move. Hairs and clothes-fibres and skin-flakes were no problem, because of course I was here every day anyway; Gerry's cute USN SpecOps cleaning stuff would get rid of any cordite and gun-oil from my skin after I dumped the shooter. But the floss could prove I had been here at this time, maybe. I fished it out of the bin and pocketed it, tutting to myself at my own near-stupidity, and sat down again, and swivelled some more.

If only.

If only it could be possible.

Maybe it was? Maybe telling Sarah everything would even be for the best? I mean, it would be tears and horrors and all, days of it, weeks maybe, but then maybe, who knew? maybe Sarah and me would find that we had been living for years like we were wearing bee-keepers' hats, or blinkers; maybe this would get us touching whiskers again, maybe our lives would be transparent and bright again, like when the old music had been new?

If you are moving on together, the wind whips the guilt from your words as you speak them; the past flies like tumbleweed, away down Memory Lane, until it is lost behind the thirty-foot concrete walls in a dark, old life we no longer recognise as ours, and which we can no longer imagine how we stood so long. So long as you are moving on, together.

I remembered Sarah's eyes when she pressed the button to make the ansaphone say THE UNIT IS ON. And I got this mad feeling that she actually might understand, that somehow the baby had changed everything: that all we had been for the last few years was two grotesque superteens, and now we had become real people with real problems to deal with really, real jobs in hand to keep the devil from making crap thoughts for idle minds. Maybe the baby, the babies, could set us free from our ingrown selves, by giving us at last some angle other than the well-known sight of our own navels.

Something that mattered.

Maybe.

If only I could be sure.

—Sure, Mr Thompson? asked the Interview Panel, which had convened at Jobson's desk, and was now laying out its various papers. – *Sure* is the one thing we can never be. To be unsure is a condition of living. The desire for certainty is merely the desire for stasis. But nothing that lives is static, Mr Thompson. What, after all, is the difference between a blade of grass and a stone? All that lives, changes. Do you desire stasis, Mr Thompson? Is that why you desire The Job?

The door buzzed; the Interview Panel disappeared as I swung round in my chair. I lifted the intercom phone.

—Hoi, said Deeny, in the street: – Glad you made it.

—Hi Sean, I said, and pressed the button. In the dead, Sunday quiet, I could hear the lock whizz open downstairs, and the door to the street slam shut again.

Then I realised that this was not just good old Sean Deeny, my crappily charming paddy-on-the-make bent accountant, coming up to piss me off yet again: this was a Sean Deeny I had never seen, coming up to blow me away for good. I thought of the light in the eye of the fighting-cow in the bullring. The look that says: the dealing's done (twang twang).

As I padded back over to the filing cabinet, I was wondering if maybe Sarah's baby and Masha's baby would ever meet, if maybe we could ever be a kind of tribe, not some crap WASP nuclear family with all the built-in cockups that entails. Or was that just a hopeless hope?

As I shoved past my desk, I saw that one of the books lying on it had a photo of a dark man in yellow suit on the back. It seemed incredible now that this book had been kicking around the office for months, meaning nothing to anyone: now, looking at his photo, I thought about a gang of fourteen-year-olds with machetes and the blessing of the State, coming to get me. The lift-gear hummed and clattered beyond the door. Through the little glass window, I could see the cables shimmering as they moved. Out of the corner of my eye, I clocked a cab going down Charing Cross Road, and looked round: for a second, I thought it was the black stretch Lada.

As I snuggled into the space behind the cabinet, I wondered how wide the Volga actually was at Samara. I could feel the towering shadow of a rusting tanker, so big behind me that I did not dare look round to see the sky being filled without pity.

As I aimed at the door, head-height, I wondered if Gerry was telling me the truth. Maybe it would be Gerry himself coming through the door to kill me, knowing exactly where I would be, because he had told me to be there. Or Mr Kant's driver with his slow, Nazi eyes. Or all three. Or some hitman hired by Gerry's bosses. Or by Deeny. Some autistic killer who would only be doing his job. Maybe the gun was fixed to jam. Or to go off in my face. I checked it for the hundredth time, but then what the hell did I know about guns anyway? I am just a normal bloody Brit for Christ's sake, I was born to mow my lawn and wash my car:

> (but) There ain't no entrance (twang)
> To Memory Lane
> (And) if you don't go crazy sometimes
> You're insane

And as I sang this to myself, I had to restrain myself from checking the gun yet again. Too late. I knew, logically, that it was set. The safety was off and the trigger cocked and there was a round up the spout: I was in condition one.

As far as I could tell.

Logically, of course, it was far more sensible for Gerry and Deeny to just stitch me up. And what about Charlie and Trevor? Maybe Charlie had done a deal with Deeny? And even Mr Kant and Masha: OK, so she was having my kid, so what? She had even said it plain as plain: I was not needed. I was superfluous.

And then the last thing struck me. It was so blindingly obvious that it had indeed blinded me right up to now, till this last minute. I felt the gun grow heavier as it hit me, my arm sank onto my knee: *Masha's kid was probably not mine at all.* Probably, she was not even pregnant. Probably, Deeny had told them about my sperm-tests and so they knew that *this* was the final way to get me onside. To line me up for the drop.

It all fitted. An image from childhood crossed my mind from right to left: the cartoon character who has gone off the edge of the cliff, but has not yet looked down. Only I was even worse: I had looked down, and seen the drop, and was still going. I was running on pure belief. No, not on belief: on the pure *need* to believe.

But then you always do, in the end. You cannot run on logic: the maths always adds up to absolute zero, one way or another, and you never lose the black stretch Lada, no matter how hard you drive. You can only live as if.

The faraway trumpets were into the Paso Doble again.

As I heard the lift clatter shut and the cage-doors slide back, I was half-wondering if it would have been better to shoot from the kitchen door; I was half-thinking of Charlie and me groping in there, and how little I had known about her, about anything really, back then, and how long ago all that seemed, and how now I knew even less, twang twang. I saw Sarah and Masha, waving to me like I was some everyday friend, as they chugged past a small island in a wide river, cutting gherkins and tomatoes, on a little green boat filled with children.

As a shadow on the landing blotted out the little mesh window and the door-handle turned softly, I raised the gun again, but I was trying not to giggle. I was thinking:

—Berni in Hell, Deeny.

As whoever it was opened the door, as the light from the landing flooded into the office, there was a sound in my head like the thunder of hoofs in sand, and I remembered again how it all started; for a second I was back in my Volvo on the wet M25, passing under a cold grey bridge, with an old dog hobbling across above me.

Then the petrochemical flares billowed, filling the horizon, and I was remembering nothing. There were no second guesses and no backup thoughts: Memory Lane was sealed as all my doors and armour whizzed softly shut; now was for ever, the world was made of ice with a hard, metal tang, rancid aluminium; and as I squeezed the trigger I was squeezing the trigger.